The Gatekeeper

of

Crystal Pond

"Not What Lies Above, but Below"

BOOKS BY DIANN SHADDOX

A Faded Cottage

Whispering Fog

Miranda

Spirts of Sacred Mountain

The Gatekeeper

of

Crystal Pond

"Not What Lies Above, but Below"

DIANN SHADDOX

EAGLE QUILL PUBLISHING

The Gatekeeper

By Diann Shaddox

ISBN -13: 978-0-9976111-2-0
ISBN -13: 978-0-9976111-3-7
ISBN -13: 978-0-9976111-4-4

Eagle Quill Publishing
www.eaglequillpublishing.com
First print Edition 2016
Printed in the United States of American
The Gatekeeper Copyright © 2016, Diann Shaddox

This book is dedicated with love to Randy, my husband.

Acknowledgment

To Marsha Tolleson Rhodes, my editor. Thank you for your encouragement, kindness, your patience, and the many hours you have spent working with me. I will be forever grateful for everything you've done.

To Carolyn Rischbieter, my cover art artist, for her imagination and her ability to bring *The Gatekeeper* to life.

The Gatekeeper of Crystal Pond

"Not What Lies Above, but Below"

Chapter 1
The Gatekeeper

Most people will say this story is unreal and could never be; nonetheless, I've seen with my own eyes that we aren't alone in the great universe. No, don't look up into the blue sky full of swirling white, cottony clouds. You see, it isn't what lies above us, but below.

Aionios, the one small word written in red on the front of the leather journal that I hold in my hands sends chills down my back. So appropriate, that name meaning without beginning and end…forever! Madeline Jean Sayers was a young innocence girl who turned into a strong-minded woman. She became a woman with conviction, whose love sent her on an incredible journey. A journey I vowed to keep secret.

You see, my Maddy, with her long, curly, red hair bright as the setting sun and a temper to boot, was a carefree country girl. I remember the first time I met her. Her coffee brown eyes stared up at me with confidence and her tomboyish ways made her more persistent with whatever she pursued.

Maddy grew up on her family's farm in Pine Grove, South Carolina with her father Jackson, a kind, but headstrong man. Aged live oaks, tall South Carolina pines, and rolling green hills covered the Southern farm. But, the old farm did have one mystery, a small pond with crystal water that terrified Maddy. She referred to it as her only Achilles' heel. A devil's pond, her grandfather Winfred called it, a pond with a secret. If you enter into the pond, you disappear and never reappear. That pond brought me to the farm years ago to help uncover its secret.

For many years, the weight of the world was on my shoulders. I couldn't sleep, and worry took over my mind. However, I'm getting ahead of myself.

Oh, you ask, who am I? Well, I'm the gatekeeper of Crystal Pond. Now the story of Maddy Sayers and the world of Aionios must be told.

Chapter 2
One Moment of Time

A blood-curdling scream, "NO!" jarred the old farmhouse from its peaceful slumber. Maddy gulped for air. Her hands wildly grabbed at her throat to free herself of a chocking sensation. Her flushed face felt the dampness of her pillow. There on the floor was her faded, rainbow colored T-shirt, raveled jean shorts and the tennis shoes, one with a broken shoestring. Her eyes darted up from the floor.

The morning sunlight flickered around her father's silhouette as he stood in the doorway of her room. His tired eyes told the story. His head moved slowly nodding yes; it was true. Maddy's head turned from him and faced the window. She felt the freshness of the breeze from the attic fan blowing into the bedroom.

It couldn't be true... she thought. Sniffles continued. There wasn't any stopping the tears.

Maddy didn't have an answer of why her perfect world on that Saturday in 1989, in just one moment, had spun into an abrupt end. She only wished that the clock could go back counterclockwise and erase time.

***

Saturday, July 11, 1989

Maddy Sayer, a young girl of fifteen, full of spit and vinegar, woke to a beautiful summer day. She lay in her white, poster bed and her eyes stared out the window into the early morning. She sat up in bed. Something was wrong. Maddy had a sixth sense. Her grandfather Winfred said she was like his mom, her great grandmother, Virginia, who had the power of perception.

Maddy's premonitions didn't happen often, but this morning, she sensed an eerie sensation.

Even so, Maddy wasn't going to allow her feelings to disrupt this perfect day. She leaped out of bed, slipped her faded, rainbow colored T-shirt over her head, pulled on her raveled cut off jean shorts, and then slid her dingy, worn tennis shoes on her feet. She tugged on her shoestrings; one broke. The strangeness in the air had increased. *It's only a shoestring*, she grumbled to herself as she repositioned the shoestring and tied a tiny bow.

Her brown eyes gazed back with confidence at her reflection in the long mirror behind the closet door. She began to laugh seeing freckles across her face making zigzag patterns. She sighed. Her mother had told her to wear her wide-brim, straw hat when she was outside, but that wasn't going to happen, and Maddy had decided years before just live with the freckles.

She took in a deep breath; it was time to leave. Maddy's wild, red hair flew behind her as she skipped down the stairs. She was motivated... chores, and then, the rest of the day with Ryan. She grabbed a fresh warm biscuit and piece of sausage off the kitchen table. She took a huge bite as she ran to the wooden, screen door. Then she closed the screen door gently, one of her daddy's rules.

She grabbed the railing on the steps of the porch. "Ouch!" she hollered, another bad omen, a splinter. She studied her hand trying to pull the thin sliver of wood from her finger as she wiped the blood on her jean shorts.

Maddy ran into the yard. Sandy, her golden retriever lying on the porch floor, jumped from the old planks scampering alongside. The warm sun hit her in the face making her face tingle. She laughed; understanding the freckles would be growing just as fast as the tomatoes in the garden.

She slid to a quick stop in the damp dirt. In front of her was the boy that she had fallen in love with, Ryan Allen Beardsley. Ryan lived across the road on his family's farm. He was her kindred spirit, her best friend.

Ryan leaned back in a green, metal lawn chair. His feet were propped upon an old stump. Ryan's hound dog Jonas was loyally sprawled by his side. The young man's arms rose over his head and he laced his fingers together as he watched Maddy begin her chores. Maddy grabbed the empty feed bucket from the fence post and let it swing on her arm as she hurried to the barn for chicken feed.

Ryan leaped from the lawn chair, zoomed past Maddy, and quickly flung both of the barn doors wide-open. He scrambled up the rungs of the worn ladder attached to the side of the hayloft and grabbed the long rope dangling from a huge ceiling beam. "Geronimo!" he screamed swinging from the barn's loft. He cleverly landed on top of the haymow.

Maddy rolled her eyes and poured the chicken feed into the bucket. When she lifted the bucket, the chicken feed started to drain out a small hole. She stomped her foot and put her fist on her hip.

"Hey Maddy, what's taking you so long!" shouted Ryan.

"I have to feed the chickens and this dag burn bucket has a hole," she growled with her eyes squinting.

He made himself comfortable on top of the hay. "Ah, that's okay. We're fine; we've got all day," he assured. His arms stretched out wide crossing above his head. His eyes closed. Ryan was tall for a boy who was almost sixteen, well…in two weeks.

Maddy crept quietly tiptoeing near Ryan, and then she slowly pulled her leg back ready to kick at his boots, but…

Ryan, always on the alert grabbed hold of her leg and she toppled into the hay next to him. His arm wrapped around her bringing her near and gently his fingers tossed her long hair from her face. He leaned his head over in front of hers, and their lips touched for the first time. His body jerked. He leaped up taking her hand in his, and pulled her beside him.

Frozen in her spot, Maddy studied the boy towering over her: high cheekbones, strong jaw, and those narrow, emerald eyes. He grinned making his cheeks even more defined as he gazed down at her.

"You finish the chores and then we'll go to the old oak at Crystal Pond," he called out grabbing another metal bucket pitching it to her. "I'll get Wild Spice ready," he said whistling for the chestnut colored horse grazing in the back pasture.

She finished feeding the chickens and hung the bucket on the fence post. She turned around and Ryan walked up to her holding Wild Spice and Jet, his dark black stallion, reins in his hand.

Maddy settled into Wild Spice's saddle. She pulled the reins up into her hands in order to follow Jet. Both horses, knowing the way to the old oak, took off trotting along the small trail that weaved in and out of the pecan trees. The morning sun flickered though the branches, and birds serenaded them as they quietly made their way along the trail. Wild Spice walked up to Jet standing next to the gnarled oak full of Spanish moss draped from timeworn limbs.

She dismounted Wild Spice and gazed up at Ryan who was already getting settled on the huge limb. He leaned over stretching out his arm to her. She put her hand in his and he hoisted her up, helping her swing onto their limb, a routine they had mastered since childhood.

Her eyes peered below them into Crystal Pond, the name her great grandfather had given Unktehi Pond, which meant *monster* or *water spirit*. A mysterious pond that had taken many men's lives over the last century, it was a pond that terrified Maddy, but intrigued Ryan.

Maddy's head turned toward Ryan and she studied him. Today he seemed different from the hundreds, maybe thousands, of other times they sat in their tree. She wasn't going to let that morning's eerie feeling get to her as she leaned her head back and felt the cool breeze touch her face.

"Well, you gonna say something?" questioned Ryan pulling off some bark from the tree and fidgeting with the Spanish moss.

"It's nice out, and the wild roses smell so sweet this morning," answered Maddy, pressing her lips together not letting her grin emerge.

"No, silly, not about the wild roses." He smoothed his long, blonde hair from his face with his tan fingers. "I mean about earlier?"

"Oh, that," she answered nonchalantly.

"Yes, oh that. Aren't you going to hit me or something?"

"Why?" she asked, her lips finally curled into a smile as she stared back at him.

His head turned to her. "You're being obstinate, aren't you?"

"You're using those big words again," she exclaimed, letting her feet dangle from the huge limb.

Ryan looked into her vibrant brown eyes and his hand reached over pulling her face to his. He kissed her again with so much passion.

Her fingers stroked his face keeping him close.

He pulled back from her and smiled playfully, "Maddy, you sure are an enigma."

"Would you stop with the words?"

"You're not mad at me?"

"No, don't be ridiculous. Why would I be mad?"

"I don't know, I guess…

"Ryan Allen Beardsley," Maddy blurted out, "you should know by now I love you."

"I can't ever surprise you, but hell, you sure can surprise me. I love you, too, Maddy Sayers. There, I said it. You happy?" he said proudly.

She grinned. "Yep," she answered staring into his green eyes.

His head shook back and forth. "I'm gonna try and catch some fish," he announced, leaping from the tree branch.

"No Ryan! Please forget this idea," Maddy begged, "I don't like this pond, and you know there ain't any fish in it."

"You don't like any deep water."

"I sure don't like Crystal Pond. There's something strange about it, Ryan. We can easily go to the small pond in the back pasture. I don't mind fishing there."

"We can go there in a little while. Stop worrying. If you'd let me teach you to swim, then you wouldn't be so terrified of the water."

"I will…someday," she mumbled.

"I wish you'd come over here and look into the water!" he shouted climbing onto the sandy bank next to the clear water.

"No, I'm not getting near that water. I mean it, Ryan, I've always been told that there's something wrong with it."

"Don't be such a scaredy-cat. It's just water, very clear water. You'd think you could see to the bottom. I wonder how deep it is?"

"Too deep for me!" Maddy hollered back. "Ryan, let's go. I'm getting a weird feeling."

"You and your premonitions, I'm fine."

"Ryan, please, most of the time my feelings are dead on. Let's go! There've been too many little things happening. My shoestring broke, then I got a splinter in my finger, and the feed bucket had a hole in it. This bad feeling just won't go away. Let's get outta here."

"Not yet, you're being paranoid. That's all just coincidences. I'm going to put some weights on the end of the fishing line and see how deep the line goes."

"Ryan, stop being so stubborn!"

"In a minute," he insisted, positioning the grey weights on the fishing line and then casting it in. "Wow, I can't believe it. I didn't feel it hit bottom. I'm going to try a longer line."

"Ryan, quit playing around," Maddy continued to beg. "Let's go to the small pond; Daddy said the fish are biting there!"

"Just one more crack at it, and then we'll go."

The sand beneath Ryan began to shift. His body weaved back and forth. His cane pole flew up into the air and landed on top of the water, floating. Ryan's terrified eyes turned back to her and with an earsplitting yell, he bellowed, "MADDY!" As the word pierced the air, blood flowing from Ryan's face. He clawed air, and then suddenly dove supernaturally into the center of the pond.

Her screams echoed throughout the forest, as Maddy ran to the side of the pond. Getting on her knees, she waited for Ryan to emerge, but nothing. She kept screaming out for Ryan. She leaned over looking into the clear, blue water and scanned the motionless surface. She leaped to her feet and continued to scream for help. She jumped upon Wild Spice. Her voice resonated across the valley as she propelled the strong horse into a full gallop. She turned Wild Spice to the backfield where her father was working. Sandy and Jonas that had taken up residence in the field, barked as they ran after her through the tall grass. Her mind was in a dream state as she continued to call for help.

Jackson stopped the tractor when he saw her racing toward him. Maddy's voice stabbed the air. "Daddy!" she screamed, "Ryan needs your help! You need to get to Crystal Pond!"

"What?"

"Ryan was fishing on the bank of the Crystal Pond and fell in. We need to help him!"

"Ya ride back an' get John, an' I'll see what I can do!"

Her legs kicked Wild Spice; the horse raced across the pasture. Her daddy's old pickup's motor grunted and moaned as it struggled to turn over.

Maddy's heart was about to explode seeing the fence ahead and the gate that was a long way to her right. She kicked Wild Spice's side, and the strong mare leaped into the air landing on the other side of the fence. The Beardsley's farmhouse was straight ahead of her. Ryan's mom was bent over pulling weeds in the garden. She stood up when she heard Maddy shrieking.

Libby Beardsley, a slender woman wearing a flowered, cotton dress, wiped her dirty hands on her apron. The woman didn't move, standing there in a state of shock, staring at the wild girl on the horse coming directly at her.

"Where's Mr. Beardsley," Maddy shouted, "Ryan fell into Crystal Pond and hasn't come up!"

Maddy's eyes scanned the area seeing John Beardsley over by the barn running to her. "Ryan needs your help at Crystal Pond. Daddy's there. Hurry we need to get back!"

The horse's reins jerked in her hands as the horse whirled around, not waiting for an answer. John Beardsley jumped into his pickup truck spinning the truck in a half circle following the racing horse. Wild Spice took off through the pasture. The horse's nostrils flared. The fence was ahead. Maddy again kicked the horse's side, and Wild Spice, sensing Maddy's anxious aggression leaped into the air and landed smoothly on the other side of the fence. Maddy ducked her head trying to miss the low pecan limbs as the horse raced through the trees. She could see her father standing near the edge of the pond. His clothes were soaking-wet.

Jackson's head shook slowly no. "Honey, are ya sure Ryan fell into the water. He's one of the best swimmers I know of. Perhaps he's playing a trick on ya."

"No, Daddy, I saw his face when the sand on the bank gave way, and he was terrified. Maybe he hit his head. He did a nose dive right into the middle of the pond," she yelled slipping off Wild Spice's back hurrying to the side of the pond.

Ryan's dad pulled up to a stop and hurriedly exited the truck. When he heard Maddy's story, he pulled off his shoes and leaped into the water. Sirens blared in the quiet morning. Large trucks and rows of cars began to arrive. Many men along with John swam in the pond searching, but no sign of Ryan.

Libby walked up and wrapped her arms around Maddy. "Honey, Ryan will be fine. He has to be. A mother knows these things," she declared, hugging Maddy even tighter.

Sheriff Burkhart reached a hand over to John Beardsley and helped him out of the water. Sheriff Burkhart's baldhead shook no.

John's face was drained of color and his hands clinched nervously in a circle. His body moved slowly over to Maddy and Libby.

"Libby, I can't find Ryan. I'm sorry. The water's so deep I can't get to the bottom."

"Ryan!" Libby screamed her voice penetrated the humid air. She ran to the pond falling on her knees. John squatted by Libby. She whispered over and over, "Ryan, no."

"The sheriff and his men will keep searching, but," John's voice cracked, as his gripped tightened on the woman. "That pond is just," his head dipped, "to damn deep."

Tears dripped from Maddy's eyes. She darted to the pond sliding down on her knees. She leaned in touching the water, closer than she'd ever been. She wanted to dive in and follow Ryan, but before she could move, her father grabbed her shoulders.

"No, honey, that's not what Ryan would want," said Jackson gently pulling her up by him.

"Jackson," Sheriff Burkhart explained, "you take her home, and John you do the same with Libby. We'll let you know if we find anything." He shook his head to the two men. His grim eyes stared at Maddy. "They don't need to be here." He turned around and walked away.

Jackson held onto Maddy's shoulders and spun her around to face him.

"No Daddy, I won't leave," she gasped trying to get air. "I'm staying right here, I can't leave, no matter what."

"I have to stay too," Libby added holding onto John's arm, "she's right."

"Honey, I don't think it's a good idea for ya to stay," offered Jackson. "But, I won't make ya leave. While ya wait, ya need to sit in the shade of the old oak. It's cooler over there.

"Daddy, stop worrying. I won't jump into the water. I know it'd make Ryan furious. I promise, I won't get close to the pond."

Her feet shuffled kicking at the dirt and rocks as she moved over to the old oak. She sat on the large limb and gazed up into the tree watching the sun still flickering through the branches as if nothing had happened. However, her eyes were quickly pulled to the clear water of the pond. There to the side of the pond was the cane pole lying on the ground with its long line twisted around it. She closed her eyes. She could see Ryan laughing, trying to get the weights onto the line. How could a few seconds change everything?

John Beardsley walked up to the oak. "Maddy," he said in a quiet voice, "what was Ryan doing with the long line?"

"He wanted to see how deep the pond was so he was adding weights to the line when the sand gave way on the bank, and he lost his footing causing him to do a flip into the center of the water. I told him to stay away from the pond." She inhaled, trying to catch her breath. "But, he was too stubborn. I'm sorry, Mr. Beardsley," she sniffed. "I should've stopped him, now…."

"Sweetie, this isn't your fault. Ryan was strong minded and even you couldn't have stopped him." His voice got quiet. He slowly walked, shoulders hunched, back to Libby. Libby stood paralyzed staring into the pond's water, waiting for her son to climb out of the water.

Hours went by, nothing.

"John," Sheriff Burkhart began, "the pond is just too deep and even the divers can't get to the bottom. They aren't equipped to go that Gawd darn deep. I've never seen anything like it, but we won't give up until we find him."

The words pierced deep into Maddy's mind.

Night came and Maddy sat, not moving, not eating, not drinking, only waiting. Silent, Jackson and John stood over to the side of the pond, both realizing the truth. They stared into the clear water with the night growing darker and search lights illuminating, reflecting on the water.

Some of the women from town had shown up taking Libby home. She didn't need to be there when they found Ryan's body. Maddy ignored the women. She sat under the tree and her mind kept replaying Ryan plunging into the water, seeing the panic in his eyes when he looked back at her for the last time. It was a sight she'd never forget, a memory of Ryan's shouting out her name for help.

Maddy sat frozen and watched the men continue the search. She already knew the answer; they'd never find Ryan. Tears flowed for hours until it seemed there weren't anymore. The night moved on and the men continued to search without success. Finally, they gave up and packed their equipment. The long train of cars and trucks slowly disappeared leaving a silence that was deafening.

John patted Jackson on the back and both men looked at Maddy. "Sweetie," John began, "you need to go home with your daddy and get some rest. We don't want you to make yourself sick."

Her head shook no. She whispered, "I can't leave Ryan."

"Maddy, John's right, we need to get home, eat, an' rest a while. We'll come back, later." Jackson leaned near her, gently took Maddy's hand in his calloused hand, and pulling her up beside him. "Can ya ride Wild Spice, or do I need to tie her to the truck?" he questioned.

"I can ride her." The words softly uttered through the sniffs into the quiet night, as she put her foot in the stirrup. She looked over next to the old oak seeing Jet's dark head bent eating some grass. She gripped Wild Spice's mane in her hand. The horse spun around in a half circle galloping after the old pickup as it bounced on the worn trail.

Her head turned around and she took one more look at the pond. "Ryan, I'm sorry. I should've stopped you. I'll never forgive myself," she whispered out into the abyss.

Chapter 3
Coming Home

It was July 11th, 2000.

The days and years had crept by with unconsciousness. Maddy's mind was numb. She had no fear of dying, since she had died before. She didn't have a tombstone or grave like Ryan, but death had come to her just the same. It's not the pain of dying she feared, but the pain of living. That damn pond had taken a part of her soul just as it had taken so many other lives.

With the gas pedal flat to the floor, the old Mustang's motor whined. Maddy's fingers gripped the steering wheel tighter and tighter. The tall pines swished by as a blur. She could see the gravel road ahead to the left. Her foot pushed the brake, and the car slid to a stop on the pavement. Rocks and clouds of dust flew out from under the car as it traveled along the gravel road.

To the left of the road was the white, framed, 1800's farmhouse standing tall with a mighty oak shading it, a protector from the dust of the road. She let off the accelerator. One rule she never forgot was never create dust when driving up to the house. The car moaned as it crept slowly and pulled to a stop next to the twisted oak tree.

Maddy turned the motor off and climbed out of the car. She wiped the sweat growing on her brow with the sleeve of her shirt as she stared at the dust-covered car. She didn't move. Her breathing slowed hearing the serenading of birds and feeling the coolness of the shade of the old oak. Gradually, she made her way across the yard and placed her foot on the bottom step of the weathered front porch causing the old board to creak. Gordon T, her daddy's dog, lay to the side. He yawned, lifted his head, and then lay back down on the porch.

She smiled, leaned down, and stroked Gordon T on the head. Gently, she pulled the screen door open and closed it, not letting it slam. She stepped into the living room.

"Daddy, I'm home," hollered Maddy walking to the back of the home into the kitchen. The sweet smell of summer flowed from the vegetables cooking in pots on the burners of the gas stove. That smell always transported her back to a simpler time.

The kitchen door swung open and she stepped outside onto the back porch. There in the vegetable garden stood Jackson Sayers. His overalls were faded, not fastened square in the front, and his wild, white hair stuck up from bending over, picking vegetables, and pulling weeds. His tattered basket, bent on one side from years of use, was sitting on the ground overflowing with produce that he'd just picked. His eyes squinted from the evening sun as he looked up. Creases appeared around his eyes when a smile emerged on his dry wrinkled face.

"Honey, I didn't hear your car. Ya must've come in slow."

"Yes, I did, just like you told me to. How ya doing, Daddy?"

"Fair to meddling, I guess. The days seem longer and my bones seem to get worn-out faster, but not bad for an old man." He lifted the basket balancing it on his arm. He leaned over, wrapped his free arm around Maddy, and they stepped upon the porch leading into the kitchen.

"Got some nice looking tomatoes and peppers from the garden," he announced, setting the basket on the round, pedestal, oak table. He washed his hands and dried them on a worn kitchen towel. "The corn'll be coming in soon."

"You sure are cooking a lot for one person?"

"Not one, two," he said caringly, smiling at her.

"Is there something you should tell me?"

"Honey, I knew ya were coming home today."

"I didn't call to tell you."

"Honey," he paused, looking over at her, "you've not missed one year."

"Am I that obvious?"

"Yep, it's not healthy. Ya need to move on."

"Daddy…I can't."

"Supper'll be ready in a little while. I've gotta heat the oven and put some cornbread on to bake."

She stood holding onto the screen door. "Daddy, I won't be gone long."

"Ya be careful out there in the back pasture. There've been a few more snakes around this summer."

"I'll be fine," Maddy assured staring back into the kitchen. "I've got my gun."

"Yep, I forgot. Ya know it's hard to think of my little girl carrying her own pistol all the time."

"Daddy!"

"I know, but still…be careful." He moaned when he bent over in front of the stove, striking a match, and lighting the oven to preheat.

Maddy stepped outside onto the back porch and took in a deep breath of fresh country air accented by pine needles being warmed by the hot summer sun. She darted along the worn path to the barn, leaped up on the fence railing, and climbed over. She whistled for Nutmeg, her horse for eight years, a blend of Wild Spice and Jet. The strong horse trotted from the backside of the pasture toward her and quickly nudged her with its head before they went to the barn.

Maddy placed the saddle on the russet horse's back and led her back out into the sunshine. She leaped upon Nutmeg and gave the horse a kick. Nutmeg didn't hesitate galloping through the group of pecan trees, past a herd of cattle, to the gnarled oak tree.

Old feelings ignited in Maddy, ones that she'd tried to keep hidden. She jumped from the horse and Nutmeg's head bent to the ground to eat fresh grass.

By habit, Maddy's hands grabbed the lower limb of the gnarled oak and she began to climb limb after limb until she got to the one limb, the perfect limb, their limb. She scooted in close to the trunk of the tree pushing the Spanish moss to the side.

Her eyes froze as she peered downward and her heart started pounding in her chest. There, lying in front of her so calm, so clear, was the water; the water she hated with every inch of her being.   She continued to stare deep into the water. The cold, cruel water, the water that'd shattered her world.

The scream from the past made her body shudder as it echoed in her mind. Ryan calling her name was just as crisp and clear as that day so long ago. Her hands gripped the bark of the tree.

The tears had long been gone, but the pain, the anger had built over the years. Her daddy had always felt it was the reason she'd became a special agent with the FBI. He worried, believing the anger inside of her was going to take over. Maybe it already had. She took too many risks on and off her job.

The fury of that day so long ago burned in her mind, but a strong breeze touched her face, calming her. She reached up pushing her long hair from her eyes and then noticed red dripping from her hands. The bark had eaten into the palms of her hands, and she hadn't even felt the pain. She quickly wiped the blood onto her jeans and the trunk of the tree. She shivered and broke out into a cold sweat.

Her body jerked when she heard the rattling and roar of her daddy's old pickup. The sound transported her thoughts back from the past, away from the thoughts of eleven years ago; her eternity… her hell!

Her eyes moved back to the clear water and fixated on the surface. She knew that she had to reclaim her life. How was she to take back all those years that the pond had stolen from her? The torment of that day, the day she lost her heart, her existence. The day she had lost Ryan had devoured her soul.

The truck door swung open. "Maddy, it has been way over an hour."

"Sorry, Daddy, time must have slipped by."

She jumped to the ground and landing by her father. She quickly positioned her bleeding hands behind her back

He reached over pulling her hands around in front of her. "Honey, this has to stop."

"I guess I was gripping the tree's bark too tight. It isn't that bad."

"C'mon you've been out here long enough. Say what ya need to say and come on home."

She nodded her head yes. Most would think the crystal water beautiful, but to her it looked like the door to hell. She heard the truck's door close and knew her dad would sit waiting. She gripped her cut hands into tight fists and moved over by the pond searching the water as it lay so calm, looking so innocent. But, Maddy knew the truth, it was horrific.

Her head dropped. "Ryan, I'm sorry!" she exclaimed. "I'm so sorry."

She turned around grabbing the reins of Nutmeg climbing upon the saddle. She didn't move for a few seconds and took one more look at the pond.

"Maddy, let's go. It's getting late."

The truck motor moaned as it started. Then they headed down the trail out through the pasture with the horse following. Maddy finally relaxed. She was home, the only place she could find some peace.

The pain of not knowing what happened to Ryan so long ago was consuming her. That pond! Could she really settle the score and find the secret it held or was the pond going to prevail, just as it had with Ryan?"

Chapter 4
A Whisper in the Wind

After supper, Maddy gently pushed open the wooden screen door and stepped out onto the front porch. She watched the sun dropping, disappearing into the west making splashes of colors shooting up from the horizon as dusk descended upon the farm. She moved by habit over to the swing that was hanging at the end of the porch, her favorite spot. Her body stiffened hearing a soft whisper blowing in the breeze. It was if it someone was calling her name, but she knew her imagination was playing tricks again with her mind. It was Ryan's voice that she was remembering, the way he said her name. No one had ever said her name with so much passion.   But, the sound of his screaming her name started repeating in her mind and wouldn't go away.

Gordon T came from around the house and up the porch's steps. Gordon T, named for one of Jackson's old friends from his army days, was a true mutt, a mixture of Sandy, Maddy's Golden Retriever, and Ryan's old hound dog, Jonas. He had long ears and wasn't very tall, the runt of the litter, but Jackson had fallen for him. The dog unhurriedly moved by the front railing, not ever getting in a rush. The dog spun slowly to lie down on the cool porch.

Maddy, now twenty-six years old, had grown up living in this old farmhouse with her father, Jackson Elijah Sayers. She had become a FBI agent a few years ago, and now lived in Washington, DC. But each July eleventh, she had to come home. Losing Ryan had eaten away at her. For some reason, she was drawn back to the old pond. Something, or maybe someone, was tugging at her heart to find reasons for Ryan's demise, and she couldn't let go until she found answers.

The screen door screeched and Jackson stepped outside onto the porch, letting the door close softly. "Nice night. I turned on the attic fan and opened the windows in your bedroom. I hope it'll be fine. I know you're used to the air conditioning in the city."

"It'll be great. I love the sound of the big fan and feeling the fresh, cool, country air. Daddy, don't worry so."

He moaned as he sat in one of the worn rockers. "I guess ya know me as well as I know ya." Gordon T stretched, getting up from the porch floor moving over to the tired man. Jackson took the old dog's head in his hands. "I guess we're the end of the line ole boy."

"Daddy, stop it."

"I figure with you living in the city and John and Libby getting rid of Ryan's old hound dog's pups, I suppose there won't be any more of us old dogs around."

"Daddy, it's not that bad, and you know that's just hog wash. Now, I'd like to stay a couple of weeks…if you don't mind? I have some vacation time coming."

"Honey, this is your place. Ya can stay as long as ya want."

Maddy leaned her head against the back of the swing letting her toes gently push the swing back and forth. "I forgot how bright the moon and stars are out here. Back in DC, all the city's lights make the stars fade away."

"It does seem brighter tonight. Maybe it's having ya home."

"Well, Daddy, stop worrying about this place. Even if I don't live here all the time I'd never sell it. This farm will be ours, forever."

"I see." Jackson slowed the rocker and leaned over. "It's the cemetery out in the back pasture, and ya ain't gonna let your mama down."

"I guess you do know me very well."

"I should. You're so like me. Katy always said ya were me made over, so stubborn and strong minded with so much determination. Your mama sure was just so kind."

"I still miss Mama too. She kept me calm and safe," added Maddy taking in a deep breath, "something difficult for me," she sighed, "now, anyway."

"Yep, she knew how to take care of us both, just the right thing to say," he agreed. His head ducked and his old hand reached over petting Gordon T. "She shor' loved life and also loved each summer going to

Charleston and the beach," he said. "I shor' do miss those trips ever' summer."

"I loved going to the beach, too. We did have a lot of fun. Mama used to take walks out on the beach with me, knowing how scared of the water I was. She kept telling me the water wasn't my enemy, fear was. I wasn't afraid of anything, except deep water.

He pushed his hair back with his hand, a habit he was always doing when he was nervous. "I know and I blame myself for ya being scared."

"Why would you blame yourself?"

"That episode when ya were six scared ya to death and ya never got over it."

"Yep, Rufus Jones is an idiot and he sure doesn't want to get around me now."

"He's married with a slew of kids and lives on the old family farm down the road, but he won't come around ya, not now…if he's smart," he added, laughing. "He's been getting himself into trouble lately, still not very bright. I don't trust that boy. Ya know, he's gotta lot of meanness in him."

"Ryan did get Rufus good that day. He was always protecting me," said Maddy squeezing her lips together, her voice faded into silence.

His eyes peered up at her. "I hadn't yet," said Jackson shaking his head back and forth, "seen so much blood coming from a small nose ever in my life. Rufus bled like a stuck pig."

"I won't ever forget that Fourth of July picnic," she began. "All of us kids were having fun playing by the old city creek. I squatted next to the water to pick up a shiny rock to give to Ryan. You know, he was always collecting rocks."

"Yep, he shor' was."

"Someone hit me in the back and the next thing I knew I was under the water sinking deeper and deeper. I couldn't breathe. I panicked until I felt a hand on me, pulling me up to the surface.

I gasped getting some air, seeing Ryan holding onto me." Her eyes looked at her daddy. "Then you grabbed me lifting me out of the creek.

"I won't ever forget that day." His hands twisted fretfully in a washing movement. "Ya were like a wide-eyed, wet dog."

"I stood there cold and shivering even in the warm sun. Ryan climbed out of the water and stepped up to Rufus. Even though Rufus towered over Ryan, Ryan punched him square in the nose; blood flew everywhere."

"I remember…I held onto ya taking ya over to your mama. I shor' was proud of Ryan. Rufus, Sr. stood up, a giant just as his son, but I put a stop to him going after Ryan. Telling him in front of the town how his son had pushed my six-year-old girl into the creek. John stepped in front of Ryan and me and the Jones family packed up and left, but not without leaving ya scarred, terrified of water."

"Mom was so mad. I'd never heard her cuss before. I guess she was more of a fighter than I thought."

"Katy wouldn't let anyone get the best of her or her family. She had a way of getting ya good, but ya didn't know what was happening until she was finished. She did have spunk." He laughed, bent his head staring at the old plank boards of the porch.

"I miss her so much."

"It's hard to believe it's been fourteen years."

"I know, Daddy."

He smoothed his hair back and stood from the rocker with tears brimming in his eyes, trying inconspicuously to wipe them. "I'm tired. I'll see ya in the morning, honey. It's good having ya back where you belong."

Maddy's toes slid on the grey painted, porch floor stopping the wicker swing and going to her daddy. Her head leaned against the old man's chest. She could smell his aftershave, Old Spice, the one he'd used her entire life. "Good night, Daddy."

"It's nice to have ya home, honey," he said gently patting her on the back.

"It's nice to be home."

Jackson pulled open the door and Gordon T strolled over next to the white haired man going into the house, their routine each night.

Maddy wrapped her arms around the large pillar on the end of the porch feeling the coolness of the night air. The full moon beamed on the old weathered barn with its gray cedar shingles.

She closed her eyes and remembered so many good times from the past. A light wind touched her face. She could hear Ryan's laughter as he ran ahead of her to the barn that July day.

No, she'd never sell the old farm. This place kept her memories alive, good and bad. The grandfather clock in the living room bonged ten o'clock telling her it was time for some rest. She let her arms fall from the post.

The wooden front door closed, and she made her way up the stairs. She lifted her suitcase onto her bed and felt the breeze coming from the attic fan blowing her hair. Her suitcase didn't contain much, jeans, shorts, tops, bras, panties, and only a little makeup. Since she was a teenager Ryan had told her not to wear makeup, always saying what he thought that she was pretty and didn't need any of that stuff.

She went into the bathroom and slipped her t-shirt and shorts off. The hot water warmed the room as she pushed the colorful fish-pattered shower curtain back, the one she'd picked out from a catalog when she was eleven. She slid deep into the water massaging her sore muscles. Her hands stung from their cuts as she rubbed the shampoo into her long hair. Reluctantly, she stepped out of the tub. She shivered. The attic fan had cooled the home bringing in the damp night air. She dried her straight body and stared into the mirror. She wasn't very tall, about five foot six, and she'd hoped that when she grew older, her body would become curvier, but it never happened. She was stuck with a slat-like figure.

She gazed back in the mirror with a cold glare. She finally smiled, but her eyes stayed emotionless. She could see her face was like her mama's, round with a small nose covered in freckles, a daily reminder of her mother. She may act like her daddy, but she sure looked like her mama. Except, her mama's hair had more red, making her mama seem even more head strong with that fiery temper. Maddy knew her mama kept this old farm running. Katy took care of her husband and made him think he was in charge, but she really was. It was the same for Maddy. She had always thought she was the pig headed one, but Ryan was their leader, keeping the two on the right path most of the time. She brushed her long, thick hair letting it fall down her back.

She switched on the lamp on the nightstand. Sitting on her dresser was the small, wooden music box, a gift from Ryan for her fifteenth birthday. Her fingers wound the key on the back.

The music box, with its tiny painting on the inside of wild flowers blooming on a sloping hillside, began to play and she quietly sang along with the music. She caressed the box letting the music fade. Carefully, she set it back in its place of honor on the dresser.

Clicking off the lamp, Maddy noticed how brightly the moonlight shined in. The curtains danced around the window because of the attic fan, so Maddy could see out into the night. Crickets chirped, a lone owl hooted, but there weren't any sirens, horns honking, or jets roaring like in DC. Tranquility and Mother Nature were doing the talking, but sleep wasn't coming. Her head leaned on the headboard.

"Ryan," she said softly into the dark night, "I miss you." She smiled. She could hear his voice gently calling back to her. "Good night, Maddy."

The pillow caressed her head and she thought of those teasing eyes. Ryan's zest for life was unending, until…that damn pond entered into their lives.

A breeze coming from the window hit her in the face. Tears gently flowed. Tears that hadn't fallen in years spilled from her eyes. She looked at the picture sitting on the dresser. The one taken of her and Ryan, the April when she'd turned fifteen. Ryan's eyes stared at her from the picture not helping her move on. It was as if his eyes were trying to tell her a secret.

It'd been eleven years since that July day, but it felt like yesterday. The search and rescue teams never found Ryan's body or any sign of him in the pond. It was, as he would say, an enigma. Maybe if there had been some closure then she might have moved on. All the men in town still talk about Unktehi Pond. At least for the last century, folklore about the pond kept many people believing a water spirit was hidden inside, a monster eating the poor souls who fell in.

John and Libby Beardsley had a memorial for Ryan at the old Baptist Church in town and everyone in the county came to say their condolences. Most of the people were shocked that a young boy like Ryan could drown in a pond. "So sad," many of the older women said, shaking their heads with empathy. Everyone stared at Maddy, and she felt like they all believed it was her fault. If she'd known how to swim, she could've saved him just as he'd saved her so long ago at the picnic in town by the creek. Jackson tried along with John and Libby to tell her it wasn't her fault, she had to live her life, and keep the good memories of Ryan alive. But, nothing seemed to help, except time.

Her mind wouldn't allow her to imagine a life without Ryan. In the beginning, she'd felt she had abandoned Ryan, not saving him. As time moved on, however, her feelings reversed. She felt that he'd abandoned her leaving her with a void in her heart that just could not be filled.

Time had taken some of the sting away and some of the guilt, but the anger of not knowing what happened haunted her. Her life has been an emotional rollercoaster wrenching at her insides. It was a vicious cycle, she was sad, angry, and then sad again, but now anger was building again.

She remembered the stories her Grandpa Winfred told of so many people drowning in the clear water of Crystal Pond, but never finding any bodies. With an investigation, she'd have to relive the pain time and again of seeing Ryan falling into the pond. If it meant a conclusion of what really happened to Ryan, she'd confront her memories and conquer her fears. She was a trained investigator with the Bureau and she should be able to find closure for herself. She wanted her life back.

Her eyes pulled to the open window. She bit her lip, a bad habit she had started after her mama died. The moonlight illuminated the yard. Her mind started playing a movie of Ryan in full color making her feel fifteen again. She gripped her cut hands bringing reality back. Then, she heard Ryan whisper her name in the breeze. Her stomach tightened. She knew her imagination was growing with so many reminders of Ryan around her, but maybe finding out the truth about that awful day would bring peace to them both. Tomorrow she'd begin her search for the answers she needed.

Chapter 5
Memories

The morning came and with it new questions. Maddy climbed out of bed, pulled on her navy shorts, and a top with the words FBI across her chest. She could hear Jackson keeping busy clanking pots in the kitchen. Losing Katy and then Ryan wore on the man. He was so energetic, but the deaths made him older than his years. The comforting aroma of fried bacon and fresh biscuits saturated the air, embraced Maddy's senses, and brought a calming flood of memories to her.

She swung the bathroom door open, retrieved a washcloth from the cabinet, and washed her face. Her eyes looked expressionless. Her entire demeanor lacked compassion. She hadn't loved anyone since Ryan. She'd dated and even been engaged once, but it was all a farce. She had been going through the motions and trying to do what she thought everyone expected of her.

Her bed-head, red hair was finally detangled and she laid the hairbrush next to the sink. She twirled her hair on top of her head and used a black clip to hold it up.

She raced down the stairs. "Good morning, Daddy," she called out going into the kitchen. "It sure smells good in here, but you're cooking too much."

"Gnaw, your mama always said we needed a good breakfast to start the day off right and I ain't gonna let her down now. How many eggs ya want, they're fresh this morning?"

"One is all I'll need, with biscuits and bacon."

"How did ya sleep last night," he asked, sitting across from her seeing her swollen eyes.

"I slept great; the cool air was so refreshing."

"Uh um," he said as he scooped the last of his egg with his biscuit letting honey ooze out onto his plate. He knew better; her memories weren't letting her sleep. "What do ya want to do today?"

"Mama had some old boxes full of papers about the farm that she showed me when I was little. I think some of Grandpa Winfred's papers. I thought I might go through them, just curious."

"I ain't thrown anything of your mama's out, so you're welcome to go through her things." Jackson anxiously rubbed his hair. "I think it's time."

"You really don't mind, do you?"

"No, honey, they're your things now. I just couldn't do anything with them. I have some work out in the back pasture," he said closing the dishwasher's door. "A fence post has cracked and needs to be replaced."

"Do you need any help?"

"Nope, not with just one post, and then I need to check on the cows back there and be sure none of them have gotten out."

"I can help around here. I do know some about taking care of a farm."

"How about ya seeing to the horses, the trough out from the barn; the one in the corner has been losing its water and we need to be sure it's full. I plugged it the other day, but I haven't had time to check it."

"I'll make sure it's holding."

Jackson stood wiping his hands fretfully on the dishtowel. "Honey, your mama's things are still in her closet; I packed everything and slid the items inside. They haven't been touched in years."

"I'll find them," she called out as she went out the back door. She stepped off the back porch feeling the sun hitting her face. The air smelled of warm dirt and fresh vegetables from the garden. The tomato vines were pungent as she came near, seeing them overflowing with tiny green balls and many red ones that were ready to pick.

The two lawn chairs with chipped green paint and worn, white, metal arms sat under the old maple tree waiting for someone to sit in them just like Ryan did that July morning. The clothesline sagged in the center with a stick propping it up in the middle. Maddy stopped walking and closed her eyes. Her mind replayed her mama singing in the early morning sun as she'd shake the wet clothes from the basket, and then she'd skillfully drape them over the clothesline.

Maddy's life was simple when she was young, so carefree. She'd climb up into a freshly painted lawn chair and help her mom by shelling peas. Her afternoons would be full with Ryan, who was always thinking of so many escapades: building forts in the back pasture, riding horses, and going on wild safaris, something new each day. But today, she had a water plug to check.

She swung open the barn door and hurried through to the corral. The trough behind the barn was full of water, the plug had held. Nutmeg came running from the back of the pasture ready for a ride. The horse nudged her.

"Okay, I know what you have in mind. Let me see if Dad left you anything in the barn bin."

The horse nudged her again as Maddy stepped back inside the barn to check the bin.

"You're in luck, Nutmeg. Dad has some nice carrots for you and the others."

She fed each of the horses one by one. However, one old horse stood in the back of the pasture not moving.

Maddy leaped over the railed fence running to the horse near the back fence. The big brown eyes of the light auburn horse stared at her. "Good morning, Wild Spice," Maddy called out, reaching her arms around the horse's head. She leaned in handing the horse the last carrot. Maddy's hands continued to rub the old horse lovingly with memories flowing of how the horse, that hot July day, had jumped the fence both times with ease. Wild Spice was not trained to jump; the horse just intuitively knew the urgency that Maddy was feeling and did what needed to be done. The horse's mane was silky, without tangles. Maddy understood that her daddy still brushed and babied the horse, his pride and joy. This was his other girl, born the same year as Maddy. Both, so beautiful and strong minded.

Time passed quickly and she finished adoring the horses and some chores in the barn. Maddy made her way to the farmhouse; another mission to work on. She pulled open the kitchen screen door.

She stepped inside but didn't move. There on the kitchen floor was dirt left by someone who had tracked it inside, another rule never to break. She could see the leftover food from breakfast on the kitchen table was gone.

"Daddy," she called out. Hearing a creaking noise, she unclipped her gun that was hanging on her waist and cautiously walked into the living room. She turned around. Her eyes peered down at the carpet seeing the dirty tracks were going up the stairs. She hurriedly climbed the stairs and checked each bedroom. Nothing, it was quiet. She slipped her gun back into its holster. Some vagrant had been in the old farmhouse, an on-going problem with living out in the country and leaving doors unlocked. She washed her hands in the bathroom and rushed into her parent's bedroom.

Nervously, her hands twisted together, so many memories today. There, to the side by the front window was a small dresser with a flowerily stool slid underneath. Maddy closed her eyes. She could see her mama so clearly in her mind sitting on that stool and combing her hair. Her mama would motion to Maddy to sit by her, and then she would take Maddy's long hair in her hand and gently brush it, making Maddy feel like a princess.

Maddy took in a deep breath and turned the closet doorknob. In front of her were her mama's clothes hanging in the closet just the same as they had that inconsolable day in May. Maddy was only twelve years old the day she and her daddy picked out a special dress for her mama to be buried in.

She slid a shoebox from the top shelf and sat down on the bed with it. The lid lifted off, the shoebox was full of all of her mama's jewelry. She lifted a small, black, velvet box out of the container and slowly opened it. Inside the tiny box was her mama's wedding ring. That must have been such a final act for her dad, a realization his wife was gone. Maddy snapped the tiny box shut, put it back in the container, positioned the lid back on the shoebox, and slid it back onto the shelf. Her trembling hands picked up the next shoebox.

The lid of the other shoebox opened and it was piled full of pictures of her mother, her baby pictures, and other family members' photographs along with Christmas and birthday pictures with Ryan. She pulled the box to her, hugging it. Those pictures she wanted to keep out, so she sat the shoebox on the bed.

She got on her knees in front of the closet and could see a small blue box was nestled in the back of the closet. She lifted up the lid. The stale scent of old papers flowed in the air. Cards and letters were in this one, all of the mother's day cards she had given her mama along with anniversary cards her daddy had given her. Old letters her mama had saved from her family, cousins, Aunt Karen, her mama's sister who lived in Charleston, and friends her mama had grown up with. The letters were stacked in neat bundles tied in soft blue ribbons. She smiled; her mama never had a chance to use email. *People now don't have these kinds of memories,* she thought to herself. They'd all be saved in cold, stark, computer files, not hand written letters lying in an old blue box in a closet waiting for the next generation to find. She pushed the box behind her as she slid out another box covered in purple velvet. She heaved a sigh. This box had letters tied together in purple ribbon. They were all from her daddy when he was in the army. Her parents were not married then. Love letters? Probably. She'd never read them, not yet. She felt intrusive; these were her mama and daddy's memories, not hers.

She scooted the purple box back into the closet and began to dig deeper. There in the very back of the closet was her mama's wedding dress. Maddy pulled it out into the light. She held up the satin and lace dress in front of her and stared into the mirror on the back of the door. She spun around in a circle letting the bottom of the dress flow. Then, she carefully spread the beautiful dress covered in soft, white, tiny pearls upon the bed.

She crouched in front of the closet and stuck her head deep into the bottom of the closet. One more box, a little bigger than the others, had been pushed to the very back. She tugged on the white box until she could see inside. It was stuffed full of papers, birth certificates, her mama and daddy's wedding license, so many important papers. She lifted the old documents out of the box. Her head moved back and forth. No, not what she was looking for.

She kept digging through the pile of newspaper clippings and such. She lifted up one more envelope and took in a deep sigh. There lying at the bottom of the box was a large manila envelope with the name Winfred Sayers written across the middle in black magic marker. She scooped the envelope from the box and leaned back against the foot of the bed. Her fingers unhooked the clip on the envelope, and she carefully handled the papers, newspaper clippings, and notes. As she started reading headlines from the old clippings, her heart started beating faster.

She was correct. She had remembered the stories about Crystal Pond that Grandpa Winfred had told. Article after article of yellowed newspaper clippings continued with stories of so many people that'd just disappeared into Crystal Pond. The stories were the same; none of the bodies were ever recovered. How could that be? Why didn't each person just swim out of the pond like her daddy and all the others who searched for Ryan? Why didn't Ryan just swim out?

As she read and reread the articles, she found the same story with different victims. Each person had lunged into the pond hitting the water hard or had fallen into the water without being able to swim, which logically meant the bodies had gone to the bottom of the pond. They weren't like her father or the other men swimming around. But, most drowning victims float to the top of the water eventually. Ryan had dived into the center of the pond and wasn't able to come up quickly. What could be at the bottom of the pond? She sighed. Maybe, some kind of quicksand was clinging and hanging onto its prey. She shuddered with the thought of Ryan stuck on the bottom of the pond in the thick sand, fiercely fighting to free himself. But, he'd screamed out her name before he went under.

"I see ya found the papers and other things," a caring voice from the doorway startled her.

"Yes," Maddy answered looking up at her daddy.

"Oh," the man took in a long sighed. He walked into the room with his eyes fixated on the wedding dress lying on the bed. "Your mama was beautiful that day, and I sure was a lucky man," he added reaching up smoothing his white hair.

"I'm going to get a nice bag to keep the dress in, one that won't let it yellow anymore."

"It'd be nice if ya would use it someday. I'm not getting any younger, and some grandkids would be fun."

"Daddy, that's not gonna happen…at least not for a while."

"Well, an old man can wish, can't he? Ah, some pictures, what ya going to do with them?"

"I want to put them in a nice photo album for safe keeping."

"Sounds like a lot of work."

"It'll be worth it."

"What's in the large white box?"

"Oh, this box is full of birth certificates and important papers. I'm going to get a small safe and put them in."

"There's more," he said ducking his head at her, "than certificates in that box. That's the papers ya're looking for?"

"Yes, I found this large envelope in that white box. It's Grandpa Winfred's papers about all the drownings."

"Yes, Papa was always worried about Crystal Pond and said it was really the devil's pond. I always felt like he knew the secret about the pond, but he'd never say."

"I remember he forbid me to ever go near it. I just wished I'd listened. Daddy, I've been thinking and I believe the pond has some quicksand at the bottom trapping people in it."

"You might have something there. Don't know, but many people have disappeared in its waters, just vanished." Jackson's eyes continued to stare at the white dress. His lips squeezed together. "I remember Papa was curious of why Jacob Carson sold this farm to our family. It really worried him. There's a paper somewhere in that pile about the sale."

"What in the world did the article say?"

"Not shor', but Jacob Carson was almost willing to give the land away. He called the land, Satan's torture. He'd already moved his family from the land and didn't want to come back here. The transaction, I think, is in the box somewhere in that stack of papers."

"Here, this is it." She began to read the small piece of paper. "Wow, Jacob Carson traded this land for two strong horses and a wagon, nothing else."

"I told you. Papa was always curious why a man would leave everything he and generations of his family had worked for and just up and go," Jackson anxiously rubbing his forehead. "Very strange."

"I agree. I wonder why the man left in such a hurry."

"I think it had to do with the pond. Maddy, I don't like that pond and ya stay away from it. I mean it. That pond isn't safe and Papa knew it. He told me the same thing and forbade me to go near it."

"I won't let it take me. Don't start worrying."

"I'm getting hungry." Jackson turned around going to the bedroom door.

"Daddy, someone was in the house this morning when we were out doing chores."

"Yep, I saw the footprints. I've had some eggs and a few leftovers missing along with milk from the refrigerator. We do get drifter's once and a while"

"Anything else missing?"

"I can't find my paring knife."

"The small one you always keep sharp?"

"Yep, but I haven't noticed much else: a few magazines, books, and papers from the living room have gone missing, and some volumes from that old set of encyclopedias. Really odd, a drifter who's a reader."

Both chuckled at the thought of a scholarly drifter. Most just worried about where the next meal would come from.

"All the same, you need to be careful, Daddy."

"Don't worry about me. I've messed with hobos for years; they'll eventually leave. Let's eat."

"Okay, I'm going to put the dress in my room. I'll be down in a few minutes."

"Alright," he called out, "how about a BLT for lunch?"

"Yes, that sounds good. With fresh tomatoes, of course," she called back in a hopeful voice. Then she moaned and puckered her lips at the mess she had made. She slid the other boxes across the floor back into the closet and closed door.

She could hear her daddy's boots clomping down the stairs. She panned the room and softy whispered, "Goodbye, Mama."

Maddy lay the wedding dress over her arm and carefully carried it to her bedroom. Then, she clutched the shoebox containing the pictures and Grandpa Winfred's envelope in her arms and dashed down the stairs to the living room.

To prepare for her investigation she had a lot of work ahead and was determined the pond was going to tell its secret. It wasn't winning this time.

Chapter 6
Sherriff Jameson

She pushed the kitchen chair back from the table. "That sandwich was great," she said licking her lips. "Those tomatoes…ooh; they tasted so good."

"What are ya going to do this afternoon?" her daddy questioned.

"I thought I'd drive into town and talk to the sheriff. Who is the sheriff now?"

"Johnny Jameson, didn't ya go to school with him?"

"Yep, he was a year older than Ryan and he and Ryan were good friends."

"He just got elected last year, so he's new. I think he might be able to help ya. I still don't know what you're looking for?"

"I don't either, Daddy, just some answers."

She put her plate in the sink playing in the sudsy water. Her shoulders squeezed together and she suddenly felt stress cinch up her neck.

Jackson moved over by her placing his hands on her shoulders. He patted her gently. "Honey, someday ya gotta let this go. I know how hard it is to move on, but ya are young and ya got your entire life ahead of ya. Ryan wouldn't like ya spending all ya time thinking about that accident. It's eating at ya, and it's not healthy."

"I just need to do some checking. Then, I promise to let it go."

"I hope so. I'll see ya later. I'm going to sit outside on the front porch with Gordon T and rest for a spell. It's a lot cooler out there."

"I won't be gone long," she assured, giving her daddy a hug.

She closed the bathroom door and placed the cool wet rag on her warm face. She stared into the mirror and unclipped her hair letting it fall onto her shoulders. She slipped on her jeans, clipped her badge and gun onto her belt, and picked up her car keys. The screen door squeaked when she swung it open, holding it not letting it slam.

"Bye, Daddy, see you in a little while," she called out hopping off the porch's steps.

The red mustang convertible backed out moving slow down the dirt road. The car stopped at the end of the dirt road and turned onto the payment. Her foot pressed the gas pedal flat to the floor making the car zoom along the long country road. She pushed the button on the radio and KBHC came on. Her head tilted back against the headrest and she started singing along with the old country song. Her face tingled from the heat of the sun and the warm wind blew her hair. The music flowed as the car bounced across the railroad tracks. Pulling up to the stop light in the small town of Pine Grove, South Carolina, she saw the familiar Piggly Wiggly on the right and the post office building on the left. Things hadn't changed in this small town in fifty years. The traffic light dangling on the wire across the road turned green and she turned right, headed to the sheriff's office. She really didn't know what she was looking for or how she would explain herself to Johnny.

Maddy pulled into the parking lot, shifted the car to park, and turned the motor off. The music died. She pulled the office door open, walked into the air-conditioned splendor, and over to a desk in the middle of the room. She stared. "Jennie Sue?" Maddy questioned.

"Yes, can I help you?" The girl with frosted blonde hair looked up. "Oh, Maddy, I haven't seen you in a while. How you doing?"

"I'm doing fine. I was wondering if the sheriff could see me this afternoon. I know I should've called and made an appointment."

"I'll see. This isn't police business, is it; I did hear you were working for the FBI."

"No, I just want to talk to him for a minute. Nothing that important."

"Just a moment," assured Jennie Sue walking to an office in the back of the building.

Maddy wandered around the large room seeing trophies that little leagues had won at the ballpark and pictures hanging on the walls of all the sheriffs over the years. Her eyes were pulled to a picture, that of Sheriff Burkhart, a face she'd never forget. So many people had been affected by Ryan's death. She recalled those bluish gray eyes so grim with so much anguish telling John and Libby that his police department couldn't find their son and that he was calling off the search for the body.

"Maddy Sayers, now this is a surprise! Do I have it right? You want to see me? Maybe you want to join a real law enforcement agency," a tall, hefty, young man said jokingly walking into the main room.

"Hi, Johnny! As much as Dad would like for me to stay here, I'm not leaving the Bureau. Not yet, anyway."

Maddy could see the boy from her youth in the man standing in front of her. He had curly, reddish-blond hair that was beginning to gray around the edges. She smiled that he had more freckles than she did.

Johnny was about six feet three inches tall, thick shoulders and chest, a true football player. Her mind wondered thinking about Ryan. He'd be a man now just as Johnny and might even have some gray hair mixed in his hair. He'd be a little shorter, and she was sure not as husky as Johnny.

"C'mon back to my office. Now, what is it that you need from me?" Johnny said interrupting her thoughts.

"I've been doing some research on Unktehi Pond, and I wanted to see if you could pull up some police reports of all the accidents that occurred out there over the years."

"Maddy, not the old Crystal Pond," Johnny said with his head ducked. "Ryan." His head shook. "My gosh, I still miss him."

"There's never been any conclusion about what happened back then, so I decided to see what I could find. I'm here on vacation for a couple of weeks and I just wanted to do some checking. It's no big thing. It's just nagging at me."

"You could've had the Bureau dig up the old files."

"I know, but I didn't want to involve them."

"But, you will if you need to. Right? The info I have is right here at my fingertips; everything is on the computer. I'll do some checking and let you know what I find. I agree the whole episode about Ryan was strange. He was so strong and could out swim me for sure. Maybe it's time we all knew the answer. I'll help you however I can."

"Thanks Johnny. How have you been doing?"

"Well, I married Paula Owens and we have two boys and a little girl on the way, and I did get elected sheriff, not bad I guess. How's your Daddy doing? I see him once in a while at church, but not often."

"He's getting around pretty good, stays way too busy working on the farm, but maybe that's a good thing."

"He was our Boy Scout leader when we were kids and he was always coming up with fun things to do." Johnny's face turned redder making his freckles brighter. "I'm the Boy Scout leader now and I'm trying to copy your Dad. You know, I need to get out there sometime and talk to him."

"Oh, he'd like that."

"We'll see what we can turn up. Maddy, it's nice to have you home and if we have any problems around here, I may be calling on you to help." Johnny smiled.

"Sure, I'd be glad to help. Here, this is my cell phone number and you've got Daddy's number. If you need me, my email address is on the card. Thanks for helping." Maddy stood from the small leather chair. "Bye, Johnny. Give my best to Paula."

The desk chair rolled back and Johnny moved around to the front of the desk. "No, problem, I'll be in touch. Bye, Maddy," he said anxiously rubbing his temple as if he might be getting a headache.

She could see the expression on his face, sadness. She'd brought up a lot of memories from his past. He was another victim of Crystal Pond.

"Bye, Jennie Sue," Maddy called out, pushing the front door open.

"Bye, Maddy."

She shifted the car into drive and turned onto Main Street. Maddy found a parking spot in front of Tollett's Gift Store; she smiled loving the diagonal parking. The door chimed when she walked into the old store. She quickly found all her purchases, the bag for the wedding dress, safe for the papers, and a large photo album.

She set the items into the backseat of the car. Maddy backed the Mustang out from its parking space. She drove down Main Street looking at all the old brick buildings that lined the road, the bank, the pharmacy, the barbershop and other small businesses that'd taken over many of the old buildings. She made a circle around the small town, and then she headed home.

She slowed the car on the gravel road with the dust barely blowing. She could see her daddy sitting on the front porch with Gordon T lying by his feet, just where she had left him an hour ago. He was working way too hard and not sleeping enough; loneliness was getting to him. His body shuddered when the car motor woke him from his nap.

"Well, I see ya went shopping. Did ya talk to Johnny?" he called out stretching his arms.

"I sure did and he told me to tell you hello. He said you were his Boy Scout leader when he was a kid. He's the Boy Scout leader now and may come out here and talk to you. I think he could use some guidance."

"I don't know if I really did anything that great, but I did enjoy those boys. A visit would be nice. You didn't mind me hanging out with the boys since Libby worked with you girls. I guess a tradeoff."

"You know, I need to go see John and Libby. It's been a while. How are they doing?"

"About the same…I know they'd like a visit. They stay to themselves most of the time. I haven't seen them in ages. Libby brings me some leftovers or a piece of cake occasionally." He smoothed his hair back with his hands. "I don't see John often. He stays home and just works out in the fields."

"It's sad. They were both so outgoing. Oh, that damn pond has ruined so many lives!"

"Now honey, don't get started; it'll just get ya riled up."

"I know, Daddy." Maddy sat pushing the swing back and forth with her bare feet.

"Let's eat, I'm starving," he said standing.

She followed her daddy into the house, but stopped in the living room. It was still so peaceful; this was her mama's favorite room. A bookshelf full of dust-covered books stood next to the oversized fireplace, blackened from years of use, cold now with the hot summer heat. The extensive windows across the front wall looked out under the front porch roof and revealed the land so prized by her daddy. The old oak desk her daddy had given her for her seventh birthday sat in a back corner of the room behind two large flowery chairs with an antique, rose-colored, glass lamp that was sitting on a small table in between them.

After they finished lunch, Maddy picked up the bowls of leftovers and slid them into the refrigerator. "Daddy, let's sit outside for a while."

Jackson walked out onto the porch; his wrinkled hands grasp the front porch's post and he stared up into the sky. "We sure could use some rain. The garden's gettin' a little dry, but those clouds don't have much rain in them."

Maddy gave the swing a push with her toes feeling the cool wood from the porch floor. "Daddy, you know, the water of the pond is odd. It never has had any ducks or any other birds land on it that I can remember. I don't think I've ever seen any insects on it either. I wonder why not."

"Nope, all these years I've never seen any birds or insects near that pond."

"One time when it was so hot, Ryan tried to get Jet to drink the water, but the horse bucked and snorted and pulled back like there was a snake lurking around."

"I've always thought the pond water was poison and that's the answer of why no plants would grow or any animals would come near. Jet was a smart horse."

"Maybe that's all this is about: the water is poison and people swallow some of its water when they dive in and it gets into their system. But...that doesn't explain where the bodies go. Could the poison pull the bodies to the bottom?"

"Honey, I don't have any answers, but ya stay away from that pond and don't try any experiments with it, ya here!"

"I won't," she assured curling her feet up under her, becoming quiet.

Jackson leaned back in the rocker. A worried look came on his face as his eyes studied Maddy's determined face.

Maddy reclined against the swing and looked up at the stars. She started trying to remember the constellations.

Jackson, changing the subject, began telling old tales about her mother and himself back when they were young, how they met and fell in love.

Maddy's memories flowed about how strong love is and how she'd always loved Ryan that way. That day in the barn, she knew she wanted to spend the rest of her life with him.

"It's getting late. Ya get some rest, honey," said Jackson. He stood from the rocker and leaned over kissing her on the forehead. "Stop this worrying. What's done is done and ya can't bring Ryan back."

"I know. Night, Daddy," she said.

The screen door closed.

Maddy's head lay against the back of the swing and her eyes closed dreaming of what her life could've been. She could see Ryan standing so tall, his long, blonde hair with a tint of gray blowing in the breeze and those green eyes staring at her. He'd laugh and then leap onto the porch. He'd sit next to her in the swing and whistle an old song while slowly pushing the swing back and forth with his long legs. Then, a little blonde-haired, green-eyed boy about five years old would run up to the porch trying to leap the steps like Ryan had done. Of course, he would miss the top step and get frustrated swinging his arms in the air. Ryan would leap from the swing and swish the little boy up in his arms. Swinging him around in a circle, the little boy would giggle delightfully.

Maddy's felt a stabbing in her chest and tried to catch her breath. Reality was cruel to interrupt a perfect dream of what could've been.

The smell of gardenia bushes blooming along the front of the porch engulfed the air with calming sweetness. Nonetheless, she knew this was only a dream that'd never be.

Her bare feet slid on the smooth porch floor stopping the swing. All right, first a shower and then work. The front door closed and she raced up the stairs to the bathroom. She believed the envelope from Grandpa Winfred held her answers.

Chapter 7
The Investigation

Later that evening, she sat at the oak desk in the living room. Collecting her thoughts, she rocked back and forth in the desk chair. She pushed the button on her laptop turning it on. The clippings from the yellow envelope lay beside the printer. One by one, she scanned them into her laptop. When she slid the final paper back into the envelope, she closed it with the metal clips and put the envelope into the new safe, locking it.

The lamp flicked off in the living room, leaving only the moonlight streaming in from the front window. When an occasional breeze blew through the trees, it caused shadows to dance on the floor. She stopped at the top of the stairs and could see the flickering of light coming from her daddy's TV in his bedroom. She worried that he hadn't been sleeping enough, but sleep didn't come easy for her either.

She climbed into her bed with the laptop still in her hands. She doubled clicked the mouse bringing up the file she'd named *Crystal Pond*. Her hands gripped the laptop tight. Thoughts crept into her mind. Did Grandpa Winfred know the secret of Crystal Pond? The pages scanned past very slowly as she read each one and put them in timeline order. She scrolled and added a chart of each occurrence: date, time of day, weather conditions, victim's name, his or her age - anything that might have changed the incident. Then, she tried to chart what the deceased had in common, but nothing appeared to be the same. They seemed to be random accidents. *But, there has to be a connection*, she thought to herself.

She read one article about a straggler from Texas, Clayton Montgomery, who lived on the farm back in 1956. She shivered reading the article. It was worn more than the other clippings and looked as if it had been folded and kept in a wallet.

Another article about the drownings told about a young boy named Emmitt Sullivan who'd been visiting his Grandpa in the summer of 1930. And yet, another incident had occurred back in 1933 concerning the Walden boys who lived on a farm north of the Sayers farm. One hot day, Tom, Jeffery, and Billy Walden snuck over the fence in the back pasture and made their way to the pond. Tom and Jeffery bet each other about how deep they could dive and how big of a splash they'd be able make into the pond. They left their younger brother Billy to be the judge of their dives. Billy watched as each brother dove simultaneously into Crystal Pond. Maddy's heart pounded and her hands squeezed together; she understood how Billy felt that day standing waiting for his brothers to pop up from the clear water. Their bodies, like the rest, were never found.

She clicked the button and the laptop moaned shutting off. That was enough reading for tonight. She'd wait until she heard from Johnny to do more research. The stories whirled in her mind, each one so different, but with the same ending, none of the bodies were ever found.

She lay back in her bed letting the calming sounds of the night serenade her until she fell asleep.

She woke from a deep sleep when the sun shimmered across her face. Maddy felt energized. She hurriedly dressed and ran to the kitchen. Jackson sat at the table drinking his coffee. She grabbed a cup filling it with the hot liquid and poured cream and sugar into it.

He laughed, "I see ya still drinking baby coffee."

"Daddy, it's not baby coffee. Starbucks gets a lot of money in the city for coffee like this."

"Well, people must be getting even more dim-witted if they pay a lot for coffee."

"Glad you're in a good mood," Maddy teased.

"I slept great last night. Maybe our talk about each of us moving on paid off."

"Do you have a lot of work around the farm to do today?"

"Naw, just need to weed the garden and tie up the tomatoes."

"Do you need any help?"

"Nope, it won't take me long. Ya want any breakfast?"

"I'll take a piece of hot buttered cornbread. I've missed your cornbread."

He shook his head chuckling, "I may have to go into business in the city serving baby coffee and cornbread for breakfast."

Maddy had her mouth full, but she laughed, "I think you may be on to something, Daddy."

"What ya going to do this morning?" he questioned.

"I think I'll take a ride back out to the old oak and no…don't worry…I won't get close to the water. I just want to sit in the tree and think. I hope I hear from Johnny soon."

"I don't like the thought of ya near that dad gum place. I'll be worried till ya get back. Ya watch your step out there."

"I promise," she took a slow sip of coffee. "Daddy, do you remember a story about Clayton Montgomery?"

"Yep, sure do. Mama told me about him. Daddy just kept everything a secret. A few years after Mama and Daddy got married (I was about four, maybe five, years old), Clayton Montgomery came to the farm to work. Granddad Sayers was always helping people and he gave Clayton a job. Clayton was saving up some money to go to college. Mama said he was a very smart and ambitious man. It seemed Daddy and Clayton quickly became good friends. It was another sad story, like so many before him. Clayton decided to go for a swim, and you know the rest. Mama never told me anything else about the pond. I always believed there was more to the story, but Mama wouldn't finish it. I know there was more by the way Mama acted and looked when I pressed the issue. My mama couldn't lie very well."

"You never learned anymore about Clayton from Grandpa Winfred?"

"No, it was the same story; they didn't find his body, just like all the others. Why?"

"Inquiring minds like to know," she joked, squeezing her lips together as she set another serving of buttered cornbread on the table.

"Honey, you aren't having one of those bad feelings, are ya?"

"I don't know, Daddy. I just get a chill when I think about the man."

He shook his head. "Well, I don't know any more to tell you. I better get my chores done before the sun warms things up outside," he groaned slowly getting up out of his chair as he walked to the back door. "Come on Gordon T. We've gotta lot of work to do. Now Maddy, I mean it, ya be careful out there by that ol' pond."

"I'll be fine."

The morning air was crisp with a little coolness, not like the stuffy, sweltering city this time of the year. Nutmeg didn't hesitate galloping towards Maddy. The russet horse's muscles flexed with her mane softly swaying. The mare stood still as the saddle fell on her back. Maddy put her foot up in the stirrup and holding onto the reins, she swung up into the saddle. She let the horse slowly trot along the worn path through the pecan trees.

She jumped from the horse and left Nutmeg next to the massive oak. Something caught her eye, so she drew her gun from its holster. She ran over by the wild rose bushes and guardedly walked around the pond.

A tree branch snapped. Maddy darted through the trees. Standing about twenty feet from her was a man holding onto a rifle, staring with the same cruel eyes she'd seen before. She lifted her gun and a shot rang out.

"Damn it, Rufus Jones, you son of a bitch, I just nicked you but next time I won't miss!" Rufus dashed through the woods screaming and cussing at her.

She slipped her gun back into its holster and her lips tightened together. *Why is Rufus Jones hanging out here?* she wondered.

She climbed up limb after limb sitting on her and Ryan's special limb and stared into the water. The clear water wasn't moving with the breeze, not even a ripple. So strange! The bank surrounding the pond was smooth sand cascading into the water; no plants had ever grown on the side, an oddity no one had ever figured out. She sat there remembering Ryan's body weaving back and forth with the sand giving way. A movie was flowing in her mind of each person jumping into the water; so many lives changed because of the disappearances.

A noise startled her, but instead of her daddy's old truck driving up, it was the sheriff's patrol car pulling up.

The car door swung open and Johnny stepped up. "Jackson said this is where you were."

"Johnny, Rufus Jones was spying on me a few minutes ago. I fired a shot at him and I might have nicked him, that dumb-ass idiot," she said fuming. "He did have an old rifle with him, so he's looking for trouble."

Johnny gazed up at her perched on the huge limb. "He's an idiot for sure. Reports are he's been stealing chickens from some of the farms. He's probably just hungry, but I don't like him running around with a rifle. Carrying a rifle isn't normal for him. He's always been harmless, just stealing for food. There must be something new going on with him."

"That bastard is always up to no good," she snipped. "I should've taken care of him years ago, but we'll meet again and next time I won't miss."

"He'll be back. That weasel'll forget gettin' shot at, especially after he starts drinking," Johnny assured. "But really, Maddy, don't kill Rufus without cause, and don't be saying that to people. If that drunkard turns up dead, I don't want you being a suspect."

"Oh, okay. By the way, we also have a drifter hanging out around our farm. Apparently, he has taken some food and a knife from Daddy; oh, and some papers and magazines, too."

"You don't think it could have been Rufus, do you?"

"No, he's smart enough not to go inside the house, but too dumb to read." They laughed.

"I'll keep an eye out for a stranger hanging around, but you can handle a drifter."

"Yep, or Daddy will," she added.

"Maddy, you aren't obsessed with this pond, are you?"

"No, I just don't know an ending to these drownings. I need some answers," she said ducking her head and getting quiet.

"Here, maybe this'll have something in it that'll help you," he said as he handed her a large manila envelope. "I decided not to email all of this. Someone might notice, and I didn't want to stir up any speculation about what I was doing. I copied everything that I could find in the files."

"Thanks, Johnny. Did you read any of it?"

"Some, not all. But, it is curious how so many people have disappeared into the pond," he shook his head. "That pond certainly is a strange mystery 'round here."

"These reports may just have the answers. Thanks," she announced. "There has to be a connection."

"Changing the subject, I had a nice talk with Jackson, and I told him I might bring the Boy Scout troop by. We do need a good place to go camping and my backyard isn't any fun. He didn't have any objections. He'd be a lot of help to me and those boys."

"Daddy'd like that and it'd be good for him." Then there was an uncomfortable pause.

Johnny tilted his head to the side and his body tensed. "So, that's Crystal Pond. I've always wondered what it was like. Guess it hasn't changed much for you since that awful day in July?"

"No, I don't think it's ever changed; nothing changes about it. It sits there all smooth and blue, waiting to devour another soul. The devil's pond, that what my grandfather called it."

"It's so peaceful out here and the water is so cool. It's real inviting. I understand why so many have gone swimming, especially on hot summer afternoons. I also understand curiosity about the pond. That appealed to Ryan, I'm sure." Johnny's cell phone began to ring; he shook his head. "So much for relaxing. See you later, Maddy."

"Thanks," she called out.

Johnny closed the patrol car's door. He sat there talking on his phone.

Maddy held onto the papers. The file was huge, but she wasn't going to read it now. Johnny backed out and turned around. He stuck his arm out the window to wave goodbye.

Maddy climbed from the tree and just stood there. The smell of the wild blooms surrounding the pond brought back reminiscences of that July day. She moved over by the water and squatted down. "Ryan, I'm not going to sit around and say I'm sorry anymore. I'm going to find out what happened," she said confidently. Her head bowed with tears stinging her eyes, "I love you."

The leather saddle creaked as she swung up into it. She gave Nutmeg a kick and the strong horse galloped along the path.

Jackson was sitting on the front porch. "I see Johnny found ya."

"Yes," Maddy called back, stepping up on the porch, "he gave me this file. Hope it supplies some answers or at least clues." She laid the file in the seat of the other rocker. "I'll see what it says after I put Nutmeg back out in the pasture."

"First, it's lunch time and then ya can see about those papers. What ya want to eat?" he called out to her.

"A BLT sounds good again, if you don't mind."

"That'll be fine; I'll put some bacon on to cook."

"Oh, Daddy…Rufus Jones was hanging out watching me. I fired at him but I only nicked him. We need to keep an eye out for him; he was carrying a rifle."

"That Rufus Jones shor' is a dumb-ass. Can't stay on his own property. I'm shor' ya scared the hell out of him for a while, but I'll watch out for him." Jackson laughed. "I know he wasn't expecting you to be here. I would've like to seen the look on his face."

"And don't forget, we need to watch out for that drifter as well," she added.

"Aww, that drifter is probably long gone," he said dismissing thoughts about the rambler. "See ya in the kitchen in a little bit."

"Okay, it won't take me long. Come on, Nutmeg," Maddy called back, whistling for Nutmeg to follow.

Maddy rushed into the house and washed her hands. "Johnny said he had talked to you about the boys from his troop coming out here and camping out. Sounds like fun," she called out from the bathroom.

"I told him I'd consider it. The boys always loved to make camp over by the group of oaks in back of the yard. The leaves would blow in the night breeze, crackling and making rustling noises. I loved it when an owl would begin to hoot in the dark. That made those cubs a little uneasy, for sure. Ryan was the only one who wasn't bothered by the sounds of the night, but he grew up out here. He'd lean back on his elbows listening to the ghost stories that were being told and watch all the boys cringe, but not him. Johnny was one of the first of the boys who was scared. He never did like being out on the farm, at least not at night. He always believed the ghost stories," Jackson laughed, "and now he's the sheriff. Ya never know."

"He doesn't seem bothered now with anything on the farm," she injected walking into the kitchen.

"He's not out on a dark night alone on this old farm," Jackson chuckled. "Aww, but he's all grown up now and, I'm sure, has had to deal with plenty of critters at night…drunk ones, and such."

"Yep, I bet he has. The sandwich was great. Thanks. I'm going to scan in the papers Johnny gave me and put them into my laptop to see what they have to tell me."

"I'm going out front and sit for a while. Don't work too hard; remember, ya'r on vacation."

"This isn't work to me."

She scanned in the papers one after another. There were many notes that the officers had handwritten, their own stories. The final paper lay on top of the printer. She picked up her laptop and sat down in the flowerily chair in the living room and began to read.

Each story was the same as the newspaper clippings from her grandpa, but they did have considerably more information. Each of papers described in detail what had occurred the day each person had drowned. She came to the last paper. She took in a deep breath reading out loud.

"Ryan Allen Beardsley, fifteen years old, drowned July 10th, 1989 in Pine Grove, South Carolina at Crystal Pond. His body was never recovered. A sophomore basketball player at Pine Grove High School…" Every detail of that day was right there in front of her making her relive each agonizing minute of her own experience.

She snuggled back in the chair. She knew what she had to do. She clicked her email and began typing. She needed help and there was only one person to help, Terry. He knew her story about the old pond, and he was a forensic scientist with the FBI. He'd be able to find some answers. Terry was also the only person who'd take a chance doing research under the auspices of the FBI. She finished the email and pushed send. Now, she'd just have to wait to see what he said.

That evening after supper, she sat on the porch with her laptop on the small table in between the rockers. She had turned its volume up loud hoping to hear the beep for an incoming email, but it was quiet.

"Honey, a watched pot won't boil any sooner."

"I'm just anxious to hear from Terry."

"You think that Terry will be able to help ya?"

"Yes, he can do some testing and we might find out why the water is so clear, but nothing grows on the banks. He's really a great guy. And no, don't start thinking, Daddy. We're just good friends."

"We'll see," he winked at her smiling. "Anyway give him some time. If he's a good friend, he'll help. I'm tired," he groaned as he stood and stretched. "My ol' bones get stiff when I sit too long. I'll see ya in the morning, honey."

"Good night, Daddy," she said picking up the laptop. "I need to plug the laptop in. Its battery's getting low."

The attic fan was pulling in the cool night air making the house creak from retraction. She pushed the plug into the laptop and laid it on her nightstand. A long bath sounded soothing.

Her t-shirt and shorts dropped to the floor and she stepped into the bath water. She lay back against the side of the tub. Her tired shoulders relaxed from working too long on the computer. Her hair swished, floating in the water. Ryan would be shocked that she could put her head completely under water for a few seconds. That was one thing she had learned, swimming, not as well as Ryan, but she could swim, part of her FBI training. Her body rested not making any waves as she soaked in the warm water. Her mind wouldn't stop searching, "Ryan, why couldn't you swim back to the surface?"

The house was so peaceful with the hum of the huge fan. Her eyes closed as she slid under the water letting it flow over her head again. Time moved on, and she reluctantly stood from the tub drying off her thin body. She slipped on her boxer, balloon-printed shorts and pulled on her green top. Then she used a blow dryer to half-way style her hair.

Her anxiety came back, and she hurried to the nightstand to check her laptop. Touching it revealed no new emails. She clicked off the lamp. The pillow swallowed her head as she listened in the quiet night to the crickets serenading her. She sat up and stared outside watching heat-lightning flashing in the west. Tomorrow would be another day to try again for some kind of logical resolution.

Chapter 8
A Floating Body

Waking early the next morning, Maddy promptly searched for a new email. Maybe Terry would answer the email from work since it was Monday morning. She reached over touching the laptop and stopping the swirling colors. Zilch! She quickly got dressed and pulled on clean shorts and a t-shirt. She finished brushing her hair and tying it up on top of her head.

"Breakfast is ready," her daddy yelled from the kitchen as she ran down the stairs.

"Well?" Jackson asked peering over the Pine Grove weekly newspaper.

"Nothing," she answered shaking her head sadly.

Swallowing a sip of coffee, he maintained, "It hasn't been that long. Honey, stop worrying. He'll get back ta ya. He'll at least tell you *yes* or *no*, don't ya think."

"Yep, you're right; he must be busy."

"Sit and eat some breakfast. I made some waffles."

She nodded her head yes as she picked up a waffle and some bacon. "Anything happening in the paper?"

"Nope, they're adding a stop sign by the old school and they've had a few break-ins. That's about it. Got quiet around town after the Fourth of July celebration. They're gearing up for school next month. It starts earlier and earlier."

Jackson shook the newspaper and then folded it. "Ya can read it later if ya want," he said laying the paper on the table. He stood, filled the sink up with warm water and began to rinse the dishes. "There, the dishes are done," he said. "Honey, what ya doing this morning?"

"I think I'll take a ride on Nutmeg and clear my mind. I won't be gone long."

"I have a few chores to do. See ya in a little while," he said going out the back door.

She walked to the barn and prepared Nutmeg for their ride. She jumped upon the horse and they raced across the pasture. She slowed Nutmeg when she felt the coolness coming from the creek that curved and wound by Ryan's farm. Her body leaned back in the saddle and her eyes looked up into the sky as she watched the soft white clouds float by, some in animal shapes. Serenity was overtaking her, and she wasn't worried about the email right then. By habit, she turned Nutmeg and began to ride back to the pond. There in front of her was the old oak standing tall. She took in a deep breath and then gasped.

In front of her was Rufus Jones, dead as a doughnut! She slipped off of Nutmeg and walked near. This couldn't be true. This was the first time the pond had a body floating in it, but she could see, Rufus didn't die from drowning. The body lay face down in the water with watery bloodstains on his shirt and his hair was matted in partially dried blood.

She pushed speed call. "Johnny, this is Maddy…Rufus is back, but this time he's not leaving. No, I didn't shoot him, but someone took care of him. He's floating in Crystal Pond. All right, I'll see you in a few minutes. No rush, he's not going anywhere."

She vaulted up on Nutmeg and sped to the farmhouse.

"Daddy! Dad-dee!" she shouted running to the garden in the back of the old farmhouse. "Rufus has pissed off someone," she asserted, "worse than me. He's dead… floating in Crystal Pond."

"What?"

"Rufus Jones has been killed, stabbed, I think. Couldn't really tell."

"Stabbed! Oh, Maddy, my kitchen knife. Maybe that drifter still IS around. Maybe he killed Rufus with my knife. You think?"

"Yep, maybe."

"Did ya call Johnny?"

"He's on his way," she assured. *At least I know bodies can float in the water,* she thought to herself.

After a few minutes, they heard tires crunching rocks in the gravel driveway.

"Johnny's here," Maddy hollered running around the house to the front yard. "He's got a crew with him."

Truck after truck pulled into the driveway.

"Maddy," Johnny yelled, "you coming out to help?"

"I'm not missing this," she yelled opening the passenger door of the patrol car and sliding inside. "Let's go."

The parade of vehicles rolled along the winding path to the old oak. There, just as she'd left him, was Rufus floating on the water with his arms and legs spread out wide. She stood to the side letting Johnny and his officers do their job. She was impressed with their work, as she watched them pull the lifeless body from the pond.

"You're right. He was stabbed and Abe, the medical examiner, thinks it was a small knife."

"Johnny," called out the medical examiner waving his hand in the air for Johnny to come over.

"What's the problem, Abe?"

"Johnny, take a look at this," said Abe pulling Rufus's shirt back.

"Oh man! That's gnarly!"

"I'm not sure until I get him back, but this ole boy is missing his heart, I think."

"His heart!" Maddy screamed out, "Why?"

"That's the big question," Abe said. "I don't understand why they sliced him up like this just to take out his heart."

"Way too many questions at this point," Johnny snapped. "Abe, get Rufus back to your table and see what his remains have to say."

"Why would a drifter kill someone and cut out his heart?" questioned Maddy. "I guess Rufus really did piss him off."

"If the drifter did kill Rufus, I can assure you that he's not hanging around. He's probably headed to the Bahamas or Mexico by now."

"Well, at least the pond gave up the body this time," she said watching as the team put Rufus's body into a black bag and slid it into the back of the medical examiner's truck.

Johnny stopped the car in the front yard next to the Mustang. "Maddy, if you find any more evidence, like maybe the knife," he said grinning, "give me a call." He became serious.

"There's more?" she replied as she sighed.

"Sorry, but yes. I found out a reporter named Robert Brennan from *The Examiner* is looking into the case of the missing bodies and the pond. I did some research and he doesn't give up. He also has the reputation to twist stories around."

Maddy stared at Johnny, "Do you think Brennan could be watching me?"

"If he is, this could mess everything up for you."

"Do you know what the man looks like?"

"He's about my height, thin, with short, grey hair."

"This news isn't good. Daddy and I don't like people snooping around our place."

"I'll do my best to keep things under wraps."

"Thanks, Johnny. How do you think Brennan found out that I'm checking on the pond?"

"Not sure," he answered shaking his head. Maddy understood he wasn't going to tell her who his snitch was.

"I'll keep watching for a knife to turn up," she grabbed the door handle. "Bye, Johnny," she called out shutting the passenger door of the car. She stepped up on the porch and stood next to Jackson as they watched Johnny drive away.

"Well, Rufus won't be bothering ya anymore."

"I know. Daddy, if he hadn't terrified me of water, then I might've tried to save Ryan."

"Then I'd have lost ya both," Jackson added looking at the floor. His stomach growled. "Guess it's time for lunch."

She started to warn him about Brennan but didn't want to stress him out. She would have to take care of that reporter herself.

Jackson turned around going to the screen door. He stopped and looked at her.

Maddy grinned. "Yep, a bacon and tomato sandwich," she called out laughing.

She followed Jackson inside but detoured to go wash up. Before she made it to the kitchen, she heard a loud motor. She turned and hurried outside on the porch.

Pulling up next to her Mustang was a huge FBI crime truck. A tall, slender man in his early thirties stepped out on the driver's side.

"Terry," Maddy screamed, as she hopped off the porch and hugged the man.

"Alright, I like these welcomes," said Terry with a big grin on his face.

"Why didn't you email me?"

"I know you, and you don't have any patience, so I packed everything I thought we'd need and here I am," he declared, spreading his arms out wide.

"Oh, Terry, you're going to get in trouble bringing the truck."

"Nope, Kevin knows. I told him your story and he's onboard with this. Plus, I guess it didn't hurt since you two were engaged for a while."

"He said it was okay?"

"Yep, he said for me to check things out. This is now an official FBI case, and we have FBI equipment to use."

"Why would he do such a thing over a small pond?"

"Not just any small pond, Crystal Pond. There have been too many drownings in such an out-of-the-way place. This is official FBI business."

Jackson coughed. "Oh, Daddy, this is Terry Maples. Terry, this is my father, Jackson Sayers."

Terry stepped up on the porch extending his hand. "It's a pleasure, sir."

"Nice to meet ya, son, and thank ya for coming down here to help Maddy," Jackson grinned, noticing the strong handshake.

"I'd do anything for her; she's great and has helped me out with cases on many occasions."

"We're getting ready to eat a sandwich. Come on in and join us," Jackson explained.

"I grabbed a hamburger a little while ago, but something cold to drink would be nice. It sure is hot here," Terry said gesturing by outstretching his arm.

Maddy started laughing. "Well, you're in the real Old South now. C'mon in."

"Here's a cold glass of iced tea," Jackson assured placing a tall glass on the table. Then he turned back to the stove to fry bacon.

"Wow, sweet tea," Terry announced. "Boy, it smells good in here."

"Everything is sweet here," Maddy admitted smiling at him. "Daddy's cooking a pot roast, potatoes, carrots, onions, plus some cornbread for supper tonight."

"A real home-cooked meal in the real Old South," Terry said with enthusiasm. "Who could resist?" He was a round-faced man who wore dark-rimmed glasses, had a thick, dark mustache, and hazel eyes.

The bacon sizzled in the skillet, but she noticed Jackson's eyes glancing over studying Terry. She shook her head no, which only made Jackson smile as if to say, *Don't get your dandruff up, just doing what any dad would do.*

Terry eyed the plate full of bacon, lettuce, and tomatoes.

"Here," Maddy said, handing him a plate, "one sandwich won't hurt."

Terry laid two pieces of bread on the plate, scooped out some mayonnaise, and layered his sandwich up high. He took a huge bite and moaned with his mouth full, "Mmmm…oh man, this is good."

Jackson continued to smile, not saying anything.

Finishing up, Terry wiped his mouth with a paper towel. "Now, where's the old pond?"

"Out in the back pasture," answered Maddy. "We can go out there when I'm finished with lunch."

Jackson shook his head back and forth.

"You don't like this idea, do you Mr. Sayers?"

"Nope, not a bit, we should leave well enough alone, and not mess with trouble. The old pond is dangerous. Always has been, always will be."

"We'll take every precaution. Don't worry about Maddy; I won't let anything happen to her."

She leaned back in the kitchen chair, finishing her sandwich remembering Ryan telling her the same thing. "Daddy, we'll be fine. Terry has all the equipment we need."

"Except one thing, I didn't bring a boat and THAT we could use."

"We have a small fishing boat that we can put in the back of the pickup," offered Maddy. "I'll drive the pickup out there and you can follow me in the truck. Well," she scooted her chair back, "you ready to go?"

"Sure, as soon as I call and get a hotel room in town."

"No sir, ya can stay right here in the guest bedroom. It's not fancy, but clean," Jackson, answered.

"I don't want to impose on you," Terry added earnestly.

"We won't take *no* for an answer. It's fine, Terry. We've got plenty of room, and then we can work on evidence we collect later… plus…remember, you get roast tonight." Maddy grinned.

"That sounds good to me. Thank you; I accept. Let's go, Maddy." Terry pushed his chair back from the table. "Thanks for lunch, Mr. Sayers."

"Son, call me Jackson. Mr. Sayers was my father."

"No problem, Jackson it is."

"Daddy, I need the keys to the truck. If you need to go anywhere, my car keys are on my dresser."

Jackson pulled his truck keys from the pocket of his overalls. "Here, honey. I don't need to go anywhere. Don't forget she gets stuck in second sometimes."

Maddy and Terry stepped out on the porch.

"The small boat is over there by the barn. I'll get Daddy's truck. You can follow me, but try and stay on the path. It can get even bumpier and soggier off the trail. Don't want you getting stuck."

The huge FBI truck growled following close behind the black pickup. As Maddy and Terry drove down the winding trail out through the pecan grove, they bobbled in the vehicles because of the rough terrain.

Maddy parked the truck and turned the motor off. She gripped the steering wheel nervously and then hit it with the palms of her hands to push off her emotions. Now she'd get her answers. Crystal Pond couldn't keep its secret from Terry and the FBI.

Chapter 9
The FBI

The massive FBI truck's engine churned. Terry climbed out and closed the driver's door. He swung the two back doors wide open and exposed lights and hums coming from the equipment and computers that were still running inside.

He spun around but didn't move as he surveyed the crystal water. "That's Unktehi Pond, aka Crystal Pond, I presume."

"Yep," Maddy replied.

"It's something! I don't think I've ever seen anything so extraordinary. The water is so clear and blue. I see why so many have wanted to swim in it, especially in this heat," Terry said wiping the sweat from his forehead. "The banks are strange for the South; they look like some kind of sand dunes."

"They do look like sand dunes. Nothing has ever grown on them, not even a weed."

"Alright, that's bizarre. Weeds grow everywhere."

"Not on those banks."

"First, safety! Let's put life vests on and wear oxygen tanks," he assured handing her gear. "We'll take every precaution."

"You really do mean business."

"Too many mishaps have happened here. I also want some lines attached to the truck and then we're going to connect the lines to our belts, just in case. I don't trust that water," said Terry pulling out three ropes.

"Why three ropes?"

"One for each of us and one for the boat; everything has to be secured."

"What do we do first?" she questioned.

"I want a sample of the sand from the bank and a sample of the water. Then we need to take pictures and measure the circumference of the pond."

"Let's get to work," said Maddy moving over by the bank. She stopped as she listened and looked up.

"Maddy, what's wrong?"

"I thought I heard something coming from behind the pecan trees. It's probably a deer."

"You think it could be that reporter, Brennan? Or that straggler that you talked about?"

She shrugged her shoulders as she scanned the area and unclasped her gun holster. "I don't think it's the straggler, that guy has to be gone. He wouldn't stay around here, but it could be Brennan. I'm going to check it out. I'll be right back."

Terry stood by the truck quietly watching her. His hand moved to his gun and unclipped the strap.

"I didn't see anyone," she called hurrying over to Terry. "I did find this small piece of material caught on wild rose bush that was over on that ridge. It feels unusual."

"Let me see." Terry flipped the gray material around in his hands gently rubbing it. "This is different. I'm going to run some test on it. Maddy, this fabric hasn't been out here long."

"It's probably from the drifter, but I'm not giving Johnny the evidence, not yet anyway," Maddy stated possessively. "I want you to have first crack at it. Well, don't just stand there."

Terry grinned, "Still the same, no patience. Here, you get a sample of the sand and I'll move over on the other side of the pond," he said anxiously. "Hold onto the tape and I'll measure the pond while I'm over there."

They both filled the small glass containers with the sand and Terry pulled the tape tight, writing the measurements very carefully as he gradually circled the pond. "I haven't ever seen anything like this," he called out pulling the tape in. "It's an exact circle, not off by even an inch." He turned around. "Let me have your sample of sand," he said climbing in the back of the truck. He grabbed another small jar for a water sample. He squatted by the sandy bank and filled the jar with clear water then tightened the lid. He dipped his hand in the sand and spread his fingers letting it filter through. "This sand isn't normal. It's all the same size, small grains, as if it's been through a coffee grinder. It's like industrial sand that you buy at Home Depot. There aren't any rocks, not even any dirt. This stuff won't pack like normal beach sand."

"I told you; this pond is different."

"I have a theory of my own, but first I need to run the samples and then we need to get the boat out of the truck."

Maddy didn't move; she looked like she was in a trance.

"Maddy, you sure you're up to this? You don't have to get into the boat. I just want you to stay on the bank."

"I'm not worried about myself. It's you I'm worried about. Remember, I've stood here on the bank before…"

"I know, I know," answered Terry sympathetically stepping out of the back of the FBI truck. "Let me get the pole and camera. I want to do some searching on the bottom of the pond with the camera and then I want a sample of dirt from the bottom."

The boat slid into the water. Terry stepped in and sat in the middle of the boat. Maddy's heart was beating so hard she thought it might explode. Memories of Ryan's curiosity about the depth of the pond kept flowing in her brain. She hoped getting Terry involved wasn't a mistake.

The oars splashed in the water.

"This water is so crystal clear that I can see deep, but then it gets dark as pitch." Terry laid the oars to the side letting the boat float in the center of the pond. He picked up the long pole, clipped the sonar device to sturdy the line, and slipped the contraption into the water. The monitor came on. The boat wobbled back and forth a little. He swished the small sonar around in the water to get images. He pulled the line out and snapped the underwater camera in its place. The line kept sinking, going deeper and deeper. "Wow! I'm not even close to the bottom. I haven't seen a pond this small so deep. There isn't anything in this water, no fish, plants, nothing, not even a turtle."

He pulled the line out of the water. "I can extend the pole one more time, but the line's not going to be long enough right in the middle to reach the bottom. I think I'll try more to the side. Maybe it isn't quite as deep there."

"Terry," Maddy called out, "please, be careful."

"I'm fine, if something happens just reel me in like a fish," he yelled back, laughing.

"Not funny!" she hollered back at him.

"There, I think I have it. We have pictures of the bottom or at least close and this time the pond's not winning."

"You really have some pictures?"

"Yep, now I want some samples from the bottom." He pulled in the line and changed out the camera for a claw. He let the line slide into the water and he maneuvered the claw with expertise.

"Wow!" he yelled.

"What's wrong?"

"That was strange. The claw seemed to sink into the sandy bottom and something almost pulled the pole out of my hands," he yelled. "There, I've got a sample."

"Good, then you're done. Get out of that pond!" Maddy fretfully paced back and forth along the bank.

The paddles swished on top of the smooth water making the boat weave from side to side as it moved to the bank.

Maddy grabbed the edge of the boat tugging it onto the sand. Terry jumped landing next to her.

"Alright," Terry called out anxiously, "we did it; we'll find some answers now."

"You said the line went taut when you hit bottom?"

"Yep."

"I've always thought there was quicksand at the bottom and our victims were sucked in by it."

"That's a good possibility, but I think…" he paused with caution.

"Well, spit it out. What do you think?"

"I'm not sure, but we aren't that far from the ocean and maybe this is a passageway back out to sea, you know, like Salt Lake in Utah. There could be an opening in the bottom sucking its victims into an underwater channel or cave."

"I hadn't thought about that, there might not be a bottom and you could slip through out to the sea. Oh, that is horrible," she said shuddering, her eyes filling with tears.

"Maddy," Terry assured, "don't start losing it now. We don't have any answers yet."

"Well, let's get them," she said shaking off the tears. They took the samples into the truck.

The equipment grunted and lights flashed, as Terry ran test after test. Maddy's eyes were glued to the mechanical claw's hand full of sand. Underneath all the pretense of her FBI façade, she believed like her Grandpa Winfred: Crystal Pond is the devil's pond. She pulled her legs up in the chair holding onto her knees as she watched Terry work. As the sun slipped in the western sky, shadows of the tall pines crept into the truck.

"It's getting late. We can move back to the house and you can keep working there," Maddy announced. "We can't get any more samples of anything until morning, anyway. I'm also getting hungry, and Daddy will have supper on the table. He'll have Johnny out looking for us if it gets dark."

"Sure, sorry, I get preoccupied when I start working. You know me," Terry declared as he turned to her. "Maddy, is something wrong? You're acting strange again."

"I have an odd feeling like someone is watching us. I'm sure it's anxiety, though, nothing else."

"You know your premonitions are usually correct. I admire that alert sixth sense you have," he gushed. "Let's get back to the farmhouse. I'll follow you." He quickly began flicking switches and pushing buttons. "Let me secure everything."

With the FBI truck close behind, Jackson's old truck lights flickered in the dusky evening as it slowly led the way along the bumpy path.

Terry walked into the kitchen. "Wow, smells good in here."

"Sit down, son, and help yourself," Jackson assured. "We ain't on any formalities here."

The three sat down and passed around bowls and platters of food, without saying a word. Maddy's mind kept thinking of possibilities of what happened to Ryan. She could see out of the corner of her eye that Terry was also absorbed in his own thoughts.

"Well, ya going to tell me what happened out there?" questioned Jackson.

"We took samples of the sand and water and samples from the bottom of the pond, at least the bottom near the side. It sure is deep. There isn't anything in that pond, not fish, plants, nothing; so strange. It's also a complete perfect circle," Terry announced.

"It's always been just like that, never changing. What did your findings say?"

"Not done with them yet, but I'll keep checking. I also was able to get some pictures with the underwater camera."

"Now," asked Jackson curiously, "what else are ya going to do? You don't have to go back out there, do you?"

Terry swung his head back and forth. "I don't need anything else from the pond, not right now. I have enough information and I want to do some research on the computer. I can put my information into the computer tonight and get my data back in the morning. I read what Maddy found out, but my research is more in depth and it'll have more details. We'll find out more tomorrow."

"I hope ya do find some answers. I wouldn't mind knowing myself. It has been a thorn in the family for years," Jackson stood picking up the dishes.

"I'll help you clean the dishes tonight," Maddy added standing by her father.

"I'll see to the kitchen; ya go on, Maddy. The dishes are no problem."

"Thank you, Jackson. The meal was delicious," Terry said gratefully sliding his chair back under the table. "Now, Maddy, let's go see what the computers have found out."

"Oh," Terry moaned standing on the porch, "the night's so dark without street lights, but so bright with the moon and stars. This is something. I see why you like it here. This, I could get used to, I think. But, it might be a little too quiet for me."

"Not like New York when you were little, huh?"

"No, it's not like the city of New York and it's not anything like DC," he added laughing.

Terry pulled the doors open stepping up into the back of the truck. Lights from all the electronics chirping inside were glowing, making flashes, and sending colors on the sidewalls. He flicked a switch and the back of the truck lit up. He smiled. "All the tests are done. I'll send the results to my laptop, and we can go into the house and read what we've found today. I'm going to do a full search on the history of the pond and we'll have the information in the morning."

"I can't believe you already have some of the results."

"There wasn't much to decipher, but figuring out what we do have may take a long time." He pushed his chair back. "There, I'm done; let's go." He turned the main light off, closed the truck's doors, and locked them. His hands held onto the porch railing, and his eyes, like a slow motion camera, panned the porch.

"We can sit out here later when we get done," Maddy said, smiling at him.

"That'd be nice."

"Oh, one other thing, Daddy doesn't use the air conditioner in the house, except on rare occasions when the temperature gets over a hundred, so he'll be turning on the attic fan tonight."

"Attic fan?"

"Yes, a whole house fan, it brings air in from the windows, so you'll have to leave your bedroom door and windows open tonight to get cool air. It's like a backwards fan pulling in the cool air from outside."

"Sounds fine with me. I'm tired since I didn't get a lot of sleep last night and got up early this morning."

"Sorry about that," Maddy teased.

"I think you're onto something and I'm surprised it has taken so long for someone to try and figure it out. I'm still worried that someone may be keeping tabs on us," Terry said shaking his head. "I don't like being spied on."

"Don't worry; I'm sure it's my imagination. I'm a little jumpy thinking about finding my answer to the pond. This has been a long time coming for me. I know a few people have tried to find the answer, but even the local police didn't have the resources you have. Let's go and see what the reports say."

The screen door squeaked when Maddy pulled it open.

Jackson sat reading in his overstuffed chair in the living room. "Well, did ya find out anything?"

"Let me get my laptop turned on and we'll see," Terry offered unzipping the black bag tugging the laptop. He sat the laptop on the ottoman in front of him and turned it on.

Maddy slid to the floor by Terry, anxiously staring at the laptop's screen.

Terry leaned back in the chair when pages began to appear on the laptop. "Well, I was wrong."

"About what," questioned Maddy?

"There isn't any salt in the pond water or mixed into the sand, not more than what might've come from rain being this near the coast."

"So, your theory of an underground cave to the ocean didn't pan out," Maddy answered, cinching up her mouth. "What else does it say?"

"Not a lot, but your idea doesn't work either; the sand isn't a form of quicksand, just loose sand."

Maddy leaned in closer. "So, do you know why your line seemed to be pulled deeper toward the bottom?"

"Another mystery," Terry confessed.

"So, you're saying ya don't have anything?" questioned Jackson lifting off his reading glasses from his nose, his eyes staring at the two.

"No sir, we may not have our answers right now, but we've eliminated many questions. The water is the purest water I've ever seen. No chemicals, except, what has been added by rain, but it seems that the sand purifies the water."

"So, Daddy, the pond water isn't poison. But, what on earth is it?" Maddy asked leaning in next to Terry still reading the findings.

Terry fell back in the chair rubbing his mustache with his finger. "Like I said, we'll get more from the research tomorrow. I guess we could pump the pond dry and see what is really there."

"Daddy tried," began Jackson wringing his hands together, "draining the pond with a big hose one time. He guessed that it was on a spring because the pond continued to fill back up with water as soon as the water flowed out. He kept trying, but that time, it didn't work."

"That's interesting, another ambiguity. I need to add that information to my notes. Well, you know, we may need to get the divers out here."

Jackson laid his book he'd been reading on the table. "The sheriff had divers out here when they were searching for Ryan. But they couldn't go deep enough."

"Well, divers today can go deeper and are highly trained. They'll find what we're looking for."

"Oh, I didn't want so many people involved -- draws too much attention. But, if it's the only way to find our answers," admitted Maddy taking in a deep breath, "then that's what we'll have to do."

"These guys are capable of going to the bottom. We'll see what we need to do after we get all the information tomorrow. Then we'll make our decision about the divers."

"Okay, you gonna tell me what else you are hiding?" questioned Jackson.

"Daddy, what do you mean?"

"Honey, you've never been able to keep secrets from me, so tell me what else is bothering you."

"Johnny found out a reporter named Robert Brennan from *The Examiner* is looking into the case of the pond. He found out I was checking things out about the missing bodies. He may be snooping around here."

"I see," replied Jackson leaning back in his chair. "If I catch him on my property, he won't be talking."

Maddy stood and gave Jackson a hug. "You sure are something, you *big talkin'* man." She turned around. "Terry, you look tired. Enough research. Let's go outside and sit on the porch."

Terry nodded his head yes, shut off the computer, and put it back into its black bag.

Jackson continued to sit and picked his book back up.

"Jackson, aren't you going outside and sit for a while?" questioned Terry.

"I was going to read, but on second thought, I think I'll go upstairs and watch TV in my room." Jackson stood from the chair and winked at

Maddy. "I'm opening the windows in the guest bedroom and turning on the fan to cool things off."

"Daddy," Maddy insisted, "Come outside with us. It's nice."

"Honey, ya go ahead. I'm tired. Goodnight, Terry. Make yourself at home," Jackson said as he moved slowly up the stairs to his room with Gordon T following behind him.

"Thank you, Jackson," Terry called back. He turned around to face Maddy. "Alright, what was that about?"

"Oh, Daddy's trying to be a matchmaker. He wants me to move on and forget Ryan. Sorry about that."

"That's a compliment. Most people think of me as a computer nerd and not husband material," he said laughing. "Don't worry; I get the same thing when I go home. My mother won't accept that I'm not married with kids."

Maddy pushed the screen door open and sat in the swing.

"This is nice," announced Terry leaning back in the rocker. "I can hear so many crickets, what's that other noise?"

"Aw, a few katydids and some bellowing bullfrogs that live by the creek," she answered pushing the swing with her toes. "They'll get louder in August."

"You really do miss Ryan; he must've been special."

"He knew me so well and how to handle me… keep me calm."

"How old was he when he died?"

"Almost sixteen. He couldn't wait to turn sixteen so he could drive. I also knew he was going to ask me out on our first date. His mother told me. She was so excited, almost as much as he was. Everyone knew we'd end up getting married, but fate stepped in."

"I can only imagine how hard it's been on you losing Ryan. I hope we'll get some answers soon."

"The unknown has driven me crazy. I understand dying and saying goodbye, like when my mama died, but… Ryan was a great swimmer and it seems so many of the others that drown were too. That damn pond! Maybe Daddy's correct; it's why I became an agent. I have to have some closure to this mystery."

"You know, I see what you mean about the mystery. If Ryan's body had been found," he said, leaning over in the rocker lacing his hands together, "you would have had closure with the funeral. And the others, we'd have known they'd drowned. Then this would be a different mystery about why so many drowned and not where did they go. Where and why did they disappear? Why didn't they float to the top in that clear water like that one guy, Rufus? Too many unanswered questions."

"See! That pond brings you into it and somehow you've got to figure out the answer."

"Yep, I'm beginning to understand. I can't stop thinking about that crystal blue water and what secrets it holds.

"Since he couldn't figure it out, Grandpa Winfred said it was the devil's pond. Maybe he was right and there isn't another answer."

"Well, I'm a scientist and I'm going to find a real explanation." Terry leaned back in the rocker and took in a deep breath. "Boy, this is nice," he assured, rocking slowly. "Oh, the piece of material is still running; my equipment hasn't come up with an answer on it."

"It's just a regular piece of material, right?"

"I don't think so," answered Terry nervously tapping his fingers on the rocker's arms. "It's not a common fabric of any kind here in the United States. It looks very expensive. You know, some foreign countries incorporate gold and silver into fabric. We'll see in the morning what it's made of and where it came from."

"Expensive? Why would a drifter be wearing expensive clothes?" Maddy slowed the swing staring at Terry's worried face. "Look, we'll work on all this in the morning; you don't have to stay up for me. I see how tired you are. I hope we have a profitable day tomorrow."

"I think I'll call it a night. I might just sleep like a baby with that fan on and listening to the soft sounds of the night." He stood up from the rocker stretching his arms out wide. "Good night, Maddy...you need to get some rest too."

"I will now that you're here. I don't feel alone anymore. I thought maybe I was exaggerating about the pond," her head bowed and eyes drifted to the porch floor as her words became soft, "making it more than it was."

"Nope, I don't think so. It's very curious that your grandfather tried to drain the pond and it couldn't be done. Boy, that pond is a conundrum. See you in the morning."

"Good night, Terry," she whispered, letting the swing gently sway back and forth. Maddy's mind continued to churn. She sat in the quiet evening letting time tick by, reliving that one day so long ago. Her feet slid to a stop on the porch floor. Enough! She needed to rest.

"Crystal Pond, you've met your match," she said softly.

Chapter 10
The Man Who Drowned in Crystal Pond

The cool air blew into Maddy's sunny bedroom from the window. Her eyes peered at the clock: wow, nine o'clock in the morning. She leaped from the bed, Tuesday morning, a new day, and new answers. She pulled on her navy shorts and top and hurried to the bathroom to comb her hair. As she made her way down the stairs, she could hear her father and Terry in the kitchen talking.

"Good morning, sleepy head," Jackson called out when she walked in. "Did ya sleep alright? I was getting a little worried; ya never sleep in."

"I slept all night, the best sleep ever," she assured, pouring herself a cup of coffee.

"We already had breakfast, but there's some biscuits and gravy left," Jackson said, standing getting her a plate. "Do ya want an egg?"

"No, this will be just fine." She laid a biscuit on the plate tearing it open, carefully dipping the creamy, rue gravy over the warm biscuit. "How did you sleep, Terry?"

"Great, with the cool breeze blowing in my window and the darkness, it was very relaxing. I feel energized and I'm ready to see what information we have."

"Well, I'll be done in a minute," she replied.

"Don't rush with your breakfast. It will take about fifteen minutes to get the computers up and running. I'll see you in a little while." He stood. "Thank you, Jackson, for the breakfast."

"You're welcome, son." Jackson sat in his chair with a contented smile on his face.

"Alright, Daddy, don't start."

"He's a nice young man and sure does like ya and maybe there's more to this than ya think."

"No, Daddy, there's not," she protested, trying to be convincing.

The biscuit slid around in her plate sopping up the last bite of the gravy. She sat her plate in the sink, swished it out with hot water, and dried her hands.

Jackson sat quietly at the table looking out the window. She gently put her hands onto her father's shoulders. "I think today, we're going to find our answer."

His tired eyes looked up at her and he gave her hand a gentle pat. "I hope so, but honey, it might not be what ya want to hear."

She nodded her head yes and hurriedly left the room. As she stepped outside onto the porch, Maddy felt the morning sun on her face. She walked up to the huge truck and could see Terry engrossed in reading the reports.

"Well, did you find out anything?" called out Maddy climbing into the truck and scooting over next to him. "What about that piece of grey material?"

"Nothing, its makeup is different than anything I have ever seen. My cloth analyzer must be having trouble. I'm running it back through to see if I can find anything new. I hope I don't have to send it in to an FBI tech for examination."

"The material won't matter so much to our case. It might help Johnny with his Rufus Jones case. If anyone comes around, though, we'll catch him."

"Last night, I did get a lot of reports, some of them going back to the Civil War. This came from a farmer named Trenton Carson. Listen," Terry began to read. "Trenton wrote part of this when he was an old man."

"T'was a hot summer morning, that August 19th, 1863. A band of Confederate soldiers come a'marchin' up the dirt road yonder with dust a'flying ever'wher. They was a'beating them drums in a soft, slow rhythm. An eerie feelin' done come over me when I seed them young faces a'comin' at me, not much older'an my own son. Their uniforms was wored out, tattered from many battles. Thar wet brows was a'covered in sweat. My heart done broke fer'em. Many o' the young men

done had their arms in slings an' some done had bandages wrapped around their chests er heads. They was a'limping along an' all had theirselves drawed an' expressionless faces.

The commander done rid his thin horse up chere to the porch. "Sir, I'm Sergeant Bill Thornton from Georgia. My men are weary and need rest before we move on into Virginia. Would ya be so kind," he ast, "as to allow us to camp out here on your land for a few days?"

"Yore mighty welcome to stay rat chere," I replied, "iffen yore so a'mind. I've done got some food hid yonder in them thar woods in the back pasture. I seed yore men could use a meal an' need ta rest a'spell."

"Thank you, Sir, that's very kind," he ansurd, a'turnin' his horse around an' a'movin' back to his troops.

Along tords four o'clock that afternoon, theres'as'a ruckus among 'em. I drawed near 'em and seed one young feller a'soaking wet. I done had to take myself a soulful sigh for I knowed what'ad done took place, that he and some others had gon'an' taken' a dip in that dreadful pond. They knowed they'd disobeyed orders by a'leavin' camp, but must've a'spotted the crystal pool when they'as a'helpin' brang back my hidden victuals. The two older'uns decided to dive straight 'way into the pond an' they'as never seed again. That boy, he swum around some but couldn't find nary hide nor hair of them other two. They'd disappeared. I knowed the story'as true. I'd done witnessed the same thang years a'fore. I seed fer myself a good friend disappear into the heart of that there pond. No sir, I didn't say nary a word to no one 'bout my tale of woe. I jest a'whispered a prayer fer them lost souls.

I've done kept the story to myself until now. I'm an old man this year of our Lord 1896. Many a change has done occurred in this here great land of iron, but one thang has stayed a constant, that old pond. It'as a'haunted me fer a lifetime. I've done warned my children and grandchildren 'bout that evil thang, an' now I must tell my story of them missin' young Rebels who didn't lose thar lives on no battlefield, but rather by that sparkling water. Titus D. Jones an' Jargon A. Taylor nary made it home after the war. I ast the commander fer their families addresses an' sent notes to both, a'telling how sorry I felt fer thar losses.

This here story has done disturbed me fer over thirty years. I've done kept a secret only them soldiers a'camped out on my farm knew about, but they never knowed the whole story. That thar devil's pond has a 'taken many a life, an' it keeps them bodies an' thar souls.

Now, that damnable pond has done took one of my own, my youngest grandson, Jordon, only thirteen. Warnings, they didn't strike a chord o' fear in him none; no siree! The allure of that evil pond is worse'an a painted saloon girl. The pond has did a heap mor'an violate my family; it's done gone an' tore the hearts out o' my son an' his wife...an' me. I'll soon be leaving this realm fer eternity, an' maybe then, I'll larn what done happened to them young soldiers, my childhood friend, an' my grandson. --Signed and sealed by Trenton W. Carson

"Wow that was the Carson family. Trenton's son, Jacob Carson was the man who sold the property to my family. I understand now why Jacob sold the property and left so quickly; he'd lost his son to Crystal Pond. I guess I'm not the only one that pond has frightened for years."

"I'd say not. There are more stories," Terry offered. "Most are the same ones you have, including one that is about a young man named Clayton George Montgomery who lost his life in the pond in 1956."

"Yes, he was the young man that my Grandpa Winfred knew. I still wonder if Grandpa really did witness the man diving into the pond. I think Grandpa was hiding something, not telling us for all of those years. It seemed to worry him more than it should."

"Well, listen to this, Clayton George Montgomery; born 1939 in Leander, Texas," Terry got quiet and stared at her, "lives in Savannah, Georgia."

"No, Terry!" Maddy shouted and then she whispered, "That couldn't be the same Clayton G. Montgomery...or could it?"

"I don't know, but the age is the same, place of birth, everything." Terry offered. "I think we need to drive to Savannah and talk to Mr. Montgomery. Maybe it's only a coincidence or someone made a mistake."

"I don't think it's a coincidence, just strange. Let's go," she said jumping from the FBI truck. "It doesn't take long to get there, a little over two hours. You need to program the address into my navigation system in the car, and I'll tell Daddy we're leaving."

Terry shook his head as he picked up all his papers and turned off the equipment in the back of the truck.

"Daddy," Maddy called out opening the screen door and running into the house.

"Back here, I'm still in the kitchen. I picked some more tomatoes this morning and I'm going to can them this afternoon." He stopped talking, turned, and quickly summed up her expression, "What's wrong, honey?"

"Terry found some information on Clayton Montgomery, the young man that Grandpa Winfred knew. We're going to drive over to Savannah to see if we can find some answers. We should be back by late this evening, but I'll call if we have to stay."

"Oh sure. Have fun," Jackson grinned.

"Daddy, this is business. We have some new information that could help us with the investigation. I have to grab my gear."

"I'll get you some bottled water."

Thanks," she called back going up the stairs to her room.

Jackson stood on the porch with Gordon T by his side. He leaned in and handed Maddy a small cooler full of cold, bottled water. "Be careful and call later to let me know what's going on. I know you're not a little girl, but you're my little girl," he added pointedly, getting quiet and stepping back.

"We'll be fine, sir," Terry assured. "This information really needs to be checked out and could help us immensely."

"I hope so, son. I hope this'll be over soon," Jackson said swiping his hair back as he turned to the screen door with Gordon T right behind him.

Maddy threw their gear in the trunk while Terry programmed the navigation system with Clayton Montgomery's address.

The Mustang moved slowly not kicking up dust. But when the tires hit the payment of County Highway 70, Maddy pushed the gas pedal and the car took off like a rocket.

Terry laughed. "Should I drive?"

"No, I know my way to Savannah. I'll slow down, I promise," she said chuckling. "I would have never figured on this. How could this be the same man? Did my Grandpa make up the story? Why would he? Oh, he hated the pond as much as I do."

"Stop fuming. We'll know the answer soon enough."

"We don't even know if the man still lives there or is alive or even able to talk to us. Maybe we should've called."

"Nope, I didn't want to give him a head's up. He might leave and we wouldn't be able to find him. It's against the law to falsify a police report."

"I can't believe my grandpa had anything to do with anything like that."

"Maybe Clayton Montgomery went for a swim and didn't come up, so your grandpa thought he drowned and went to get help. Then Clayton climbed out of the pond while your grandpa was gone. Maybe he wanted to disappear."

"I hadn't thought about his wanting to disappear. If that's the case, he wouldn't have any answers for us, and we'd be wasting our time."

"We'll know soon the way you drive." He laughed leaning his head on the back of the seat closing his eyes.

"Hey, turn some music on," she suggested. "I do love to drive around these parts in a convertible. I feel free."

"You sure you don't need me to keep the navigation system on?"

"No, I've been to Savannah so many times that it would just get onto me for going a different route than it has plotted. We'll turn it on after we cross over the bridge into Georgia."

"Alright," he said, tuning into KBHC. Then he closed his eyes again and rested his head on the headrest.

The tall pines stood guard with music flowing from the Mustang, as small town after small town swished by. All too soon KBHC was out of range, so Maddy dialed into a Georgia station. The Savannah River Bridge was only a couple of miles away. Maddy leaned over pushing the navigational system's button. A woman's digital voice began telling which way to turn.

Terry moaned stretching his arms. "Where are we?"

"We're in Savannah, Georgia, not much farther now."

"Wow! You should've woke me. I can't believe I slept," he grinned, "especially with you driving.

"Ah," she said grinning at him, "you're just getting used to my driving."

"I don't know about that," said Terry checking out his map. "Let's see, we turn on Richford Lane on the next block to the right."

"Yep, that's what she's been saying over and over."

"There, it's the house with the red brick, 1407 Richford Lane. Well," he said laying the map on his lap, "we're here."

Maddy pulled the Mustang next to the curb and she shut off the motor. She didn't move. She sat there, mulled things over in her mind, and stared at the house with azalea and hydrangea bushes. Her right hand felt for her gun. "This man may not want to be found, so we need to be careful. Let's go," she said opening her car door, quietly pushing it closed.

The small porch had two rockers and some pots of ferns near the front door. Terry knocked. They both stepped back from the door, prepared.

The door opened slowly. A tall, thin man stood in front of them. He had wild, grey, curly hair, light brown eyes, and was leaning on a carved oak cane.

"Mr. Clayton George Montgomery," asked Terry.

"Yes," the man with the stern face said, not moving.

"I'm special agent Maples and this is special agent Sayers from the FBI," said Terry, showing his FBI badge. "May we talk to you for a few minutes?"

"Yes," the old man said, slowly backing up. "What is this about? Did you say Sayers?"

"Yes, I'm Madeline Sayers and we need to ask you a few questions."

"Have a seat," offered Clayton as he sat down in a chair. "My knees and back don't let me stand long." His piercing eyes followed them as they sat on the blue striped couch facing him.

"Mr. Montgomery," Terry began, "how long have you lived here?"

"I moved here after I retired from NASA space program. I went to school up here when I was young and enjoyed living in the area." He sat up leaned over in his chair and glared at them. "Does this have something to do with my work with the space program? Cause if it does, I can't talk about that."

"No sir," said Maddy. She handed the man the worn, folded clipping that she'd found in the white box tucked away in her mama's closet.

"Oh," he said nodding his head, "you're from the Sayers's farm. What does the FBI have to do with the old farm?"

"We want to know how you survived Crystal Pond," Terry snapped back.

"I see," Clayton gripped his hands lacing them together in a praying position. "Not much to tell. That report is wrong. I went swimming in Crystal Pond, but as you can see, I climbed out. It's only a story."

Maddy stood from the couch. "Then why did the police report say you drowned and why didn't my grandpa Winfred throw this clipping away."

"I don't know," Clayton answered, turning his head from her not able to look her in the eye.

"Sir," she insisted pacing the room, "there's more to the story, isn't there?" She stopped walking and turned to him. "More than you're telling! I can see in your face; you're hiding something."

"Nobody in all these years has ever asked me about what happened back then."

"Why didn't NASA do a background check when you started working for them?" questioned Terry. "They should've found the police report on your drowning," he paused looking at his notes, "back in '56."

"They did check in 1956 and every five years after that, but that story was back in the fifties in a tiny town that never got around to putting old editions on a web page. I never thought about it much. I let the past go, and I moved on with my life. Sorry, I can't help you."

Maddy sat and leaned back on the couch. "Mr. Montgomery, this isn't the FBI wanting to know," she explained pulling her shoulders tight together staring at the man. "I too have seen what the clear blue water can do." She took a deep breath trying to get her composure back. "I lost a good friend of mine when we were young, and I have to know what happened in the pond. I have to have some closure. Please…sir, tell me what went on. How did you escape?"

The man took a deep breath. He stood even though he said it hurt. His feet shuffled on the carpet moving over by the window. He stood quietly for a few minutes looking outside.

He turned to face Maddy. "I understand how you feel, but I don't want any problems, not now. My wife and I are old and want to live peaceful the rest of our lives. This story could destroy me."

"There IS more. I knew it," Maddy's voice trembled as she watched the old man.

Clayton nodded his head yes.

"Please, tell me," she begged.

A silence fell over the room.

Terry walked over to the man. "Sir…how about off of the record? We won't put what you tell us into our file. Maddy needs some closure. We give our word that this information will stay between the three of us and Maddy's dad."

"Yes, please, I just have to know," pleaded Maddy trying to hold back her emotions.

The old man rubbed his head with his hands and he sat back in the chair. He stared into Maddy's eyes. "You do look like your granddad, the same kind eyes. Winfred was a good man and if you're half as good as him…well," Clayton shook his head. "Alright, I'm taking a huge chance here. My wife won't be happy if she ever finds out I talked to you."

With his brown-speckled hands gripping the chair's arms tight, Clayton leaned back in the recliner and readied himself to recount the events that had been hidden for decades. Maddy tensed, wondering what could destroy this man if his story got out.

Chapter 11
Clayton Montgomery

"I guess," said Clayton taking in a deep breath, "I'll start from the very beginning. I was born in the year of 1939; my mother died in childbirth, and my father was killed a few years later while in the army. I lived with my aunt and uncle in Leander, TX; they were all the family I had. I graduated high school at the age of 16. I'd have to work my way through college, so I decided to travel instead and work along the way to see America. I worked for cash and lived in small boarding rooms as I traveled from Texas to South Carolina.

One spring day, I came upon your farm. Your great grandfather Sayers was a pleasant man and offered me a job. He said I could stay in the old barn out back. He'd provide meals and pay cash for my work. Not a bad deal, especially since your great grandmother was an amazing cook. His son Winfred, his wife, and young son lived in the old farmhouse with his parents. He was as kind and honest as his father, and we quickly became good friends.

Winfred warned me to stay away from Crystal Pond, but I didn't like to follow rules. So, one sizzling, August day, I decided to go for a swim. I was an excellent swimmer and didn't worry about the stories that the old men in town told. But that hot day, changed my life forever." Clayton took in a deep breath and looked up at Maddy.

"That summer day was unbearably hot, even got too warm for the mule to keep working in the blazing sun. It was three o'clock when

Winfred and I decided to stop plowing the field. He went inside the house, and I went back to the barn. The barn was smothering, so I decided to take a walk. I remembered how cool it was under the shade of that magnificent old oak by Crystal Pond, so I ambled out to the cool water. I slipped my pants and shirt off along with my socks and boots setting them to the side," he smiled. I stepped upon the bank's edge and, without a second thought, extended my arms out in front of me. I dove in dead center into the clear water. My body hit the cool refreshing water soothing my sweaty skin, but…" Clayton stopped talking, pausing for a moment.

"My body went through the deep water so easily, but my body didn't stop there. I felt my fingers and hands and then my arms glide into the sand of the pond. I thought I was going to break my neck and die at the bottom of that pond. I'd been warned. What a dumb move on my part! Astonishingly, my body didn't stop when it hit the sand. Deeper and deeper into the belly of the pond I went. It became black as midnight. I needed to breathe. I tightened my eyelids feeling the sand crystals rubbing my face. It seemed like hours, but it was only terrifying seconds. Then there was light so bright that I could hardly see. The light grew. I finally took in a deep gulp of air. The pain from my lungs was excruciating from the first gasp. I felt a fine mist hit my face. I felt weightless. My arms spread out as if I were floating through the air like a feather. Had I gone to Heaven?

The mist dissipated and the light grew brighter. I screamed seeing I wasn't in the pond anymore. I was falling from the sky; trees and the ground were coming at me. I continued to descend downward, not like a parachutist, but more like a leaf floating gently on a breeze. My body was literally gliding. I was in the sky and the mist had been a cloud that I'd come through. How? I didn't know.

My body jolted when my feet touched the ground, and I looked back up into the sky from where I'd come. I stood not moving looking around trying to figure out what had occurred. My hands grabbed my throbbing head; it felt as if it might explode. I thought I'd died like the rest of the people who had drowned, and this was Heaven. I believed that I'd hit sinking sand and my body would never be found, just like the others.

THE GATEKEEPER

Heaven was unusual, not what I had presumed it to be, so normal like our world. I thought there'd be blooming flowers, people greeting me with songs and smiles, but nothing. I was disorientated but understood that this wasn't the Sayers Farm. A forest full of giant trees was to my right. They were strange with green bark, not brown, and their leaves were like large ferns dropping down.

I scanned the area and spotted a large farmhouse made out of the wood from the tall trees. I began walking toward the farmhouse in a dazed state still believing I'd died.

A short, squatty man with gray, curly hair walked out of the barn that was a few yards from the house. He saw me. Panic came over his face when he noticed I was half naked and dripping wet. His pitchfork fell to the ground and he ran to me.

Anxiety showed all over his face. 'Son,' he said pulling in a deep breath, 'did you happen to come from the Crystal Pond?'

"I was at a loss for words, so I just nodded my head yes.

'C'mon in the house and let's get you some dry clothes and shoes. My name is Jeffery Walden.' Of course, I told him my name."

Maddy gasped. "Oh," she whispered, hearing the name of one of the other men from the newspaper clippings.

"The farmhouse door opened and this woman about as round as she was tall, her hair pulled tight in a gray bun, stood in the kitchen busily cooking. She was making some fried pies that smelled delicious. I later learned they were made from franberries that grew on bushes similar to blackberries that we grow.

'Martha,' said Jeffery, 'I've gotta get this young fellow some dry clothes and something to put on his feet.'

Martha's round body turned from the stove and her head nodded yes. 'I see.' She left the kitchen, not saying anything else.

I stood on the rug by the back door trying not to drip on the wooden floor.

In a few minutes, the woman walked into the kitchen holding clothes in her hand. 'Here, ya go. These pants will be short on you for sure, but I'll cut them off to make shorts out of them later,' said Martha in a sympatric voice. 'Your feet are bigger than Jeffrey's too, but maybe these sandals will work until we can do better. You can change in the back room. Jeffery will show you where it is.'

In a dazed state, I followed the man into a bedroom. Jeffery didn't say anything just turned and left closing the bedroom door. I dressed with my mind still in a haze. I held my underwear in my hands and walked back to the kitchen. Martha reached over and kindly took them and put them in a *washer* with liquid soap. I'd never seen *the like*. Then she dried them in a *dryer*. It sure was different from a wash pot and a clothesline.

Jeffrey sat at the kitchen table. 'Have a seat; I've called for my brother Tom to come over. Don't look so worried; you're fine.'

In a few minutes, this short, thin, balding man, who looked similar to Jeffrey but older, opened the kitchen door and he slowly stepped into the room. His eyes peered over at me as he pulled out a kitchen chair and sat.

'My name is Tom.' He looked at his brother. 'Jeffery, give this young man, a cup of warm, strong coffee,' Tom finally smiled. 'He may need something stronger when we're done talking.' He smiled. 'This coffee is a little different than what you're used to, however, it does the job.'

Jeffery sat the cup of coffee in front of me and I tried to sip it, but my hands were trembling and I sloshed hot coffee onto the table.

'We too,' began Tom in a deep but soft voice, 'came from the pond. We lived with our family next to the Sayers Farm. One hot scorching day back in 1933, we decided to go for a swim in Crystal Pond with our younger brother, Billy. We'd heard the stories of the pond and had been told to stay away from it, but obviously, we didn't. We had made a bet about which one of us could dive the deepest. Like you, we never came back up out of the water, just kept going through the sand, ending up here.'

Where's here? I asked them.

'Well, that is a hell of a big question!' Tom stopped for a moment and sipped his coffee, his eyes on me.

'It seems we are in a new world, one so like Earth, but a world blended with futuristic technology. Most of the people do speak English, or a form of English. A few speak a different dialect that we don't understand very well. Sorry, we don't have all the answers. We quickly found this abandoned farmhouse along with some old papers.' Tom paused and looked over at Jeffery."

Clayton stood, opened a desk drawer, and pulled out a sheet of paper.

"This is a copy of the letter that Jeffery handed me," Clayton began to read,

I, Titus D. Jones n Jargon A. Taylor, Confederates soldiers in the southern army with Commander Sergeant Bill Thornton have died, or so we believe, this August 20th, 1863. We've left our homes n our families n we're ta live here until eternity. We've been punished fer disobeying orders n not staying with our troop that hot August day. We'll live here as well as we can, not understanding wos around us, where we are, or how we come ta be in this strange world. We've built shelter n had plenty of food; we'll survive until the end of time. Titus D. Jones n Jargon A. Taylor, Confederate soldiers.

The letter began again at the bottom of the page in scribbled handwriting.

Years have gone by n in our time, I believe in our world it'd be 1916. We've grown older, n it's strange, no questions have been answered of where we are or how we came ta be in this world. We each met young women n we've married n continue ta live our lives, having children, watching them grow n move away. We built our home and furniture just as we had back in Tennessee. Our lives have been one of fulfillment n love, but lonely missing our family n our world we left behind. Where are we? I still can't say.

Jargon A. Taylor passed last evening, so we aren't immortal n this ain't Heaven. I miss my buddy so much, but understand my time'll be coming soon. My wife, Lilly passed a couple of years ago n this life has now become very lonely. I wish I'd some answers ta leave ta ya, my friends, but I'm sad ta say I don't.

There've been a few more of us that've fallen through the sand over the years, again without answers. Many have left us going exploring never to be heard of again. I leave this letter for the next one of us ta find n maybe someday they'll find the answer of where we are. God bless ya, my friend, n keep ya safe on this adventure. Titus D Jones, a Rebel soldier from Shelby County, Tennessee, Confederate States of America.

"I asked looking at the two men whether they ever found out exactly where we were. They shook their heads no.

'This world is similar to ours back home; there is a city, or what they call a polis, not far that's full of people like us. They have more technology than in our world. The stories have gone on about strange beings falling from the sky. They don't deal with people like us, and if they find out you are one of the people that fell from the sky, you'll be put to death."

Maddy gasped, "No!" She stood walking around the room.

"My dear, I'm sorry to worry you more," Clayton, insisted.

"I'm sorry," she said sitting. "Mr. Montgomery, please continue."

"I sat there at that kitchen table staring at the men, feeling like the Confederate soldiers believing that maybe I'd died.

'Don't worry so," Jeffrey insisted. 'You'll be fine if you follow the rules of this world. The polis is called Macrobi. We met our wives, Martha and Joyce one day in Macrobi. We were being naive and talking to one of the police officers trying to find out where we were, asking for help. Martha overheard what we were saying. The officer went back to his QLR, or flying car, to call for help. Martha grabbed hold of me, pulling me inside a door and Tom followed. We ran through the small building out the back and into the alley. She led us to the bank of a hill and over to a small cave. You see, this is a cruel world, and it's controlled by one mean son of a gun. Like I said before, death is the alternative if you don't follow the rules.'

'So, this is my life to live here forever?' I asked, looking over at the two men.

'Yes, we're sorry. There's no way to get home.'

'Jeffery, did you say a flying car?'

'Yes, a flying QLR, jet aero car. Like I said, their technology is more advanced than our worlds.'

'Do you need that drink? I do have something more powerful than coffee,' Jeffery assured.

I sat at the kitchen table staring at the writings of a Confederate soldier. 'No thank you, sir, but thank you for your help. I'd like to stay here for a while until I figure out what to do.'

'No problem, but you just keep a low profile,' Tom added. 'We don't need any problems.'

'I'll be careful, sir.'

The two men sat there at the kitchen table asking me questions about my time. I had to tell those two men that their mother was still alive, but their father had died along with their brother Billy who had died of polo a few months before. They stood when I was done with their faces drawn and tears in their eyes.

Days went by and the day did arrive when I packed a bag with food and water and I headed out to the small cave they'd told me about near the city.

I studied this world as I walked. The sky was just as ours, but the grass was moss like with red dirt, however it wasn't my world. Strange birds flew over my head; the cattle, similar to our cattle but a whole lot larger more like elephants, were out in the fields. I could hear dogs barking or what I'd call barking in the distance. I walked through the pasture staying out of sight as I made my way to Macrobi.

My heart pounded in my chest. The will to survive was in me and I knew I should surrender and live here for the rest of my life, but I wanted to find a way back home. I kept a diary each day of my journey while I camped out in the small cave.

I took short walks each day into Macrobi City watching people hurrying everywhere. It was difficult for my mind to comprehend the small flying cars zooming past. I did notice one such vehicle coming at me with lights blinking all over the craft and I remembered the story told by Tom. I quickly ducked into a building. The aroma in the room was overwhelming full of fresh baked bread.

A young beautiful girl with long, curly, dark brown hair came up to me. 'May I help you?' she asked in a sweet voice. I stared. I'd never seen such stunning blue eyes. I couldn't find my voice. She smiled at me and went behind the counter. There she pulled out a warm, thick slice of fresh baked bread, handing it to me.

I found my voice. 'I can't afford to buy any bread. Thank you anyway.'

'No, this slice of bread is for you to try, no charge. It's buttered.'

I took the warm bread and butter letting it melt in my mouth. 'Thank you,' I blurted.

'My name is Bayle. My father owns this store. You aren't from the city, are you?"

'I'm from the country; my name is Clayton,' I said wondering what she was going to say. I should've turned around and left the store, but I kept standing there hypnotized by her blue eyes.

'I figured,' answered Bayle. 'Now, who are you?'

My heart stopped, she was so beautiful, but had I let beauty do me in?

'I told you my name is Clayton.' I turned around to leave. 'I need to go. Thanks for the bread.'

Bayle grabbed my arm with her soft fingers.

I tensed not wanting to hurt her, but I kept trying to pull away.

'I know most of the people from the farms, and I also know Jenny Walden who lives on one. You're one of those people, aren't you? Don't worry, I'm not telling anyone.'

'What gave me away?'

'It'll be hard for you to hide, you're so different. You'll need to be careful. Don't think others won't notice.'

'Great,' I answered sighing, feeling even more lost.

'I live in the back of this building. You can come to the back door that is in the alley if you need anything and I'll help.'

'Why,' I asked.

'Just say I like you. Isn't that enough?' Bayle added grinning.

'You might get in trouble. I can't take that chance.'

'You do care about others. I am a good judge of character. Now, Clayton, where are you staying?'

'Out in the country in a cave not far from here,' I answered knowing I was talking too much.

'Yes, I know the cave. Jenny and I played there when we were young. I'll meet you there in the morning and bring you some food. You need to leave and go straight there. Don't hang out in the city.'

I left Bayle, closed the door to the building, and stepped around into the alley. I ran not stopping until I made it to the small cave. I sat at the entrance trying to catch my breath. That night I wasn't able to sleep. I just kept worrying.

Time moved on and Bayle did as she promised and kept me fully supplied with everything I needed, including information on the flying QLR. When she was with me, my fears heightened. I was so worried for her, afraid she was going to get caught by the patrols. But day after day, she'd come to the cave bringing me more supplies and statistics on the crafts.

Sam, a man about forty-five, a friend of Bayle's owned a shop that worked on the QLRs. He didn't worry that I was different, and he agreed to let me work with him. I quickly learned how the machines were made. I was able to take one of the crafts apart making it lighter and faster, supercharging it. I'd come up with a theory that if I could build a rocket, I might be able to send the jet car up into the clouds and back into the bottom of the pond. I worked diligently experimenting each day. I needed more power to make my small rocket lift off.

Bayle and I spent more and more time together, and I soon realized I'd fallen in love. My heart broke questioning if I really wanted to leave. I could stay and live my life in her world, work with Sam, and never go back to my time. But, something inside kept drawing me home; I couldn't stay in her world.

The day did arrive. I believed my craft was strong enough to reach the sky and skyrocket me back up into the clouds and through the bottom into the sand and water. Bayle had convinced me to take her with me even though I knew I could be killing us both.

I modified the craft to hold us and made each of us helmets. I flew the craft out to the exact spot I had entered this world the year before. I said goodbye to Jeffery and Tom leaving them my journal to put with the letter from the Confederate soldiers. They didn't want to come out and watch, believing Bayle and I were going to die.

I kissed Bayle. We climbed onto the craft, the motor started, and the large engine began to whine. I leaned the craft straight back letting the motor rev. I said a prayer, and then I hit the supercharger. The craft became a bullet flying straight for the cloud. My head throbbed and everything went black. I couldn't breathe. Then…I felt the cool water on my face. I grabbed Bayle letting the craft slip from under us falling back to the other world. I swam to the surface clinging to Bayle. I pulled her out of the pond and we both lay on the ground. I began to laugh hysterically staring up into my sky. We'd made it back to my world. I couldn't believe what'd happened. Was it a dream? No, there was Bayle beside me.

I helped her off the ground and I lead her to the Sayers's farmhouse. Winfred was standing to the side near the barn. He turned pale seeing me walking up, both of us soaking wet. I told him my story and he didn't judge me, knowing something had happened. He told Judith, his wife, my story and she wasn't quite sure she believed the story, but she helped Bayle out of her wet clothes and gave her some dry ones.

I stood looking at my best friend in this world. We both knew Bayle and I couldn't stay on the farm. We couldn't answer any questions about where I'd been for the last year or who Bayle was. We had to move on. Winfred drove us to a small town in Georgia. I found a job and was soon able to go to school just as I'd hoped."

Clayton's head moved back and forth slowly. "I never talked to Winfred again. I didn't want to get him into trouble, but I sure missed my friend. I studied at Georgia Tech here in Savannah and became an astronautical engineer. After college, I worked at NASA as an aerospace engineer in Florida. I literally became a rocket scientist. I worked on aircrafts and even a spacecraft or two. Workings on that small craft in the other world helped significantly. I've lived my life designing and building many types of spacecrafts and wondering what else was out there above or below us. I've tried to study about the pond and the phenomenon it is, but even with my resources at NASA, I haven't been able to find an answer.

Well, that is my story. You may or may not believe it, but it is true. I admonish you again, no one should ever know about my experience. The world would think I was insane, and the press would ruin my life." He sat back looking at the two young people in front of him.

Maddy leaped up off the couch, "I have to go into water and find Ryan. He could be alive."

"Wait a second; if he's alive, Maddy…you have to think," Terry snapped. "He might not want to leave. He could have found someone else and started a life. It has been over ten years, and he's a grown man."

"I understand and that would hurt, but I could live with the knowledge, knowing he is alive and well. I need at least to say goodbye."

"My dear," Clayton began, "it's not that easy to leave that world. It could be impossible to do again."

"I have to. We could take some kind of small rocket with us," Maddy said excitedly. "We could go prepared!"

"Maddy," Terry began, "we don't have any idea what that world is or how it came to be. We have to do some research first and I don't know what kind of craft we could use to fly back into the pond. I'm not trained to fly, and I'm not sure I want to go into that pond."

"He's right, young lady. I got lucky, but you might not be so lucky. It has been many years. It was a strange world and could've changed. You could be falling into something that could get you killed."

"At long last, there's hope. I have to see for myself that Ryan's alive. I'm determined to go into the pond."

"He might not be around that area, many of the pond's people left to go exploring and never came back," Clayton argued. "I don't know what is out past the city. Bayle might know."

"Mr. Montgomery you could help us design someway to fly back up into the sky. You understand what we'd need," Maddy begged.

"My dear, I'm an old man, and I don't know whether I could produce anything that would be of use to you. There are materials and costs involved. This project would be too hard on me."

"Well, not for one person," this soft voice came from behind them. A woman with the bluest eyes stepped near.

"Bayle, how long have you been there?"

"Long enough to hear," she said. "We need to help this young girl. I once was in her position not wanting you to leave. Remember?"

"Yes," Clayton assured, smiling up at his wife.

"You took the chance for us to be together and she needs to know, or at least try…I understand. I still don't comprehend what went on back then, but I'm glad you fell into that pond." She patted Clayton lovingly on the back.

"Mrs. Montgomery, what did you mean, *one person*," Maddy asked.

"Well sweetie, and call me Bayle, our son is an astronautical engineer at NASA and he'd be able to help you. He also knows the story of where I'm from. He is part from this world and my world. He's talked about trying to find a way back to my world, but hasn't ever tried. He might be interested."

"Bayle, it's too dangerous for Michael. We could lose our only son," Clayton protested wringing his hands.

"Clayton," she continued, "it'd be up to him. We don't have the right to stop him from learning about his heritage. He'd have help now and not be going alone. Even if he didn't go into the pond, he could assist these two. He's studied what they'd need to take with them. You two worked on a plan years ago."

"Please, Mr. Montgomery," pleaded Maddy. "Let us at least talk to your son. She's right; he doesn't need to go into the pond. I'll go."

"Dear, I don't want to lose my son, but I don't want to lose you either. I'd never forgive myself, and then when I die, I'd have to face Winfred for letting his granddaughter go into that pond."

"Well now, it's too late, I'm going into that pond with or without your help. I have to have more answers, and if it were the other way around, Ryan'd be coming after me, no matter what."

"Oh, you're as stubborn as Bayle," Clayton said grasping the arms of the chair. "Alright, I'll call Michael and let you know what he says. Give me your phone number. It may be a while; he does like to think things over."

"I'll talk to him, sweetie," said Bayle in whispering voice looking at Maddy. "My son is as stubborn as me."

Maddy looked at the women. "You really came from a different world?"

"Yes, one so similar to yours, but so different in many ways."

"I still don't know about this plan," said Terry. He stood shaking his head. "This is more than I bargained for."

"Look Terry, you don't need to go into the pond either," Maddy assured. "I'm a trained agent and can handle myself, but I'd feel better if you helped me get ready."

"But," Terry said in an exasperating voice, "I don't know how much I can hide from the Bureau." He shook his head back and forth, "Another world!"

"Don't look so worried, Mr. Montgomery. We'll keep your secret. This'll be a fishing expedition on our own, and we won't involve you. Terry, we don't have to tell all, just part, but we'll keep good records if this ever came out. I'll take full responsibility for this assignment."

Terry didn't say anything else he just stood shuffling his feet.

"Here's, my card with my phone number," offered Maddy handing it to Mr. Montgomery.

"Now, young lady, you don't do anything foolish, when you get home. I've done enough foolishness in my life. You need to plan this out very precisely to get this done right. You don't want to go into that world and not be able to come out. Your young man might not be around. I don't want you to get stuck there. You're needed here more than there, and that, I'm afraid, is something you are failing to see. Take your time."

"I will, Mr. Montgomery," Maddy replied leaning over giving him a hug. "Thank you for trusting me with your story. It's also a great love story, and I hope my story will have a happy ending, too."

"Sweetie, never give up, but do as Clayton said. This is dangerous, and it's been a long time since we were there," said Bayle pulling Maddy close. "But, I do understand."

Terry walked to the door and then waved. "Thank you, sir," he called back turning the knob on the front door.

Bayle softly whispered to Maddy, "Michael will help you; don't worry."

"Thank you," Maddy turned from the woman and followed Terry to the car. The motor started.

Terry rubbed his mouth with his fingers, tensing his shoulders.

"Stop worrying so," Maddy called out pulling the car away from the curb.

"I don't know, Maddy, this isn't just some strange pond. This is about finding another world. We need to tell someone."

She pulled the car over pushing it into park. "Terry, no, we can't have this become a circus. The government will do something stupid, and then I wouldn't be able to go into the pond and find Ryan. They'd destroy my father's farm. Please, don't say anything."

"Maddy," Terry became quiet letting his voice fade away.

She slid the stick shift into drive and headed toward the Savannah River Bridge. Terry sat quietly as they drove home.

Her mind spun; saying repeatedly in her head, *Surely Ryan is alive.* Libby had kept saying a mother knows these things and her son wasn't dead, but no one believed her. Maybe that was why Maddy couldn't let this go either.

Maddy's body trembled. Ryan could be alive. Again, she knew that he might've moved on finding a new love, and she'd have to deal with the knowledge of Ryan loving another. It would break her heart, but knowing he was happy and alive would help her handle the pain of losing him. She wanted to shout not worrying about the other world, maybe not thinking clearly, but saying it repeatedly in her mind, *Ryan is alive.*

Chapter 12
Michael

The Mustang pulled to a stop next to the old farmhouse. They'd made it home about seven thirty. Jackson sat in a rocker out front. He watched them as they stepped up on the porch and sat down. "Well, by the looks on your faces, ya must've found out something. Honey, did you eat?"

"No, Daddy we didn't have lunch or supper, but we'll get something in a little while," she admitted, pushing the swing back and forth by habit.

Terry sat in the other rocker. He bent over gripping his hands together. "Tell him, Maddy. Tell him the story; I think he's going to agree with me."

"Tell me what?" questioned Jackson "What did ya learn?"

"Daddy," Maddy began, "this is a long story and one you won't believe. We found the answer to the Crystal Pond, but we found some more questions with it."

"Alright, well…start talking," Jackson said looking at his daughter.

"We found Clayton Montgomery, the man who supposedly drowned in the pond years ago. The man Grandpa Winfred knew, his best friend."

"What! How can you find a dead man?" questioned Jackson.

"Well, he *ain't* dead, Daddy. He lived his life working for NASA and not telling anyone his story. But Grandpa Winfred knew it and Grandmother Judith did too."

"What did Papa and Mamma know? Why didn't they ever tell me any of this?"

"For one thing, this is a hard one to believe, sir," Terry answered. "Your parents, I'm sure, didn't want you to get into trouble, knowing the story."

"Go on, tell me," Jackson insisted rubbing his hair.

Maddy began the story of Clayton Montgomery and Jackson kept shaking his head that this couldn't be for real. He was shocked when she brought up the Walden boys. She finished with Grandpa Winfred taking Clayton and Bayle Montgomery to Georgia and never seeing them again.

"No, honey," Jackson said before Maddy could say anything else. "Ya ain't gonna go into that pond after Ryan, I forbid it!" he snapped. He stood from his rocker not saying another word, going into the house, letting the screen door slam.

"I knew he'd feel like me. This is too much for us. You can't go into that pond," Terry announced, taking in a deep breath.

"I'm not going to argue with you or him right now. I'm starving and fixing me some left over roast and cornbread. You do what you want." She stood biting her lip getting irritated at Terry.

Terry sat for a few minutes in the rocker. Finally, he followed her into the kitchen. He smiled. There, on the table were two plates with warm roast and cornbread, along with butter. He sat across from Maddy knowing she was going to have her way no matter what. She was a grown woman and no one could stop her.

Maddy picked up their dishes putting them into the dishwasher and turning it on. "I'm going to take a long bath, and think things through. See you in the morning."

Terry scooted his chair up to the table's edge. He sat quietly, elbows on the table, hands supporting head. He seemed lost in thought.

The warm water flowed over Maddy's body as she soaked in the old, claw-footed tub. Thinking of Ryan, her counterpart, was as soothing as the warm water to her. Ryan could anticipate her thoughts. She didn't even have to talk; he could read her mind always knowing what she was thinking. Her finger touched her lips feeling the one kiss, their first kiss. Her mind wouldn't stop. She stepped out of the tub, drying off. She slipped on her boxer shorts and top, hanging her towel on the hook to dry. She opened the door. She could hear the TV in Terry's room. Her father's room was dark and quiet, but she knew he wasn't sleeping. He was sitting in his chair looking out the window into the darkness, worrying.

This was complicated. She picked up the picture of Ryan. Thoughts raced through her mind like a movie. If she'd known how to swim and had dove in after Ryan, they'd been together this whole time and maybe found their way back out of that world. So many scenarios of what could've been! What had happened to Ryan when he arrived in that world? Were some of the Walden's children living in the old farmhouse? Did he stay there with them or move on? She had to know the answer hoping Michael Montgomery would call and agree to help. Of course, then she'd have to deal with her daddy and Terry.

"I've got to get some rest," Maddy said out loud to herself. So, she closed her eyes and listened to the crickets. Her head sank into her pillow and the next thing she knew, she was waking up with Ryan's picture lying next to her. She jumped out of bed, closed her door, dressed, and was ready for a new day. A day to convince her daddy and Terry she'd be able to survive going into another world.

She sighed when she walked into the kitchen and saw her dad and Terry at the breakfast table talking in hushed tones. She knew she was the topic of their conversation.

"Good morning." She picked up a cup and poured hot coffee inside.

A frown of concern grew on Jackson's face. "Were your ears burning? We've been talking about..."

"Now, Daddy, don't start. I'll be careful."

"Well then, would ya like some breakfast? Terry, here, just wanted some cereal."

"Cereal is fine with me," she assured, not wanting to discuss the pond.

Her cell phone began to ring and she jumped pulling it out of its case.

"Hello...yes. Michael... I'm at the farm in Pine Grove. Late today would be fine. I know your father's worried, so is mine. Alright, see you this evening, bye." She clicked the off button looking at the men sitting in front of her.

"I guess that was Michael Montgomery?" questioned Terry.

"Yes, and he's coming later today with everything we'll need," she answered.

"I don't like this a bit," Jackson said, giving her a look.

"Let the man get here. Give him a chance, and then we'll see what you think."

"I won't think any different after talking to him. I don't want ya to go into that pond."

"I'm taking every precaution I can, Daddy. I promise to be careful. Stop worrying."

"This whole mess isn't right; we should leave that pond alone. My daddy knew about this and didn't tell me. He knew better." Jackson stood going out the back door letting it slam, a sign of his frustration.

"Well, aren't you going to say something too?" asked Maddy giving Terry a sarcastic look.

"Why, you've made up your mind and I can't stop you, but you should leave this to the professionals."

"Professionals, like who, the FBI, or a rocket scientist. Terry, we're the professionals," she said, getting up putting the dishes into the dishwasher. "Now, you're not going to change your mind and put any of this into the files of the FBI, are you?"

"No, would you stop asking. I gave my word, but then again if anything happens to you, I might have to tell the story."

"Well then, I'll have to complete the mission and come back. I promise. Oh, it seems I'm making a lot of promises. I'll write down the entire story. Satisfied? Then, I'm also going to try and figure out where or what that other world is."

"What are you going to do today before Michael gets here?" Terry asked.

"Try and think this through. Maybe we should do some research on strange happenings in the world with ponds or unexplained disappearances."

"That I can handle," Terry added getting up going to the front door. He stopped and looked back at her.

Jackson stayed busy in his garden only coming inside to fix lunch. Maddy could see the worry on his face, and it hurt knowing she was the cause of it. Terry intensely searched data bases for bodies of water associated with unexplained deaths and evidence from Crystal Pond.

Maddy climbed into the huge FBI truck. As she watched the monitors and lights blink, she saw Terry absorbed in his work. She sat there quietly. He finally turned around and faced her holding onto the gray piece of material.

"You know, I still can't get any hits on this fabric," he said taking a sharp breath. "This fabric could be from the other world."

"What did you say?"

"This," Terry snapped tossing the piece of fabric to her, "could be from the world Clayton described. It's not from this world."

"Terry, oh…"

"Yep, that'd mean someone else has come through the sand and into our world. Maddy, this is bigger than the two of us, we need help."

"We're getting help with Michael."

"No, we need more agents, ones with more experience with phenomena like Crystal Pond."

"Don't put yourself down; you're the smartest person I know. You can find the answers for us."

"Maddy…"

"No, not until we find Ryan, and then if we have to, I'll bring in more people. Like I said, the government would mess this up. It has to stay a secret."

"It might not be a secret if others have found out about the portal to another world."

"Then let's find our answers. Maybe Ryan can help. You promised."

"Okay, okay. I'm not going back on my promise," Terry answered turning back around flicking switches.

Maddy held onto the small piece of fabric biting her lip. She left Terry working in the back of the truck. She sat on the porch trying to figure out how this was to play out.

Around seven o'clock that evening, a black SUV came rolling slowly up the driveway, not stirring up dust. Maddy stood from the porch swing. Terry and her father didn't move and just kept sitting in the rockers. A tall man with broad shoulders in his early thirties stepped out of the vehicle.

Michael's dark, wavy hair curved around his tan face just like his father's, but his eyes were vibrant blue eyes like his mother's. He stepped upon the first step and stopped.

"Michael?" Maddy asked moving over to the porch steps.

Michael smiled showing his deep dimples. "Yes, and you're Maddy Sayers?"

"Yes," she answered stepping back, so he could step up on the porch. "Michael Montgomery, this is my father Jackson Sayers and this is Terry Maples."

Terry stood from the rocker standing a few inches taller than Michael who was about six feet tall. Terry thrust his hand out to Michael and they shook hands giving each other cold steel stares. Michael turned toward Jackson, and the old man reluctantly stood to shake hands. Maddy saw a slight grin come on Michael's face when he turned back around facing her. He understood immediately the nervous undertones of the two men.

"Please sit," Maddy said, patting the swing for him to sit next to her. "How was your drive over from Savannah?"

"Fine, it's not a long drive over here, but it did take me a while this morning to get prepared. I had to take some time off from work. Boy," added Michael taking in a deep breath of air, "it's nice and quiet out here."

"Yep," snapped Jackson, "and we want to keep it that way."

"I understand how you feel and my father feels the same. He wished he could've come with me to see the old farm. He hopes to come out later and meet you, Mr. Sayers. He sure did like your father."

"I'd like to meet your father," Jackson declared his voice calming, "and he is welcome out here anytime."

Becoming quiet to study the men sitting in front of him, Michael leaned back in the swing.

"Did you eat?" Maddy asked.

"Yes, I'm fine," Michael assured looking at her, "but thank you anyway."

"In the morning, I'll show you around the farm," Maddy offered staring up at Michael. Something about him made her feel calm even though his being at the farm was going to cause a lot of turmoil.

Jackson stood; I'm going to my room for a while to watch TV. Michael, do make yourself at home. Maddy'll see to you," he said going into the house with Gordon T following.

"Seems like my arrival has put people on edge," Michael replied leaning over in the swing stopping it with his feet.

"Well, Jackson doesn't like the plan of going into the pond," said Terry.

"Terry, what do you think about it," Michael asked point blank, not beating around the bush.

"I don't know yet, but I'm not sure about dealing with the pond. Maybe Jackson is right," answered Terry raising one eyebrow with his eyes on Michael.

"I brought all the data and plans that Dad and I drew up years ago. I also brought two jetpacks that I've worked on for years. Dad helped with their designs. They're waterproof and have enough thrust to get us back to the pond from the other world."

"Us," shrieked Maddy raising her voice, "you're going with me into the pond?"

"Yes, of course," explained Michael, "I wouldn't let you go alone, and you don't even have to go if you don't want to. I can go alone. I'm not missing this opportunity to go back to see where my family is from. Remember, I'm part of both worlds."

Terry moaned and a frown grew on his face as he anxiously rubbed his mustache with his fingers.

"You're worried about that aren't you, Terry?" added Michael. "There's more to this than not just wanting Maddy to go into the pond. Because you don't know me, you have reservations about me. Am I right? After all, I'm from the other world, and I'll be all alone with Maddy."

"What?" Maddy blurted out, looking over at Terry.

"Maddy," warned Terry, "we don't know anything about him, and we don't know anything about that world."

"Terry," snapped Maddy her voice rising, "I can handle myself. You and Daddy need to quit patronizing me."

Terry's hands gripped the seat of the rocker. "Maddy, you don't know what you'll be falling into when you go into the pond. Maybe I should go too."

"Terry, this is getting silly," offered Maddy, "you didn't want to go into the pond in the first place. I want to find Ryan and Michael wants to see his world, and besides, we need someone to stay here to help."

Maddy's eyes glanced at the piece of gray fabric lying on the table next to the living room window.

Michael leaned over and picked up the fabric gently rubbing it with his fingers.

Maddy bit her lip turning her head to the side away from Michael.

"Alright, what's up with this material?" questioned Michael.

"That piece of material," said Terry, "we think came from the other world."

"What, how? It's not worn or faded. It can't be old enough to have come from Dad or Mom." Michael leaned back in the swing stretching arm out into more light to examine the fabric. "Huh, you think this is new and someone else has found the entrance into our world?"

"Yes," said Maddy turning her face to Michael, "we think someone is spying on us."

"Guys, this isn't a good thing," Michael said briskly, shaking his head. "That world is highly intelligent and in many ways superior to ours. The dictator of that world controls all the people and would love to send his military here to take control as well."

"We have to find Ryan, first," Maddy insisted. "Then we will deal with the intruder."

"I agree; we need to finish our mission and close the entrance so no one else can come into our world. That world is capable of controlling our computers and taking over this world, not just the United States."

"See, Maddy," Terry began, "we need to tell someone. This may already be way out of our control."

"And, it may not be," she declared. "We don't know!"

"She's right, we can't let this out, not yet. We need to find out what's going on before we turn this into a chaotic mess," Michael added.

"This may already be an international mess," Terry said, standing walking to the edge of the porch with his hands tucked into his jean pockets.

"We're going ahead with our plan, and then we'll consider our options when we return," assured Michael.

"I wonder," Terry began leaning his head back staring up into the starry sky, "if we could set up some kind of communication system with you."

"Dad and I thought about that. We came up with a way to try to communicate, but we're unable to determine its reliability," Michael concluded. "I have some strong walkie-talkies in the truck, and we've come up with a plan to change channels in a sequence every few minutes and see if we could find each other. It's possible for the walkie-talkies to work, but only near the entrance."

"Yes," Terry leaned over. "That might work; we'd have to add some kind of stronger antenna to them. I'll get to work on it," Terry added excitedly.

"Good, I'll give you the walkie-talkies in the morning," offered Michael.

Maddy sat back in the swing and let Michael and Terry talk. Terry quit protesting the mission and suddenly became enamored with it. Hours went by and Maddy finally spoke up, "It's getting late and we have a lot of work ahead of us tomorrow. Come on Michael, I'll show you to your room. Daddy runs an attic fan, and it'll cool your room, but you have to leave your bedroom door open."

"Yep, it works great," Terry assured.

"That'll be fine, but I might not leave my door open. I don't have to have it that cool. I need to get my things out of the truck," he said.

Terry looked over at Maddy leaning in whispering, "There's something different about that guy. I can't quite figure it out, maybe it's because he's a creature from another world."

"Stop," Maddy said in a quiet voice, hitting Terry on the arm.

Michael stepped up on the porch grinning at her; he'd heard what Terry said. He followed Maddy into the house. They went up the stairs to the bedroom next to Terry's. Turning the ceiling light on, Maddy offered, "If you need anything, let me know."

"I'll be fine Maddy," said Michael standing inches from her. "My mom told me about Ryan, and don't worry, we're going to find him."

"Your mom is very kind. Thank you for your help. Now, get some rest, and tomorrow I'll show you Crystal Pond."

"I can't wait to see the pond. It's something I've thought about all my life. Goodnight, Maddy."

Maddy left the room and stopped by Terry's room. She whispered, "Terry, now you be good tomorrow and stop treating Michael like he's an alien."

"He is an alien, Maddy, and you need to be careful," responded Terry.

"Terry," she snipped back at him peeking into the bedroom giving him a look, "stop that." She turned and hurried to the bathroom.

The shower felt refreshing. There was too much to think about, and she didn't want to turn the water off. Her bathroom was nice place to hide from everyone. Reluctantly, she stepped out of the tub slipping on her shorts and top. Hurrying to peek down the hall, she noticed that Michael's door was closed. "Alright Maddy, don't think so much, maybe he just wants privacy," she thought trying not to let Terry's talk of his being an alien get to her. She lay in her bed but she was anxious about the next few days. Terry was right, she was going into a new world, not just going to another country, so she'd have to stay on the alert and be prepared.

Chapter 13
Mirror Image

Maddy's eyes closed and sleep came, but she was awake early the next morning before the sun. She quickly dressed and made her way silently down the stairs. It was quiet, but she could see Michael's silhouette in the overstuffed chair in the dark living room next to the front window.

"Good morning," she said quietly walking into the room.

"Oh, good morning. I hope I didn't wake you?"

Maddy moved over by a table. She clicked on a lamp letting the light show Michael's tired and worried face. "No, you didn't wake me."

"It's nice and peaceful out here," he replied. "You can get a lot of thinking done."

"You sure can. Would you like some coffee?" She asked, turning around to go into the kitchen.

"Coffee sounds good." He stood from his chair and followed her into the kitchen.

The coffee pot began to gurgle while she lifted some coffee cups out of the cabinet sitting them on the counter. "I see you're as anxious as I am to get started."

"I guess it shows. I just couldn't sleep this morning, and it's not because I'm an alien or some strange creature from Mars," he announced staring at her.

She laughed. "You do have very good hearing."

"Yes, I got that from my mom's side of the family. So, we are a little different, but not in a strange way."

"Oh, don't let Terry get to you; he's a worry wart."

"I understand and I know that he's worried about you. Again, you don't have to go into the pond. I'll find Ryan for you and send him back."

"Michael, I'm going into the pond, so no more talk about going alone. After breakfast, we'll take a ride out to the pond. You need to see it before plunging into it. It's really a very lovely spot."

"See, we aren't so different. I can tell you've been out there a lot," Michael paused peering up at her.

"I've been out there way more times than I care to admit. I can't accept it like Daddy. I can't let it go. There's just too much unfinished business for me out there."

"I know what you mean. I can't wait to see the pond. I guess I was too anxious to sleep last night. My mind was in overdrive," Michael confessed.

"Yep, that was my problem too. How long will it take to get us prepared?"

"I've planned on being ready by Saturday, July 29th. I want you to learn everything I know in case something happens to me in that other world. I want you to be able to get out on your own. You have to learn to fly the jet pack and be able to control it."

"I do want to learn everything, but nothing is going to happen to either of us; you'll see."

She picked up the hot pot of coffee and poured the steaming brew into to the stoneware cups, adding sugar and cream into hers.

"Ah, I hear the rooster crowing. Now that isn't something you ever hear in the city," said Michael with a big grin on his face bringing out the dimples.

Maddy sat across the table from Michael. Her cup of hot coffee cupped in her hands as she studied him, staring more than she should. He was handsome in a roughed way. He had strong facial features, long dark eyelashes encompassing those sapphire eyes, and deep dimples when he smiled. Something was fascinating about him; maybe it was because he was from another world.

"Good morning honey," declared Jackson walking over to pour himself a cup of coffee. "I'm hungry." He pulled open the refrigerator door lifting out the sausage, biscuits, and eggs. The sausage began to sizzle in the iron skillet, and he slid the pan of biscuits in the oven.

"Son, do you want any eggs this morning, I can fry them however you want."

"Yes, a fried egg would be nice," assured Michael looking over at the man who was scrutinizing him.

"I'll take a fried egg, too," came a voice from the doorway.

"Good morning, Terry. Fried eggs coming right up," Jackson said getting his other iron skillet out of the cabinet. "What about you, honey?"

"Sure, Daddy," Maddy answered, "one fried egg sounds good."

"I see you two got up early," announced Terry staring at Michael and Maddy. "What do we do first?"

"I have my notes in the truck," Michael began, "and. Terry, I'd like you to go over my plans and see what you think."

"Alright, I'd like to see what you've done," said Terry sitting down at the table slowly sipping his coffee.

"Michael and I are going to ride out to the pond this morning," explained Maddy, dumping the old coffee grounds into the garbage and making a new pot of coffee. "Daddy, we'll be fine. Stop looking at me like that."

Michael sighed.

Jackson set the sausage and biscuits along with the butter, homemade preserves, and honey on the table. He handed Michael a plate with one fried egg and then he handed Terry his plate.   Everyone stayed quiet as they buttered their biscuits and ate their eggs each staring down at their plates.

Jackson glared at Michael with a grave look on his face. Maddy hurriedly finished her last bite of biscuit and quickly set her plate on the counter.

"I'll be ready in a few minutes, Michael. I want to get my gun cause Daddy said there've been a few more snakes than usual out in the pasture."

"I'll meet you out front," said Michael taking his last bite of sausage. "Breakfast was delicious, sir. Thank you."

"You're welcome, son. Don't worry about your plate; I'll get it," Jackson offered.

Michael stood from the table and slid the straight-backed, kitchen chair under. He didn't move looking at Jackson. "Sir, I'm not going to let anything happen to your daughter. You do understand that she's determined to go into that pond with or without me, don't you?"

"I know and I'm sorry, son. I've been rude. I'm just worried."

"Sir, I'm worried too," confessed Michael, "but we both have to know what is in the other world."

Jackson shook his head yes that he understood as he smoothed his wild hair from his face with his fingers.

Terry stood. He didn't say anything following Michael into the living room. He stopped walking. "Michael, I want you to know that I'm going to be watching you. I can't just trust anyone I first meet with Maddy's life. Sorry, I'm not trying to offend you, just being cautious."

"Fair enough, I've been warned. I do understand, but as I just said, I don't want anything to happen to her. Plus, I also have my father to answer to," admitted Michael standing by the front door.

"Alright, are you ready," Maddy called out skipping down the stairs with her wild red hair bouncing. She hurried to the front door.

"First, before we go, I want to get my notes and the walkie-talkies and then I'll be ready," Michael said racing up the stairs. In a few minutes, he pushed the screen door and stepped out onto the front porch but didn't move. "Oh, the morning is great. Look at the light fog with the sun trying to shine through the tall pines across the hills. Dad did love it here. Maybe before we go into the pond, I can get him to come and stay with Jackson. That might help both of them."

"That's a good idea," said Maddy following Terry and Michael to the FBI truck.

Terry unlocked the back door and fired up the equipment that set bright lights blinking and computers humming.

Michael handed Terry a stack of papers. "Terry, this is the plan my father and I came up with years ago. If you think of anything else, just write it on the paper."

"Come on Michael," hollered Maddy walking out into the yard. "Terry, we'll be back in a while."

"You be careful around that pond," Terry called back.

"Alright, Daddy," she chuckled directing her remark at Terry.

"Where are we going," asked Michael following her to the barn.

"Well, the best way to see this farm in on horseback," she said whistling loudly.

"Horses!" yelled Michael running over to her.

"Yes, I see by your expression you haven't ridden a horse very often."

"No, never," declared Michael following her into the barn. He stopped by the door and intensely watched her saddle both horses.

"This is Nutmeg and your horse is Cinnamon. I guess I got carried away with spices," Maddy confessed. "Their mother Wild Spice was my horse when I was young."

Maddy grabbed both reins and walked out of the barn with the horses. "Whoa," she called out to Michael, reaching over grabbing his arm stopping him from climbing upon the horse. "You have to climb up on the other side of the horse. Put your foot in the stirrup and swing your body into the saddle," she explained. She leaped upon Nutmeg's back and watched Michael struggle to get into the saddle.

"Slow, please," Michael called out as he was getting situated in the saddle.

Maddy laughed and gave Nutmeg a big kick in the side making the horse gallop along the path.

Her head swung around and looked back at Michael; his tensed tan face had paled. She pulled on Nutmeg's reins. "Relax, Michael. The horse can feel how tense you are."

"Well, I am tense!" he yelled to her. Terror was showing in his eyes and his knuckles had turned white gripping the reins so tightly.

"Okay, Michael, breathe. Take in a deep breath and let your body move with the horse…that's right, now look around the pasture. It's a beautiful morning. Feel the light breeze."

"It is a beautiful morning," he replied and took in a deep breath. His anxiety was leaving as the horse walked in a smooth stride following Nutmeg down the worn path. Eventually, the old oak and Crystal Pond came into sight.

"We'll tie the horses over there in the shade under the twisted oak," Maddy called out slipping from Nutmeg's back.

Michael leaped from the saddle. He laughed. "Not graceful; my dad would be amused. Wow, I'm also going to be sore," he said patting his butt, as he tried to get his legs to cooperate.

Maddy grinned. "A few more times and you'll get the hang of it, now… this is Unktehi Pond or Crystal Pond. You know the Indians believe the pond was home to a water monster. I guess they were right."

"Oh my, it's beautiful, and the water is so clear," announced Michael moving closer to the bank. "This pond is the gateway to another world. This is where my mom is from and where for generations my family has lived somewhere below."

"Don't get so close! The bank is dangerous; it can give way before you know it."

"I won't get near, but it's almost impossible to believe that another world is underneath. Maddy, how can that be?"

"I don't know, but the pond does seem to be pulling you in. Michael!" She grabbed his arm tugging him back next to her. "You're getting way too close. Come on back up to the tree with me. You can see into the pond from there."

He turned looking at her with those enticing blue eyes. "Sorry, but it's strange; it's like the pond knows who I am and wants to draw me into it."

"I observed. That was a little bizarre. C'mon," she said anxiously holding onto his arm. They climbed up the limbs of the old tree.

"Wow, you're right. This is a lot safer," Michael assured getting settled on a limb. He bent over staring at the water. "How old did you say you were when Ryan fell in?"

"I was fifteen. I won't ever forget that day. It was a nice day very much like today, and we were having a good time, but he had to go near the edge of the pond." She shook her head. "The sand on the bank gave way and he slipped. He seemed to get his footing, but then he flipped into the middle of the pond. I think if he had just fallen in the shallow side, then he could've swum out."

"I think so too. That had to be so difficult for you to watch. Why didn't you jump in to help him?"

"Back then, I couldn't swim. I was terrified of water."

"Are you still terrified of water?" his voice rose looking at her.

"Of that water, yes," Maddy replied, "but of most water, no."

"Oh, this is amazing," he paused, putting his head against the limb behind them. He took in a sharp breath of air trying to get his composure back. "I've heard of this pond all my life. It was a fairytale told to me at night with a happy ending for my parents about their finding each other, a beautiful love story. My dream is sitting right in front of me, so real. Now, I understand like all fairy tales, this one has a villain. I've heard my mom talking to my dad; remember I can hear more than I need to hear, about how close they came to getting caught before they left that world. I wonder if the world is still the same, with the same cruel ruler."

"Maybe it has changed and is a kinder world now."

"You do believe in fairy tales and happy endings," he said softly, leaning over close to her.

She shivered; Maddy stared deep into his eyes, studying him. His eyes were kind, but there was something different about him.

"Okay, what is it?"

"Sorry," I didn't mean to stare. I don't know what you mean," she tried to cover up her angst.

"Yes, there's something different about me and I'm surprised Terry didn't notice, but he hasn't looked at me, like you are."

"I didn't mean to stare."

"You're fine; stop apologizing. Only a few people in my entire life have questioned me about being different. The girl I was engaged to years ago and one other person, my best friend who I grew up with. It's only been people who seem to care about me who have noticed."

"Oh, I didn't know you were married," she said overwhelmed.

"I'm not, when she found out I was different," he sighed, "she ended our engagement. She believed that I was some deformed human."

"I'm sorry," Maddy said softy, placing her hand on his arm.

"Well, aren't you going to ask me why I'm so different?"

"No, you don't have to tell me."

"You afraid to hear?" he questioned.

"No, don't be foolish. It's your business, and I'm not worried about you. I study everyone I meet, so don't take it so personally."

"Well, look at me closely," he said getting near her.

"There is something," she said letting her voice disappear in the quiet morning, "but I can't quite figure it out."

"Think about a mirror."

"Oh, are you are somehow backwards to the rest of us?"

"Yep, everything about me, even my body is opposite of most people here in your world. My biological makeup is completely different from yours on Earth. My heart is on the other side and so are the rest of my organs. I'm truly unlike you. When I was born, the doctor told my parents that I probably wouldn't live past five."

Maddy bit her lip, her mind assimilating this new information.

"I'm like the image in a mirror, not as bad as my mom's body, though. You must not have been around her very long, or you might've noticed. She tries to stay away from people."

"A mirror image, how?"

"I think my world is a mirror image of your world, kind of a yin and yang scenario. My world exists in proportion to your world."

"Could all of the people falling into your world change the proportion?"

"Ah, I've thought about that. My mom's and now my staying here on Earth could've upset the balance of both worlds. But, all the men falling into the pond and staying in my mom's world didn't seem to cause any problems, at least none we know of."

"You don't want me to tell Terry about this, do you?"

"No, how do you know," he said squeezing his eyebrows together, "what I'm thinking?"

"I don't know, but I seem to be able to read you very well."

"Terry would think I was a true alien if he knew I really was different, kind of like my old girlfriend."

"I'll write it in my journal, just in case we don't make it back here. However, I won't let him or anyone read my journal, not now. You aren't an alien to me."

"Thank you," he replied finally relaxing uncurling his shoulders.

"Anymore secrets?"

"No, not from me. How about you?" he questioned turning his eyes toward her.

"Nope. What's the name of the other world?"

"Mom said our world is known as Aionios. It means without beginning and end, eternal universe, and my favorite definition… forever."

"Aionios, alright, I don't have to keep calling it your world."

"Tell me some about growing up here on this farm, again. I want to add this part to my fairy tale," he added grinning finally relaxing.

Her stories began of Ryan, riding their horses, and preparing for Halloween and Christmas, living a simple life until that one July day.

He peered over the limb into the water. "Maddy," he sighed, "we need to be prepared."

"We will, although I'll admit that I'm scared too," she replied looking over at him.

He laughed. "You're something. Nobody has been able to read me so well."

She smiled back at him. He might be different, but she was drawn to him. "I guess we better get back and check on Terry."

"Sure, but I do hate to leave this place. It feels so familiar to me," he sighed. "I'd like to come here again soon."

"We will, but you have to promise to stay away from that water. It wants to pull you in."

"I wasn't even thinking, just moving closer," he added. He scooted over to the side of the limb jumping from it. He turned back to her and lifted her from the tree, just as Ryan used to.

Laughing, he wiggled his foot on the stirrup trying to get back into the saddle on Cinnamon. His hands tugged on the reins letting the horse follow Nutmeg. The house was quiet as they rode up to the FBI truck. Terry was still engrossed in his work and didn't notice them.

"Hey, you're working too hard," Maddy called out leaning from the horse.

"Oh, you're back. Wow, time flew by fast. I read your notes Michael, and it seems like a good plan. On the other hand, Maddy, my dear, you have a lot to learn."

"Yep, but I'll be able to teach her in the next few days."

"Did you see or hear anyone at the pond?" asked Terry.

"No, it was quiet. We're fine, Terry," assured Maddy holding Nutmeg's   reins.

"Maddy, I need to get back to DC. They need the truck. I can go back this afternoon and I'll come back in a few days. How'd that be?"

"Oh, I'm going to miss you, but I understand. Michael and I'll be busy preparing. Please, don't say too much about all this to anyone back at the Bureau."

"I know. Now, stop worrying; you're the one that is becoming like your father."

"Actually, that is a compliment," she said grinning.

"He's been busy in the kitchen," said Terry. "The aroma smells wonderful. So, I'm sure it's time for lunch."

"You're getting used to this eating all the time," said Maddy taking both horse's reins and walking to the barn.

"Do you need any help with the horses?" Michael called out.

Maddy slowed the horses and looked back at Michael. "Not this time, but next time you're going to learn to saddle your own horse. You've got a lot to learn too."

"No problem," hollered Michael stepping up on the porch. He sat down in the swing waiting for her to return.

"What did you think of the pond?" questioned Terry standing with his back against the porch's post.

"I can feel the pond's mystery. You know, it is one thing to dive in unknowingly, but for us to dive in knowing we are going into another world isn't going to be easy."

Terry smiled. "Maybe you're more like us than I thought. I've been scared to death of that pond."

"I see why everyone goes swimming in it. It's mystic. Its powers will pull you in, literally. It's still hard for me to believe there's a world beyond the water, even knowing I'm a part of it. Terry, I'm having reservations about Maddy being prepared. I've been working on this most of my life, and I'm still wondering if I'm ready." Michael stopped the swing leaning over lacing his fingers together.

"Hey, you two still out here. I thought you'd be in the kitchen eating," Maddy called out hurrying up to the porch steps.

"No, it's nice out here," Terry offered.

"Come on; let's see what Daddy's doing." She pulled open the screen with the two men following. "Alright, smells good in here," she hollered walking into the kitchen.

"You always seem to know when it's time to eat, honey," Jackson replied. "C'mon in and get a plate. I cooked up some fried chicken and vegetables."

"Jackson, after lunch, I need to get back to DC," Terry quickly added.

"Oh," moaned Jackson, "I thought ya were going to stay and help Maddy."

"Michael is going to help Maddy for a few days. I'll be back in a few days."

"Son, it's been nice having you around," Jackson declared anxiously. He sat at the table staring at his food on his plate.

"Daddy, stop worrying, nothing is going to happen without your knowing. Michael and I aren't going to take any risks."

"Honey, I don't like any of this. I wish ya'd let it go." Jackson looked at his plate scooting his vegetables around.

The room got quiet as they finished their lunch.

Terry stood from the table. "I have to get my things. Thank you again for the great lunch. Jackson, I'm sure going to miss your good cooking."

"I'm glad ya enjoyed it," replied Jackson standing and turning to the sink to rinse the dishes.

Maddy placed her plate into the sink reaching over hugging her daddy. He sighed leaning in putting the plates into the dishwasher. Her body ached. She hadn't wanted to cause him so much pain. She left him cleaning the kitchen and hurried out to the front porch.

Michael was sitting in the swing. "Your father doesn't like me being around."

"Michael, he's just worried and you remind him of the pond."

"He's afraid I'm going to take you into the pond and never bring you back. You know it could be a reality."

She wasn't going to respond to his statement, understanding he was right. "I think your idea of your parents coming here is a good one.

Maybe then Daddy would see they're as worried as he is. Their common distress could, in an odd way, be a comfort."

"I'll call them and see when they can come. Daddy would love to stay here a while. He found this place so peaceful, except for the pond," Michael paused. "It was the best and worst time of his life."

The door screeched open and Jackson and Terry stepped out onto the porch.

"I'm ready to go even with a doggy bag for a snack." Terry laughed, holding up a brown sack.

Maddy jumped up from the swing grabbing Terry. "Thank you for all your help. I couldn't have figured this out without you."

"I hope that is a good thing," Terry responded swinging his head back and forth.

"Yes, it is and even without Ryan involved, we'd want to discover what that world is like."

"Don't do anything until I get back," warned Terry.

"I won't," exclaimed Maddy. "I need you here as a level-headed cushion between our plan and our parents. Now drive safe and call and let me know you made it."

"Yes, Mamma." Terry laughed giving her another hug. "I won't drive like you, so it'll take a little longer since this truck isn't very speedy."

Jackson stepped up reaching out his hand, but then he leaned in hugging the young man. "Take care, son."

"Thank you again for everything, Jackson."

Michael stood from the rocker. "Terry, Maddy will be fine. Stop worrying; I won't let her do anything foolish," he said reaching out his hand which was interrupted by Maddy's punching Michael's shoulder. Michael grabbed his upper arm like he was mortally wounded, and the three of them laughed. The antics even got a chuckle from Jackson.

Maddy gave Terry a hug. She stood watching the huge FBI truck slowly make it way down the gravel road. Then she heard the motor shifting gears out on the payment until the truck's sound faded in the distance.

Chapter 14
Preparing

Maddy leaned back in the swing. She watched as her father stood quietly on the porch gazing out over the farm.

"I'm going out back and work a while in the garden," said Jackson solemnly. He swung open the screen door. "C'mon, Gordon T." The hound dog stretched, wiggled, and followed him into the house.

"What do you want to work on?" Maddy asked anxiously pushing the swing back and forth.

"First thing," Michael began, "you need to read my plan, and then we need to practice with the jet packs. I want you to learn everything about them even how they are made. I need you to be able to take one of the jetpacks apart and put it back together again."

"When do I get to fly one?"

"Patience, girl, first things first! When you learn everything about them, then we'll work on the flying lessons."

"Alright, but I'm not very mechanical."

"This isn't something you are going to do for a profession, but it could save your life and maybe mine."

"You look as worried as Daddy. We'll be fine."

"C'mon," Michael said standing from the rocker. He stretched. "Let me show you one of the jetpacks." He opened the back of the SUV, reached inside, and slid the jetpack to the edge of the truck. It was a silver futuristic thing with two oblong cylinders that could've come from a picture in an old comic book. "What do you think?"

"Wow!" Maddy shouted, climbing into the truck touching the strange shiny contraption. "This is one of the jetpacks we're going to use?"

"It sure is. My dad and I've worked on this since I was a teenager. We've perfected it to fly at a fast takeoff straight up into the air, not slow and smooth like what most people would want out of them."

"It's amazing," declared Maddy fiddling with the apparatus.

"Yes, and a jetpack like this would cost way over a hundred thousand dollars or more if you could buy one."

"You paid that much?"

"No, my dad and I built them. He was going to use one and me the other."

"How does it work?"

"Slow, you need to learn a lot before you mess with this one. Come over here," said Michael pulling her close to him. "Sit down on the tailgate." He scooted the jetpack next to her back. "I'm going to hold it, and you stand and try to lift it up.

Maddy leaped from the tailgate and tried to lift the contraption on her back, but fell backward as Michael grabbed onto the heavy jet pack.

"Shit, that thing weighs a ton! Oh, Michael, how'll I be able to hold it."

He started laughing, "Now, you see why I'm worried. This one is half the size of the ones on the market; it's an extra ultra-light. It doesn't even have fuel inside. Don't look so worried, I have a few ideas. Remember, I am a rocket scientist."

"How does it work?" she asked playing with buttons on the jetpack.

"These joy sticks are just like what you'd use on a video game. They control the jetpack, see," he said moving one of the sticks around.

"This is going to be a lot to learn. I don't know, Michael."

"You'll do fine. You're probably just a little overwhelmed. The hardest part of all of this is going to be dealing with g-forces." He sighed. "I've been able to work with g-forces in the past, but it isn't something you get used to easily. The thrust is going to be powerful."

"I hadn't thought about how the stress from g-forces could affect us," she exclaimed, worriedly squeezing her mouth tight.

"The acceleration will be great. Not like what you're used to in a car. It'll be hard on our bodies and there isn't any way for you to get use to the g-force before we leave."

"What happens if we fly into the air and miss the pond when we're leaving Aionios? Won't we fall back to the ground?"

"Yes, very fast, I'm afraid; however, I did add a small parachute which will help some," he said in a quiet voice looking down at the ground. "At least we won't hit the ground quite as hard. But, Maddy, there's more than falling back to the ground."

"What else?"

"We could pass out, lose vision or die from the pull of g-forces."

"Boy, you're full of good news. Anything positive about all this?"

"Yes, I'm positive it's going to be tricky for us and the odds aren't good."

She stood by the truck giving him a nasty look.

"Stop that…you won't get your way with those looks, Maddy Sayers."

She couldn't believe he'd said that. It was so odd that they seemed to know what the other was thinking. Ryan had been the only person that knew her so well.

"What else is in here?" she asked climbing deeper into the truck.

"I have all kinds of equipment back there," assured Michael scooting next to her. "That is your jetpack, the one you are going to put together."

"It's in a lot of pieces. You really want me to put that thing together, why?"

"Like I said before, if something happens to me and your jetpack gets messed up, you'll have to fix it."

"Let's just not let anything happen to you."

"Sounds good to me, but we have to be prepared for everything."

"I know, I've thought about what we need to take with us."

Maddy leaned against the side of the truck, thinking.

"I have a list in my plans. You need to read through them and then add your ideas. Mom says food and water won't be a problem, so we don't need to take them along."

"No, but I'm taking my weapons. Did you and Terry figure out a way to communicate from the other world?"

"We're still working on the walkie-talkies, the ones that my dad developed. He's a genius and has worked years on them."

She studied Michael. This wasn't going to be easy. She looked over at the other jetpack in pieces lying in a large box.

"You're wondering what happens if this doesn't work?"

"How did you know?" she asked.

"Because I was thinking the same thing. So much could go wrong."

"Not if I study and you help me."

"Then let's get started." Michael scooted a small box to him. "Come on. We can sit on the porch and sort through these items."

Michael jumped from the truck's tailgate. He reached in and lifted Maddy out of the truck. He picked up the box setting it on the porch by the rockers.

"Here are the walkie-talkies. This one can be yours. Click here," he said showing her how to work the round knob on the side. "We'll start with the bottom number and call each other or Terry by scanning the channels. You have to keep trying no matter how long it takes until we find him. Dad made them waterproof, so we can hang them on our belts."

"Do we have to wear a protective suit of some kind?"

"Yes, we have suits made from special material to withstand heat and water, along with a helmet that Dad came up with. We'll use the suits when we go into the pond and when we leave Aionios. The sand was an issue for him and mom, but he believes the suits will protect us."

"Terry made us wear breathing tanks around the pond when he was getting samples of sand and water," said Maddy turning the walkie-talkie around and around in her hands. "Do we need some way to breathe in case it takes longer to get through the water and sand?"

"I have two small tanks." He pulled one out of the box. "They are lightweight and don't have a long air span, but they'll work for a while."

Maddy sighed soulfully and looked toward the horizon.

Michael placed everything back into the box and stood from the rocker. "Too much to think about isn't it? We'll take our time. In the morning, we can begin working on the jetpack. Oh, here's your homework to start reading. The map of the city is in there. Don't overload. But first, I think you need a break, so how about giving me a tour of the farm?"

She stopped the swing and grinned. "Sure, but the only way to see the farm up close and personal is on horseback."

He sighed, "All right."

"C'mon you have to learn to saddle your own horse. If you can build a jetpack, you can saddle Cinnamon."

"Let's go," Michael said confidently, sliding the box to the side of the porch. The old porch steps creaked as he stepped out into the yard. He stopped walking, letting her catch up.

The wide barn door flew open. The coolness in the air hit them in the face along with the smell of hay and animals.

"Okay, the saddles are hanging over there on the wall. The one with the red fringe is for you to use; watch and do as I do."

She first placed the padded blanket and then the saddle onto the horse's back. She could see he didn't have any trouble catching on. Once the horses were saddled, she hoisted herself up into the saddle.

"Now what?" Michael asked.

"You," said Maddy pausing, looking at the ground not making eye contact with him. "You're so smart, and I don't know if I can learn all I need to know as fast as I need to. I don't know how you do it, remembering things the way you do."

"I inherited my dad's mind and I have a photo memory, so gaining knowledge comes easy for me, but," he sighed, patting Cinnamon, "but maybe not dealing with animals. Maddy, you're trained with weapons. I haven't ever shot a gun and wouldn't even know how."

"You don't know anything about guns! Oh, all right, tomorrow we're going out to the back pasture and I'm going to teach you. I'll get Terry to bring some weapons. Guns and knives may be as important for us as the jetpacks, since we don't know what we may encounter."

Michael smiled climbing up onto Cinnamon.

Maddy gently rubbed Nutmeg's mane, "Okay, what?" she questioned looking at Michael.

"See, it doesn't take much to get you energized. We both have different abilities that complement each other. Both of us being the same wouldn't work," he called out, gently kicking Cinnamon.

Not being outdone, Maddy raced past him out through the pasture, but Cinnamon soon caught up. They made their way down a small worn path that ended at small stream. She pulled up on Nutmeg's reigns stopping the horse near the flowing water. She slid from the saddle. "This is the creek that runs behind the Beardsley's farm, Ryan's farm a little ways over there."

"It's so peaceful here," Michael added as he hopped down from the horse and tied the reigns to a limb under a group of old oaks. He laughed. "At least this water isn't pulling me in." He sat on a large rock by the cool water and Maddy scooted beside him on the ground.

She grabbed a handful of pebbles and began throwing each of them making them skip over the water. "What was it like growing up knowing you were from another world?"

"When I was young, I didn't think much about it. I did tell a friend, or thought he was my friend, but he just laughed and called me an imbecile. He said that I'd been reading too many science fiction books. I never told anyone else in my life or discussed the other world with anyone until you," he answered kicking rocks. "I hid in my books and studies. I didn't have a lot of friends."

"It had to be tough to keep that bottled up inside of you all of these years. You didn't confess about Aionios to the girl you were going to marry?"

"No, like I said, when she figured out my body was unusual, she broke off our engagement without ever knowing about Aionios. It's nice to have someone to talk to about my hidden world."

Maddy turned toward him seeing the pain in his eyes from hiding his secret all of those years. She placed her hand on his arm with his eyes pulling her in. She shuddered and leaped up from the ground. She had to get away from him and be more careful. She hadn't felt so close to anyone her entire life other than Ryan. She squatted next to the water continuing to throw a few rocks into the creek making a splash.

Michael didn't say anything but kept watching her very intensely. "I do love it out here on this farm. Growing up in the city, well, it's so noisy, so busy. Working for NASA didn't give me very much time for myself. Maybe that is why I haven't found anyone or married."

Maddy wasn't able to look at him. "I had to go to the city; it was too quiet here for me. I had too much time on my hands, too much time to think about what might have been."

"I understand and I hope I can help take away some of that pain for you."

She looked up at the sky. "It might rain tonight. Clouds are moving in."

His body stiffened not moving.

"Michael, what's wrong?"

He held up his hand for her to stop talking.

"I heard someone walking around, but they aren't real close. Not close enough to have heard us."

"I'm going to check it out," she said pulling out her gun. "You stay right here and I mean it."

Michael sat anxiously waiting listening to her walk around. He took in a deep breath when he finally heard her footsteps coming out from the thick forest.

"Nothing, whoever it was, is gone. I'll catch them next time."

"Maddy, this isn't good. What if it is someone from Aionios is keeping an eye on us? We have to be careful."

"I can't believe it could be someone from Aionios," she whispered picking up some rocks. She smiled remembering Ryan collecting different shaped rocks. She had to stay focused on the mission and not think about Ryan and what could've been.

"It will be dark soon, so we'd better head back to the farmhouse," said Michael. He stood looking out through the trees. "Thanks for showing me around and talking. It's nice to have someone I can talk to who doesn't think I'm an alien," he added laughing.

"Would you stop bringing up being an alien?" declared Maddy wiping the dirt off of her shorts. "You know, it's been hard on me too, since no one has understood my feelings. They've all thought I'd gone insane or that I'd become fixated on the pond."

She threw one more rock into the water and then hurriedly untied Nutmeg. She smiled watching Michael jump upon Cinnamon as easy as she could. He did learn fast.

This time they both went to the barn. When they put the saddles away, they set the horses free to roam the pasture. When they reached the house, Michael opened the screen door letting her go in first.

"Daddy," she hollered walking to the kitchen.

"Yep, back here. Supper is about ready." Jackson looked over at her with his eyes squeezing tight. He could see something different in his daughter's face, but he didn't say anything.

"Can I help?"

"Sure, honey. Set the table; everything is about done."

"Smells delicious," added Michael sitting at the table. "Mr. Montgomery…"

"Jackson, son…not Mr. Montgomery," Jackson interrupted.

"Jackson," said Michael amused. "I was wondering if it'd be all right for me to invite my parents out here to stay for a while. Dad would love to come back to the farm and talk to you."

"Sure, they're welcome, and I'd like to meet Clayton Montgomery. You know, get our farm's big secret out in the open."

Maddy smiled seeing her father relaxing around Michael, at least for a few minutes.

"I'll call them and see what they say. Now, you don't need to overwork yourself cooking for them. Mom loves to cook and she'd be glad to help around the house. Of course, Dad knows how to take care of a farm, but he can't get around very well anymore."

"It'll be fine. I don't get around as well as I used to either. Aw, just know they're welcome anytime."

Michael took a deep breath, trying to figure out the man sitting in front of him.

After supper, Michael handed Maddy his plans.

"Wow, this is a lot of pages to study, but tonight I'll read over them," she said hurrying up the stairs to her room laying the papers on her bed to read later. She noticed that it had started to rain.

Maddy quietly walked to the living room. A small lamp glowed in the corner of the room. Her hand felt the worn wood of the screen door as it creaked when she opened it. "I thought you might be out here," she said in a soft voice carefully closing the door.

A bolt of lightning sliced through the sky with rolling thunder following.

"I thought I'd sit here a while and listen to the rain." Michael added leaning back in the swing. He closed his eyes. "The thunder is loud, but not as loud as the storms in Florida. This thunder has a peaceful grandeur about it." He opened his eyes and looked over at Maddy. "The lightning is so bright as it flickers every few minutes showing the tall pines."

Maddy sat down in the swing next to Michael. "I've always loved to listen at night to the thunderstorms and rain, cooling and cleansing everything."

"Is Jackson coming outside?"

"Nope, he's watching TV in his room."

"I thought he might've calmed down about my being here and he'd come on out and sit for a while."

"He has calmed, but this is bothering him and it's not all about your being here."

"I think I'll go up to my room, call my dad, and see what he thinks about staying a while out here on the farm. I hope he and mom will stay until we return from Aionios," he said getting quiet rubbing his hands together. "If we come back."

"Would you stop that, what is wrong with you? We'll be fine. With your brain and my street smarts, we'll be undefeatable."

"Oh, Maddy," he said laughing, "Girl, you're something! You know just what to say to make me laugh."

"Good, then you're not going to be such a gloomy puss anymore, right?"

"Right," he said giving her a strong stare, "I'll see you in the morning."

Maddy stood next to him. "I need to go upstairs and read your plan and study some. This is like school, and I didn't like studying or school."

"You just didn't have the right teacher, my dear," Michael commented smiling.

She closed the wooden door locking it and turning the lone lamp in the living room off. She stood for a few minutes watching the lightning flash in the front windows. Then, she followed Michael upstairs. She picked up the pile of papers on her bed. She moaned at so many papers. *Well Maddy you have to start somewhere,* she said to herself. She picked up the first page; however, she couldn't concentrate. She kept thinking, *Maddy Sayers, you're really going into another world.*

Chapter 15
A Quandary

Sun beams glistening on rain drops hanging on the bedroom window hit Maddy in the eyes. She kicked the quilt off of her legs. She didn't move when she saw all the papers scattered on her bed that she had been reading the night before. There was so much to learn and absorb, but so little time. She understood that the next few days would be trying. She dressed, dashed down the stairs, and was happily surprised to find Michael and her father in the kitchen having a pleasant conversation.

"Good morning," she called out with a grin.

"Ya sure are happy this morning," Jackson said studying his daughter's face.

She poured a cup of coffee and added cream and sugar. "It was nice last night listening to the rain. Oh, I did study. Sorry, Michael, but I fell asleep before I finished reading all of the plans."

"All that technical stuff makes it easy to go to sleep. I'll teach you everything that's in the notes. First thing this morning, we're going to work on the jetpack. You only need to figure out some of the important parts and how to put some of them back together."

"Sure, right…I only have to know how to build a jetpack," she moaned.

Jackson laughed. "Honey ya been able to do things all of your life that I didn't think ya could do. If you're determined to go through with this plan, ya gotta listen to what Michael says."

"Daddy," she said laying her hand on his shoulders. "Did you just say it was alright for me to go into the pond?"

"No, I shor' didn't say that, but I know how stubborn ya are and y'll go even if I say no. So, I want ya to be safe when ya do."

"She'll be safe, Jackson. I'll see to that. Oh, Dad said he and Mom could come Tuesday morning. He can't wait to see the pond and the farm. He's also wants to try and help. He does know a lot about the pond, and Mom knows about Aionios."

"Good," Maddy urged, "maybe your dad can calm you down."

"I'm calm."

"Like a hen with a fox in the chicken coop," she said. "This afternoon, you're going to learn to shoot a gun."

"Michael, ya don't know how to shoot?" questioned Jackson in a surprise voice.

"No sir, but it seems I'm going to learn."

"Maddy, ya need to take my old rifle. It's a good way for him to learn. After that, use your pistol."

"I will, Daddy. Are the shells for the old rifle still in the cabinet?"

"They should be. I haven't used the rifle in a spell. I used to like to go to the creek and shoot some snakes just to keep the gun lose, but I haven't in a while. Honey, do ya want some breakfast? Michael and I've already eaten."

"I'll just eat a biscuit and jelly. Then I'll go back up to my room, get the papers and then," she took in a deep breath. "I'll be ready…maybe," she laughed, "to build a jetpack."

"Thanks for the breakfast, Jackson," offered Michael pushing his kitchen chair back under the table. "I'll be out in the truck when you're ready," he added as he walked to the front door.

"He's not so bad after all, just a different sort. Maybe too smart for his own good," Jackson said rinsing the breakfast dishes.

"Yes, maybe a little too smart for his own good," Maddy said with a smirk. She placed her plate in the dishwasher. "See you in a while, Daddy," she said hurrying upstairs to her room.

Papers were strewn all over her bed. She stacked them in a pile, cupped them in her arms, and raced down the stairs. She jumped off the porch steps and dashed to the tailgate of the truck.

"I did read some of the plans," she admitted climbing into the truck. "I made it half way through them before I fell asleep."

"We'll go over the papers later. Now, let's get started on learning how to build a jetpack. I'll let you begin," he grinned, "since I'm too smart for my own good."

"Oh, I knew you could hear us. Your ears aren't big, so how do you hear so well?"

"I don't know, but at least Jackson is getting used to me. What about you?"

"I can tolerate you…I guess." She snickered sliding next to him as she peered over the side of the large box full of jet pack parts. "Yuck, there are a lot of parts to this thing."

"Yes there are. First things first, here are the instructions. Start following them, but memorize the parts as you go. Can you handle that?"

"If I have to…"

"Good, stop moping!"

"I'm not moping," she said scrunching her nose, staring up at him. She picked up the instructions reading them out loud. "Let's get going. This is like a jigsaw puzzle."

"Maddy, no, not that piece…here," said Michael scooting even closer to her. "This piece first," he assured holding a large metal piece in his hand, "and then the one you have in your hand. See how they connect. They fit perfectly. Try the next piece," he added staying next to her.

She quivered feeling him so close. This wasn't going to be easy staying this near him for the next few days. She handed Michael another round piece of metal. "This is the next piece, right?"

"Yes, that's correct," Michael added, not paying any attention to her absorbed in his work.

All right, Maddy, she said to herself, *stop thinking about Michael and pay attention. This is serious.*

"Look, the jetpack is taking shape," she squealed. "It's working. You know," she grinned, "I remember some of the pieces. That is the fuel line…very important, and that level controls how much thrust and the velocity the jetpack will have."

"See, you are learning. We'll go over the jetpack's parts again tomorrow."

"Wow! It's twelve thirty. The morning went by fast. All of this is really pretty simple once you learn the terminology." She rested her head on the side of the truck looking up at Michael. "Hey, we used all of the pieces; every time Daddy and I put anything together, we have lots of extra pieces."

Michael's head moved back and forth. He smiled showing his dimples. "No…left out pieces wouldn't be a good thing with this."

"Let's get some lunch and then I'll get Daddy's rifle. It's your turn to learn."

"And your turn to teach." He slid the jetpack to the side of the truck.

"Yes, it is," she called back to him scooting out to the edge of the truck. "Boy, I'm stiff," she declared stretching. "How do you work like that all the time in such a confined space?"

"You get used to it and get lost in the details."

"Time did fly by. Hey, I built a jetpack…with your help," she chuckled. "I do understand some about how it runs. When can I fly one?"

"Maddy, give it some time to sink in. You don't have very much patience."

"Nope, not with myself. But this afternoon, I'll be fine since I'll be the teacher and I like target practice. C'mon, let's eat," she said grabbing his arm.

"Well, how did it go?" Jackson asked putting their plates on the table.

"I built a jetpack; well…with help, but I do understand some of it…maybe…I guess," she said anxiously. "I think I could fix one after I learn to fly the thing," she added looking over at Michael.

"In time, in time. Jackson, have you ever noticed your daughter's lack of patience?"

"No, Maddy? Really? Not Maddy!" Jackson answered sarcastically. "Even when she was little, she couldn't tolerate not mastering something right away. I remember the first few times we went bowling in the city. Of course, she hit the gutters more than anything else. Most kids would have pouted and cried, but not my Maddy. She was determined to learn." Jackson told how Maddy observed and asked questions to develop her style. He finished by saying that she brought home a junior bowling trophy by the end of her first year of competing.

Maddy put her plate in the sink. "I'm going to get the rifle and some ammunition. We're going out to the back pasture and shoot some old cans."

Jackson dried his hands on the dishtowel. "Not a problem, I've got to go into town this afternoon, so I'll see you two later. Is there anything I can get ya from the store?"

"Not for me," answered Michael.

"Me either. Bye, Daddy. Ready to go?" Maddy handed Michael some ammunition. She opened the back door and stepped outside onto the back porch.

"Are we taking the horses?"

"No, they don't like the gun shots, and it's not far for us to walk." She pulled the back gate open, and quickly closed it. "Boy, Daddy's needs to bush hog out here," she said flattening the tall grass with her shoes. "Watch for snakes."

She stopped walking and laughed. "What are you doing?"

"I'm watching where I step. I hate snakes," he said as he kept taking short, funny steps.

"The snakes will run from you for sure. They'll think you're a nut."

"You told me to be careful."

"C'mon," she laughed, reaching in grabbing his arm. "It's not much further."

"Let me set up the cans. You stay there. Daddy's brings feed sacks full of old tin cans out here to shoot."

"Now pay attention. Watch how to load the rifle." She showed Michael how to push in the long bullets, snapping the old rifle shut. "You hold it up and place the gun level against your shoulder. Look into its scope and when you see the target, squeeze the trigger."

When Michael fired the rifle, its recoil knocked him backward.

"Alright, you hit one. Maybe you've shot a gun before and just didn't want to tell me."

"No, and honestly…I was aiming for the first one, not the third one," he said laughing.

"Try again."

He held the gun up on his shoulder and fired again, this time not hitting anything.

"Keep trying," she urged, leaning in by his face. "Look into the gage, and when you pull the trigger, don't let the gun shift on your shoulder. Hold it tight."

Michael didn't move. "Maddy, someone is moving around and watching us over to the right in that group of trees."

Maddy grabbed the rifle pulling it to her shoulder. Upon seeing a shadow in the woods, she fired. "I'm not giving them a chance after what they did to Rufus. He was a dumb ass but didn't deserve to be treated the way he was."

The shot rang out and Michael stood silent for a few seconds. "They're running, but I heard some sort of a moan. You might've hit them."

"Think we ought to go check it out?"

"No, you've got them on the run and they moved fast. They're not coming back today."

"Okay." She handed Michael the rifle. "Let me show you how to use the gage." She leaned in next to his face. His head turned to her and they were inches from each other. He didn't move and she didn't back away. She jerked finally stepping back from him.

"Sorry," he said, looking at her.

"No, you don't ever have to tell me you're sorry, but we can't let this happen again."

He shook his head in agreement. Preparing to fire the rifle, Michael focused his eye on his target. His finger pulled the trigger. "Yes," he shouted hitting one of the cans.

"See, you did great. Now, try for a few more. Then I'll teach you to fire the pistol."

Michael was amazingly accurate and had already gained speed between shots.

"Alright, this is different," he said holding up the pistol in front of him gripping it tight with both hands. He squeezed off a few rounds.

"Hey, not bad. You do learn fast," she said as he put a new clip into the pistol.

"You just have to calculate the distance and the angle of the shot..."

She interrupted him. "Stop, no more mathematics. Just shoot," she declared laughing.

"Just shoot? Oh no, not me. Plain ol' geometry helps with precision shooting I'm finding out." He finished up the rounds. "This has been fun."

"I'll get Terry to bring you a gun, and we can come back out here and practice. Every gun has a different feel to it, so I want you to get used to the one you'll be carrying."

"That makes sense. See, we do make a good pair, mind and body," he assured smiling, handing her the pistol.

They didn't move.

Michael's body tightened standing so close to her. "Maddy, this is becoming awkward. I don't understand what's happening. I feel so at ease with you. Maybe it's because you know my secret." He sighed, "I don't know."

She stared into his eyes with her head nodding slowly yes.

"I understand you love Ryan and I don't want to interfere."

"I do love Ryan, but... this is becoming too complicated too fast. You're so easy to talk to, and I haven't ever been able to talk to anyone except Ryan."

"I'm sorry this is getting so mixed up."

"I can't seem to hide my feelings from you. I'm confused," she said turning to leave.

Michael put his hands on her shoulder turning her to face him. She laid her head on his chest. He wrapped his arms around her and felt her breathing. Her head leaned back looking up into his kind eyes, and he leaned over touching her lips with his. Her emotions swirled; this was more than she could comprehend. She reached up putting her arm around his neck not wanting to let go. Her body quivered as she backed away.

"Michael, this can't happen again," she whispered looking in his eyes.

He nodded his head yes with his eyes telling a different story. He reached over wrapping his arm around her shoulders as they walked through the tall grass. "I guess I'll have you for a few days, and then I'll give you back to Ryan."

She couldn't talk. Her head nodded yes as they walked to the farmhouse.

"I hear the old truck. Daddy's home. I need to see if he needs any help unloading the groceries."

"Sure," answered Michael solemnly, letting go of her. He slowed his pace watching her race around the house to the front.

"Hey, Honey. Have you got Michael shooting like the Lone Ranger? How did he do?"

"Just like he does everything! He became an expert very quickly," Maddy replied reluctantly.

"Then what's the problem?"

"No, problem," she assured, sitting down a bag of groceries on the kitchen table turning her face from him.

He reached over putting his hands on her shoulder pulling her around to face him. "Honey, something's up. Ya can't hide anything from me."

"Daddy, it's that, I've fallen in…" pausing, not able to finish.

"Oh, Maddy, not Michael! Honey, after all these years of waitin' around on news of Ryan?"

She didn't say anything, just nodded her head.

"Well, what are ya going to do? He's a different sort."

"I still and will always love Ryan, but…"

"It's seems ya have yourself in a quandary."

"I have to stay focused on our mission and get it over with first. Then I'll sort out my emotions and hopefully make a reasonable decision," she paused. "Well, that's what my brain is telling me to do, but my heart sure isn't," she closed her eyes, shook her head, and changed the subject. "We need to get the rest of the groceries out of the truck and into the frig."

Jackson nodded his head, not saying anything else as he followed her to the truck.

Michael was sitting on the fence by the barn petting the horses. She hurried into the house, pulled some carrots from the refrigerator, and raced to the fence.

"Here," she said handing him some carrots. "The horses are waiting for a treat." She reached over giving Nutmeg a carrot. "Just be careful and don't get nipped. Give 'em one at a time."

"I'll be right back." She ran to the horse in the back of the pasture. She reached out a carrot to Wild Spice and leaned in giving her a hug laying her head on the horse. "Ol' girl, I wish you could talk," she whispered hoping Michael couldn't hear. "I could use some guidance. I'm in a quandary, Daddy says." She stroked the horse's head. She turned back around with Michael's alluring eyes focused on her.

"You heard, didn't you?" she questioned climbing on the fence by him.

"Sorry, it's hard not to listen. I'm here to get a job done, not to cause you any pain."

"I told you not to say you're sorry," she began. "This isn't your fault. It just happened, but like you said, we have a task to do."

"Alright," he began, "let's make a deal. No decisions until after our mission is done. Then we'll deal with the consequences of our feelings. Deal?"

"Yes, deal. After we eat lunch, I need to study the plans and send an email to Terry about your gun."

Michael leaped from the fence and turned putting his hands around her waist lifting her down. Michael's strong hands and helpful touch was almost a deal breaker right then and there. She didn't move gazing up into his caring face, but then she thought of Ryan and headed toward the house. They went into the kitchen and through the routine of eating with Jackson watching closely.

Maddy stood, scooting her chair back under the table. "I'm going upstairs, send an email to Terry, and work on the plans. I'll see you two later."

Michael sat still.

"Son, remember, I say what I think," Jackson began. "This is a predicament ya two are in. I know how much she loves Ryan, but it's been over eleven years. Life has gone on since that day in July. Even if Maddy finds Ryan, he may have changed so much…aww, who knows."

"I'm not going to interfere with her and Ryan."

"Why the hell not? I love Ryan just as if he was my son, but, Michael, she hasn't cared for anyone in all these years. Then you show up and win her over in a couple of days. Don't be foolish and give up."

"I can't believe your saying that."

"Why, does it sound cruel?"

"No," Michael chuckled, "I didn't think you wanted me around. Terry thinks I'm an alien."

"I trust my daughter's judgment, and if she cares for ya, then I'll give ya a chance."

"Sir, I won't ever hurt her that I'll guarantee."

"I know my daughter and ya need to let her have some time to think. Just let things calm down."

"I have plenty of work to do on our mission. Thanks for talking to me," Michael said, standing.

"It'll work…if it's right."

Michael went out to his truck, pulled out the other set of plans, and began a new strategy on what they'd go through on Saturday morning when it was time to go into the pond.

Maddy walked into her room. A noise startled her. She jumped up and looked out the window. A small tan car pulled to a stop next to Michael's truck. A tall, thin man with short, grey hair stepped out of the car. A shiver went down her spine. It was the reporter, Robert Brennan from *The Examiner*.

She raced down the stairs and outside. She stopped and stood by the door. Michael had climbed out of the back of the truck and closed the door before Brennan walked up.

"I'm looking for Maddy Sayers," the man said as he stared up at Maddy.

"I'm Maddy Sayers," Maddy responded in a cold voice walking to the edge of the porch. "Do I know you?" she asked.

I'm Robert Brennan from *The Examiner* and I have some questions about a pond on your property."

"There are ponds on most of the farms around here."

"This is a special pond, a mysterious pond. I think it is called Crystal Pond."

"What about the pond?" she asked.

"A deputy in town contacted me. He said there had been a lot of people that have died in that pond, and their bodies were never found until last week. So, I'm curious about the story."

"Who was the deputy?"

"Tony Sanders," Brennan replied

"Well, there's not much of a story to tell. People drown in ponds, rivers, and lakes all the time. The guy that was killed was a chicken thief and got into a fight with a drifter."

"I'd like to take a look at the pond."

"Nothing to see; it's just a pond," Maddy added.

"Deputy Sanders didn't think you'd let me check out the pond."

"Sorry, but there's not a story here. Have a nice day, Mr. Brennan," she said giving him a hard glare.

Brennan grinned. "So why has a FBI truck been here for days?"

"Have you been spying on us?"

"Just keeping up with what is going on out here."

"That was a friend of mine who stopped by for a visit, if it's any business of yours. I happen to be an agent; we work together. You better not get caught snooping around our property. Here in the South, we shoot trespassers."

"Nothing to hide," he said with a smirk on his face as he walked to his car. "We'll see." He stopped by Michael, looked down, and tried to read the license plate, but Michael blocked his view.

When the tan car pulled out onto the paved road, Michael hurried up on the porch.

"That was too close. Who is Deputy Sanders?" he questioned.

"A know-it-all deputy who wants to be sheriff. He will do anything to bring attention to himself. He was a bully in school and apparently hasn't changed much over the years."

"Nope, that reporter isn't going to give up easily."

"I've gotta send my email to Terry, and then, I'm giving Johnny a call," she replied going to the door. She stopped at the door and looked back at Michael as he walked around the yard with his head down studying the ground.

Maddy pushed the osculating fan up toward the ceiling so it wouldn't blow the papers off her bed. She pushed the button on her laptop letting it come on. She didn't move for a few minutes staring at the picture of Ryan next to the music box on the dresser. She opened the box letting it play until it wound down. The melody mocked her, breaking her heart.

That was all she'd had for eleven years, a music box and a picture, but Michael was real. She knew she'd changed since that day at the pond and had grown into a socially detached person. What had happened to Ryan after he fell into the pond? Had he grown into a cold and unfeeling man? Why had Michael swept her off her feet? Maybe it was because Michael and she'd both grown up lonely, with the secret of the pond weighing on them. Was this fate or coincidence? Her feelings were jumbled up. The laptop chimed on bringing her back from her thoughts.

She signed on and checked her emails. She did have one email from Terry, and he was worried about leaving her alone with Michael. Terry was going to need a lot more convincing before he trusted Michael. She sent back a reply that all was well, and she was learning all about the jet pack. She told him about Brennan snooping around and that he had spotted the FBI truck parked in the driveway. She also requested some weapons for Michael. She finished reading all the emails, so she laid the laptop to the side and called Johnny. She explained to Johnny that Reporter Brennan had stopped by because there was a snitch in the sheriff's office, none other than Deputy Sanders.

"Well, Sanders is trying to unseat me as sheriff in this county, and it's looking like he'll do whatever it takes to win the election, including sharing secrets from this office," explained Johnny. "I'm sorry, Maddy. I had no idea…"

"Enough said," replied Maddy. "Let me talk to your deputy. I'll give him something to chew on."

"Aww, now Maddy, I'll handle this," said Johnny, "Ya just gonna stir things up worse."

"Put him on the phone, Johnny," Maddy said assertively. "Please," she stated more like a command than a courtesy. She clutched the phone in her hand wishing she had taken the time to meet with Sanders face to face, but then she would have become even madder and might have said more than she needed.

"Okay, okay, I'll put him on," stated Johnny, giving in. A few moments passed. "Alright, Maddy, he's on the line. I told him your name and that you have some concerns about a reporter who showed up out at y'all's farm. He's all yours."

"Deputy Sanders, I understand that you sent a reporter to investigate Crystal Pond. I am surprised that a man running for public office puts so much stock in Indian folklore. If you think the pond needs investigating, why didn't you check it out yourself? That's your job, isn't it?"

"Well, er'ah," the deputy stammered giving his usual fast answer to anything he'd like to avoid.

But, Maddy didn't give him any leeway to reply. "I wonder what the voters of this county would think about your sending a reporter out to someone's private property to check out an old wives' tale. I happen to be on vacation, and I've invited some friends to the farm for a visit. We like our privacy," she said emphatically. "If I catch you or Brennan out here again, I'll have a restraining order thrown on both of you. That'd make a good news topic for reporters around here, now wouldn't it? Think about it!" Maddy asserted as she hung up before he had time say a word. She inhaled a deep, cleansing breath and assured herself that she had thrown Deputy Sanders a curve ball, but she wasn't as sure about Reporter Brennan. He wouldn't be intimated as easy as Deputy Sanders.

"Well, it's time Maddy," she whispered to herself as she picked up some of Michael's papers and began to read the plan.

Time clicked by. She heard a noise and looked up. Michael stood at the door.

"You're trying too hard; it's time for a break."

"It's so strange looking at the map of Aionios. How can it exist?"

"I don't know. Dad and I have tried to figure out the puzzle, but nothing."

"That world has a sun and moon. Is it the same as ours?" she questioned.

"I don't think so. It is its own planet, just as this one, but the people are different in their ways. I guess it's like giving two children each a toy to build any way they want. They'll each build the toy differently. Maybe one will follow directions, and the other will just build it."

She smiled.

"Did I say it wrong?"

"No, nothing's wrong. It's just that you're so smart, but you can explain abstract ideas in a simple, concrete way."

He walked over to the dresser. "This must be Ryan with you when you were young?"

"Yes," she said, "I was fifteen and that picture was taken about three months before he…I guess I can't say drowned, went into the pond.

"You were very happy then."

"Yes, I was," she agreed, seeing the pain in Michael's face. She stood. "Michael, stop worrying." She put her hand on his arm.

He set the picture on the dresser and turned to face her. "Your dad told me not to give up on us," he admitted honestly.

She grinned. "Wow! Now that is something. Daddy's gotten drawn in by you, too."

"He just wants you to be happy. What do you have to say about my not giving up on us?"

"I didn't think you would anyway, and I don't want you to either. Let's just not act on our emotions until after we return from the pond."

"I hear Jackson in the kitchen. It must be time for diner, sorry, supper." He laughed, turning back to the door.

"I'm going to turn off my computer; I'll be there in a minute."

Michael walked out of the bedroom. Maddy clicked the shutdown button on the computer. She collected the papers laying them by the picture on the dresser. She hurried into the bathroom wetting a cloth wiping her face. She looked into her eyes. A smile emerged on her face. Feeling was back in her eyes for the first time in years. "*Maddy Sayers don't let this opportunity pass you by*," she thought as she lay the face cloth on the side of the sink.

Jackson and Michael were sitting at the kitchen table laughing at stories Jackson was telling about Maddy's growing up.

"Hey now, you watch what you're telling," warned Maddy smiling at her father.

"Ya, going to study anymore?" Jackson questioned.

"No, not tonight," Michael offered. "We both have thought enough for one day, and we'll go over things tomorrow."

"My old mind couldn't take so much thinking, that's for sure."

"All the information is getting jumbled up inside of mine," said Maddy. "Daddy, do you remember Tony Sanders?"

"Wasn't he Hue Sanders's boy that live on the other side of town?"

"Yes, that's him. Well, that guy Brennan, the reporter who was here earlier, said Deputy Sanders called him and told him about Crystal Pond."

"I've heard he's running next year for Sheriff and he and his dad will do anything to get him elected. So, that's who is causing trouble."

"Yep," she said sighing.

"Do you think the reporter will give up?"

"Nope, and he will be watching us."

"Honey, this is becoming a mess."

"I know, Daddy," she said placing her plate in the sink.

"Come on," Michael urged, reaching over pulling Maddy close. "Let's go out front and sit on the porch. It's a great evening. Let's not ruin it by thinking and worrying too much."

"Daddy, why don't you come out with us?"

"Naw, I'm gonna watch some TV," replied Jackson.

"You're not going to bother us," confessed Michael.

"I'm fine. Y'all go on out front." Jackson nodded his head as he wiped the kitchen table.

Michael sat in the swing pulling Maddy next to him. She lay her head on his shoulder, snuggling. "Tell me about growing up living near NASA."

"It was an unusual upbringing; of course, my parents are both unusual. I grew up learning about space shuttles like most kids learn about long division. I knew most of the astronauts. I met John Glenn and learned to tinker and build all kinds of rockets on my own. Dad did have an advantage coming from the other world. Mom had giving him a lot of information he didn't know about for years, some things they're still learning. I guess you think I'm strange too."

"Why would you say something like that?" she asked reaching her hands touching his face pulling it to hers.

They sat in the swing in the quiet night, talking, getting to know each other. Maddy pulled out her camera holding it up in front of them clicking two pictures.

Michael's feet slowed the swing. "It's getting late and tomorrow will be another busy day."

"I'm not tired," she protested, "I want to sit longer. What's bothering you?"

"I'm worried about Dad driving here. I should've gone home and brought them back."

"Call them in the morning and we can go get them. I don't mind."

"I'll call first thing in the morning, but I'm getting tired and you need some rest too."

"Alright," she said, as he stopped the swing.

She closed the wooden door locking it and turned off the lamp in the living room. He wrapped his arm around her and they slowly walked up the stairs. He stopped in front of her bedroom and pulled her close. There was no protest as he kissed her good night.

"See you in the morning. Maddy, I love you," he whispered, saying the three words for the first time.

"Good night, Michael. I love you, too," she said in a very soft voice, knowing he could hear.

Michael walked to his bedroom door, but he stopped and turned around to beam a satisfied smile.

Maddy lay listening to the attic-fan blades pulling in the cool, night air. How could her life be so great and so complicated at the same time? She smiled thinking of Michael as a young boy working alongside his father, and she thought of him as a man working alongside her.

Chapter 16
Clayton and Bayle

Morning came quickly. Maddy bounded out of bed straighten the covers and dressed in record time. She hurried to the kitchen. "Good morning," she called out pouring a cup of coffee looking over at Michael. "Did you talk to your father?"

"Yes, and he says he's fine driving. He's feeling better today and isn't worried about getting here. He sounded different somehow, excited."

"Keeping us old farts busy does seem to make us feel young," Jackson added.

"What are we going to work on today?" Maddy questioned leaning back in the kitchen chair with her eyes still on Michael.

"We're going to do a little more studying on the jetpacks and then you might get to fly one." He smiled. "How's that sound?"

"Alright, I can't wait."

Michael stood from his chair. "Dad said they'll be here around lunch time. They're not going to hurry."

"Son, they'll be fine. I have the guest bedroom downstairs ready since your dad doesn't get around easy. I figure, I'll eventually have to move into it, but hopefully not for a while."

"That bedroom will be perfect," Michael replied. "I hadn't thought about where my parents were going to stay."

"Come on," Maddy urged. "Let's go. I want to fly my jetpack."

"Maddy," said Michael, "we have to do some more studying first. You'd be up in the sky before I had a chance to stop you. Calm down, girl." Michael said wrapping his arm around her.

Jackson stacked plates into the dishwasher. Worry lines increased on his brow. "You be careful, honey, and do what he says."

"Okay, you two," Maddy interrupted, casting glances from her dad and then to Michael. "Will you kindly stop with the condescending remarks?" Then she smirked and they smiled. "I'm ready, Michael. Let's go."

Michael clicked his truck key and climbed into the back of the truck. He slid the jet pack, to the edge. "First we're going over all the parts."

She moaned.

"Maddy, it's not going to work, so stop pouting."

She scooted over and pulled his face to hers, kissing him with passion.

"Nope, not going to work, but not bad and you can try and win me over some more later," he assured laughing.

"Alright, what are the questions?" She gave in smiling at him.

"Let's start at the beginning." He quickly asked question after question.

"Wow! I can't believe I knew most of the answers."

"See, if you pay attention, then you'll learn. Now, the joystick, this makes the jetpack go backwards and forwards and this makes it fly straight up into the air."

"Okay," she proclaimed, fidgeting with the joystick. "That's not so difficult to remember."

"This is the button that will engage the supercharger and send you into the clouds. Don't use it until you're prepared." He became quiet for a second. "One more time, you tell me all about the parts of the jetpack."

Michael leaned back against the side of the truck as she began. "Not bad," he admitted when she was done, scooting the jetpack to the edge of the tailgate filling it with fuel.

"Alright, do I get to fly it?"

"Yes and no."

"What kind of answer is that?" she rang out.

He did some adjustments to the jetpack and stepped into the straps sliding his arms through the straps.

"Hey, wait a minute; you said I could fly it," she snapped.

"You will; pay attention," said Michael. "Now step into the straps with me."

"What?"

"Come here." He pulled her close. "Step into the straps."

"We're both going to fly that thing together."

"Yep, you're getting it."

"I thought we each have our own jetpack."

"We do, but I'm not letting you fly one of these on your own, not yet. I learned to fly one when I was eleven years old with my father."

Maddy leaned back against him. He reached his arm around her pulling the belt tight.

"This is the quick release button. All the straps will drop off, and the jetpack will fall. Don't use it until it's time."

"When we're back here in this world?"

"When we come out of the sand and into the water, you hit the button and let the jetpack fall back to Aionios."

"Why?"

"It's heavy and if you wait too long, it'll take you back to the other world with it. Dad said the QLR almost pulled them back into Aionios. Mom and Dad were lucky they weren't strapped in. He grabbed hold of mom and pulled them out of the pond. You have to know the exact time so you don't get caught by the gravitational pull of the jetpack."

"So, we're letting the jetpacks fall back into the sand and then we swim out of the pond?"

"You got it."

"Oh, another thing to think about! This is too much," she said overwhelmed.

He pulled her head back kissing her gently on the cheek. "You'll be fine."

She sighed. "Now what?"

"We start the engine, and you push the buttons."

"Me."

"Yes, you. You wanted to fly."

"I'm so nervous."

"Think before you touch anything. Put you knowledge into action."

Maddy pushed the on button and the strong engine began to hum. "Alright, now what?"

"We need to position it to fly directly into the group of clouds under the pond. It's like shooting your gun, but you're the bullet."

"How will I ever be able to fly into the clouds?"

"You'll learn how to position yourself to fly straight at a target. You'll also learn when it's time to push the supercharger, but not now. First, I want you to maneuver the jet pack and get the feel of it. Slowly move the joystick. Slowly," He emphasized, "not like you drive your car. I heard from Terry how you like speed."

"Ah, he's a chicken."

"Well, slow down and learn to maneuver the jetpack. Good, okay go backwards and from side to side."

"Alright!" she cheered. "This is great. Oh, I feel so free, or I would if you weren't with me."

"You aren't going to get rid of me that easily."

"Good," she yelled back.

"Not bad. Let's see you land," he called out to her.

She pulled the joystick back towards her and they slowly floated to the ground. "I never thought playing video games would help me later on in life."

"Great job! Undo the belt and see how hard it'll be to get it loose."

The button clicked and the straps fell off as Michael held onto the jetpack.

Maddy turned around facing him. "Well, I have you trapped; you can't move away from me."

"Who says I want to move away from you," he said sliding the jetpack back into the truck.

"Well, Mr. Rocket Scientist, how did I do?"

"Not bad for an amateur rocket scientist," he said teasingly wrapping his arms around her. A car turned from the paved road onto the dirt road. Michael let her go. "Mom and Dad must be here."

"Are you going to tell them about us?"

"I'm sure I won't have to with Jackson around." He closed the back of the truck and watched the small blue car.

"I'll get Daddy," Maddy declared jumping up the steps onto the porch. "Daddy," Maddy called out going into the living room, "Clayton and Bayle are here."

"Good, just in time. I've got lunch ready. I hope they didn't stop and eat." Jackson wiped his hands on a dishtowel. "Let's go meet 'em," Jackson said excitedly grabbing Maddy's arm.

Michael led his parents up the porch steps. Clayton stopped. He stood taking in the farm. "The old place looks good," he said proudly.

Jackson walked up.

"Clayton Montgomery," Clayton said holding out his hand. "You must be Winfred's son; yes I can see you are. I remember your toddling around the farm with your mother chasing you."

"Yes, I'm Jackson. It's so nice to meet you Clayton."

"Daddy," Maddy said, "this is Bayle, Michael's mother."

"Bayle, come on in and have a seat. It's a pleasure to welcome you here."

"It's nice to see you. I, too, remember you, Winfred, and Judith. Your mother sure was a pretty women and so kind. She wasn't sure what to think of me, but that didn't stop her from helping us."

"Did y'll eat lunch?" questioned Jackson.

"No, we just kept driving," Clayton assured.

"Well c'mon in; I've fixed some fresh vegetables and cornbread. The cornbread is about ready."

"Oh." Clayton stopped in the living room. "It smells great. That's was one thing I remember about Judith. She sure could cook, and she made the best cornbread."

"Well, have a seat," said Jackson. "This is Momma's recipe, and I hope I do it justice."

Michael sat by his parents at the kitchen table, as nervous as a cat. Maddy fixed each of them a glass of sweet iced tea. Jackson set the hot cornbread on the table with the butter next to bowls of vegetables.

Jackson patted Michael on the back. "Son, calm down. We're all fine. Now, do I tell them, or do ya want to?"

"Daddy, stop picking on Michael," Maddy snapped.

"Clayton, Bayle, it seems these two have gotten, shall we say, close over the last few days, way close."

"Daddy," Maddy rolled her eyes like a school girl.

Michael rubbed his hands together.

Bayle smiled. "Good, so what's the matter?"

"Michael's worried about Ryan and me. He doesn't want to cause any problems, but we'll deal with everything when we get back from the pond," said Maddy, caressing Michael's arm with her fingers.

Clayton didn't say anything. He just smiled and started eating.

"This morning, I got to fly one of the jetpacks," she said with a sigh, "well, with Michael's help."

"Good, how did you do?" questioned Clayton.

"She did fine, Dad," assured Michael. "She surprised me. Although, there's still ample territory to cover in the next few days."

"The vegetables are great Jackson," said Bayle changing the subject.

"I do love garden-fresh vegetables," Jackson answered, "and this year the garden is doing pretty good, could use a little more rain. Alright, save room, I made a peach cobbler for dessert."

"Sounds nice," Bayle said, standing and picking up the plates.

"Bayle, I'll get those. Sit, sit; you're a guest," Jackson responded.

"Oh no, I'm not a guest. Remember, we're family and family helps," answered Bayle.

"Daddy, I'll dip out the cobbler. Who wants ice cream?" Maddy laughed seeing everyone's hands fly in the air. "Okay, it seems everyone does."

How about eating the cobbler on the front porch?" Bayle asked. "It's nice out there."

That's a good idea," agreed Jackson. "Michael, you go out back and get another chair, one of those old metal rockers, and put it on the front porch."

"Sure," replied Michael, first glancing at Maddy then dashing out the back door.

Bayle and Jackson finished putting away the leftovers and the dirty dishes into the dishwasher.

With a smile on his face as big as Texas, Clayton sat in the metal rocker on the front porch as he looked over the farm.

Maddy handed Michael his cobbler and scooted next to him in the swing.

"Oh, now this is good stuff," Clayton began. "I didn't expect to be waited on, but I should've known. Jackson, your family has always been so hospitable. Thank you."

"Well, like Bayle said, when you're here on the farm, you're family."

"Dad, what do you think about being back?" asked Michael using his feet slowly to push the swing back.

"It's nice, however, I do miss Winfred, and I wish I'd come back for a visit. Probably, no one would've known who I was, or perhaps he could've come to Florida. You know, I'd like to go see the old pond," he took in a deep breath, "maybe tomorrow."

"Sure, no problem, Clayton. We can go in the morning. I'll drive ya out there," Jackson said setting his empty bowl on the table next to the rocker.

Michael stood. "We need to get back to work." He walked out to the truck, opened the tailgate, and helped Maddy inside.

"Alright, these are our suits and helmets. You need to try this one on; it's the smallest one I have."

Her fingers rubbed the dark black suit. "The fabric feels really different." She turned around looking at him. "It's not a diving suit, so is this what the astronauts wear?"

"No, it's kind of in between a diving suit and what the astronauts wear. Dad and I came up with the fabric. It doesn't tear easily, and it's lightweight, so it won't weigh us down when we're swimming out of the pond. Slip your feet into it and your head in the hood. The suit covers your entire body, clothes and all. After that, put the gloves and helmet on; then we'll seal it."

Maddy let her feet slip into the suit, tugging the suit around her body.

"Good, it fits," Michael sounded relieved. "This is one of the suits I used when I was young, and it fastens tight around the waist and neck. Here, put the gloves on."

"This is strange," she said tugging on the suit.

His eyes stared down at her. "You do look like a small robot," he added laughing. "Let's check out the helmet. I won't seal it so you can breathe normally."

She nodded her head okay.

"It has a microphone inside so we can talk to each other. How does it feel?"

"Where does the air tank and line go?"

"Right on your side, and this hook holds the small tank and this line fits into the helmet."

"How do you know the suit is air tight?"

"After we designed the suit, I swam time after time in a pool at NASA. We needed something easy to maneuver in. It works, don't worry."

"I'm not worried, just curious. This is a great suit, and it'll keep my shoes and clothes dry."

"Dad said everyone comes out of the pond having to change clothes, but we won't have to. We can just take the suits off and hide them and the jetpacks near the entrance to the pond. Then we can explore."

"You've thought of everything."

"I hope so," he said sighing.

"Michael," she whispered holding onto his arm, "we'll be fine."

"Let's go sit on the porch for a while, and take a break, enough thinking for today."

"Good," she added, sliding the suit inside the truck.

Michael stopped on the step. He held onto the porch's post and then went inside.

"How did it go?" Clayton asked.

"The smaller suit and helmet fit Maddy just fine."

"I thought that one would be the right size," said Clayton.

After supper, they stepped outside on the porch. "Maddy, let's go for a walk," Michael said stepping down the porch steps.

She nodded her head and followed Michael as he slowly began to walk to the pasture with the horses.

Maddy raced ahead and climbed up onto the wooden fence. "You know when we go to your world you might not want to come back here to this world. You are a part of it just as you are this one. I could lose you and Ryan."

"No, if Ryan doesn't want to come back to this world, I'd never leave you," he said climbing up on the fence. "I'll stay with you wherever you choose."

"You need to think it over.

"I don't have to think anything over. Maddy, it's hard on our bodies going into the pond. That is why Dad has so much pain. Hitting the sand twice and the gravitational pull wasn't easy on his body. He said when he and Mom came back through the sand, she was behind him so he could protect her from the impact. It did damage to his back, so we need to be careful."

"We'll have our suits and helmets on; it'll be fine. Michael, you're worrying again."

"I can't have anything happen to you," he said gripping the wood on the fence. "It's getting late and I know Dad is wanting go to bed, but he's waiting on us to return," he added jumping from the fence. He reached up putting his hands on her waist lifting her off the fence.

"We're going to be fine," whispered Maddy pulling him close.

They slowly walked back to the porch. Maddy leaned her head back seeing the twinkling stars and a full moon shining down. For a few minutes, their lives were uncomplicated.

Clayton stood when he saw them coming from the barn. "I'm tired. Thank you, Jackson, for your hospitality."

"Y'll are welcome and ya make yourself at home. We don't have any fixed schedule around here. Do as ya like. I'm turning in as well. Come on Gordon T." Jackson stood from the rocker and opened the screen door with Clayton and Bayle following him back to their room.

Michael held the door for Maddy and pulled the wooden door closed, locking it. He drew her close. "I'm going to check on my parents," he said leaning in kissing her. "Good night."

"Good night, I love you," she whispered, holding onto the stair's railing.

The night was nice and cool. Maddy pulled the sheet up around her neck. This had been some day, and she'd really flown a jetpack. She also understood how different Michael was from Ryan. This other world, Aionios, was as real as Bayle and Michael, and she was going there in a few days. As she tossed and turned looking out the window, she knew sleep wasn't happening.

"Hey, you awake," a hushed voice came through the doorway entrance.

"Yes," Maddy whispered back into the quiet.

"I thought so," Michael said softly sitting on the bed by her. "Maddy, you need rest. What's the matter?"

"Nothing really. It's just, everything seems to be getting to me."

"It's not easy thinking about a new world, is it? I'm feeling some trepidation, and I've known about all this my entire life. I also realize that I'm unique, to say the least."

"Yes, that is the word, you're unique, not some monster or alien."

"Is that what you really think or are you trying to convince yourself? Maddy, you and Ryan are normal. He's not some freak like me. And, what about children we may have. What would they be like?"

"Yes, it has crossed my mind, but I think you're unique, so stop putting yourself down. It's become a habit for you." She reached over pulling Michael close. "I don't have any reservations about you or children we may have, so don't ever doubt my love. I haven't loved anyone like you."

"Except Ryan."

"No, Ryan and I grew up together; it was a different kind of love. Promise me you want ever say you're not like us. I love you for who you are. I was just thinking about Aionios and diving into the pond and going through the sand."

"I have to admit, I'm worried about going into the pond myself. Even thinking about this for years doesn't help. My thoughts of 'what if this, what if that' are overwhelming."

"As long as we're together, we'll be fine."

"Yes," said Michael in a soft voice.

Maddy reached up caressing his face in her hands. Her emotions were going wild cuddling close to his body.

"I better leave while I can," he chuckled.

"I wish you could stay. I'd sleep better knowing I'd be safe with you beside me."

"Well, your father and my parents wouldn't feel the same. I'll see you in the morning." He bent over kissing her one more time. "Good night, Maddy."

"Good night, Michael. I love you."

"I'll love you forever," he whispered leaving the room.

The next morning was beautiful and the weather was supposed to stay nice for the next few days. They didn't need any summer thunderstorms as they prepared to go into the pond.

When Maddy came downstairs, Jackson was sitting at the kitchen table with Clayton and Bayle deep in conversation.

"Good morning, honey. Ya look tired. Are you alright?" Jackson asked looking up at her.

"Yes, I was thinking too much last night. It's like the week before I took my driver's test. I had trouble sleeping then."

"I remember and you'd been driving since ya were able to reach the gas pedal."

"It's all the studying and remembering the instructions in order," she said, trying to smile.

"Well, Michael must be worried too, since he's not up," Bayle said. "You two have had a lot to think about for the last week. It's been a whirlwind for you."

"It sure has, Mom," Michael offered. "Good morning," he said pulling out a kitchen chair. "When do you want to go out to the pond?"

"When we're finished eating. You have yourself some breakfast, Michael. We're not in any hurry. That pond has been there for hundreds of years. I don't think it will have disappeared over night," Bayle assured.

"I sure do like breakfast on the farm," Clayton declared leaning over picking up another piece of bacon.

"Honey," Jackson said. "What do ya want to eat this morning?"

"A bacon and tomato biscuit sounds fine."

"Oh," Clayton perked up, "that sounds good to me too. I might have one for lunch."

"How about you, Michael?" Bayle asked.

"A biscuit will be fine."

Maddy stared at him seeing he wasn't acting like himself. Bayle stood picking up the dishes.

"I'm going out on the porch and finish my cup of coffee," Clayton added.

Michael picked up his biscuit. "I'll go out front with you," he said scooting his chair back.

Maddy started to get up, but Bayle shook her head no, so she didn't move. "I might eat one more," said Maddy smiling up at Michael. His hand stroked her shoulder as he walked by.

"He needs time with his father; this responsibility of taking care of you in the pond is bothering him."

"Bayle," Jackson said as he wiped his hands on the kitchen towel hanging it on the stove, "I'm done here. Ya just let me know when you want to leave. I'm going outback and check the garden. Come on, Gordon T."

"He's like Daddy thinking I can't hold my own, but I'm not some wimpy, little girl," Maddy assured.

"Not to him," she answered back smiling. "Well, I'm going to go straighten up our bedroom. I'll be ready in a little while. You just let him talk to his Dad. He just needs some reassurance."

Chapter 17
Crystal Pond

Maddy pushed the screen door open. She could see Michael sitting on the porch next to his dad deep in conversation.

"I'm going to feed the horses and get them saddled. We can ride out to the pond and Daddy can take Clayton and Bayle in the old truck."

"I'll help with the horses in a minute."

"I don't need any help, Michael. Visit with your dad." Maddy called out jumping off the porch.

The day was beautiful as she headed to the barn, the breeze was rustling the leaves, and the sun flickered through the trees making shadows across the dirt path. Swinging the barn door open, Maddy hurried through it to the pasture outback. She whistled loudly and Nutmeg came running to her.

"Hey girl, you ready to go for a ride," she asked rubbing the horse's neck.

She turned around and whistled again calling out to Cinnamon. She watched the horse, the color of dark maple syrup, galloping toward her. She saddled the horses, but stopped before she led them out of the barn and stared around the barn. Memories of Ryan lying on the hay waiting for her to finish her chores were flowing through her mind. She shook her head as if to send the memories away and carefully closed the barn door leading the two horses out.

Michael glanced up. He bounded down the steps and hurried to her taking Cinnamon's reins. He leaped so gracefully upon the horse. His face beamed proud of himself looking over at his father. He pulled the reins on Cinnamon and rode up beside Maddy and Nutmeg.

"Daddy, we'll be out by the pond," Maddy yelled, kicking Nutmeg, taking off with Michael close behind her, this time able to keep up. When they were out of sight, she pulled on Nutmeg's reins slowing the horse, and she turned around in the saddle to face Michael. "Okay, what's bothering you?"

"Everything, we only have a few days left, but knowing Dad is here helps," he said in a serious voice staring at the redheaded girl in front of him. "Don't worry, I just have a lot on my mind," he replied, kicking Cinnamon in the side racing past Maddy down the curvy trail dodging pecan limbs hanging over the path.

He pulled on Cinnamon's reigns, "The pond is more beautiful than ever today. It's like it knows Mom is coming to visit."

"We need to watch her; you know the pond may try and pull her in. I'm keeping my eyes on you too," she said forking her fingers first toward her eyes then toward his. With a cloud of dust behind it, the old truck and its passengers came to a stop near the oak.

A strong breeze blew the gnarled oak's leaves making crackling noises, but the pond stood deathly still, not one ripple.

Clayton stepped from the truck and slowly walked to the side of the pond, his face grim as his eyes studied the glistening water.

"Dad!" Michael shouted, "Be careful of the side. The sand is loose, and you might slip in."

"I know," Clayton laughed. "I had a hell of a time pulling your mom and myself over the sand. The sand kept sliding out from under me. I remember all too well."

Bayle stood by the truck and didn't move as tears brimmed in her eyes. She knew what lay beneath the water, her world, her family, and her childhood. She began to move to the pond closer and closer.

Maddy grabbed hold of her arm. "Bayle, the pond will pull you back into it. Don't get so close. Clayton!" Maddy declared, "Come over here and hold onto Bayle."

"Sweetie, I'm fine," Bayle assured patting Maddy's hand.

"No, you're not! Clayton you hold onto Bayle and I'll latch onto Michael," ordered Maddy reaching over taking hold of Michael's arm. Michael and Bayle started inching their way toward the edge of the pond. "Clayton, the pond is trying to take them back."

"It's the gravitational pull from the other world," hollered Clayton. "The two world's gravity meets right here. It's like throwing a ball into the air letting it fall. The pull is going to be great on them because they are from the other world."

"The pond then is literally pulling me and Mom into it?" said Michael staring into the water.

"Yes," Clayton called out, "I hadn't thought about it until now. It may be more difficult for you to leave Aionios than for Maddy. The gravitational pull for her leaving the other world won't be as intense."

"Great another thing to worry about," called out Michael tightening his fist.

"Come on let's sit in the tree," Maddy said tugging Michael's arm.

The two didn't talk they just watched as Clayton held onto Bayle and Jackson leaned against the truck. Bayle tucked her face into her hands as she let go of her emotions. Clayton squeezed his wife tight feeling her pain, knowing he was the cause. She rested her head against him wiping her eyes, nodding her head she was done, and ready to leave. Clayton led her back to the truck. He looked up and waved to Michael a sign that everything was all right, as Jackson backed up the truck and turned it around toward a safer place.

Maddy listened to the truck motor get softer and softer as she stared into the pond. "Michael, your parents have an unconditional love, one that is better than any love story someone could tell. Your mom left her parents and life to be with Clayton."

"I know and I hadn't thought about the pain she has lived with all these years. I understand now," he said pulling Maddy close. "It'd be so…." He paused. "I don't know how she did it."

"She loves your father more than herself," she whispered looking up at him.

"She only knew him a few months, not years," he added making his point.

"Yes, love at first sight. I guess it's real. It was for them."

"Well, is it for us?"

"Yes," she said reaching up touching his face. "But, leaving my daddy forever would be so…oh, Michael, please don't make me choose."

"I'm not planning on making either one of us choose. I don't want to leave my parents either, but I'd choose you," he said softly getting quiet.

She understood what Michael meant, but it wasn't her daddy that he was talking about it was Ryan. What was she to do?

"Oh," Michael whispered as he turned his head. "I hear someone."

"Where?"

"Over to our right. Someone's moving near. I'm sure they're watching us. Maddy, if this gets out about Aionios, my mom and I will be exploited in all the tabloids. We can't let these guys destroy our lives."

"We won't let them. They'll mess up soon and we'll catch them."

"They're gone. We need to get back and let you practice flying the jetpack."

"Alright, sounds good to me."

Michael jumped to the ground, reached up bringing her next to him, pulling her close, and kissing her passionately.

She smiled and pushed away. "Let's go; I want to fly the jetpack," she said quickly leaping upon Nutmeg.

"You aren't easily diverted. That's too bad for me," he laughed with his big grin covering his face. Michael pulled on Cinnamon's reins, gave it a soft kick, and Maddy and Nutmeg followed.

After they put the horses in the pasture, they hurried to the SUV. Michael pulled out the jetpack and tinkered with it. "The suit is ready for you to put it on."

"Suit, I thought I was just going to fly the jetpack."

"I want you to practice with everything on," he said smiling, "just for a while. You need to get used to wearing the suit and helmet."

"Alright," Maddy reluctantly added, stepping into the suit.

"See that forked limb up there at the top of that pine tree. I want you to fly up there a few times and touch the limb with your helmet. You have to learn to control where you're going."

"Okay, I should be able to handle hitting that big limb."

"Slip your feet into the straps."

"Aren't you flying with me?"

"Nope, you are going to solo."

"Oh, Michael…you sure."

"Yes, I wouldn't let you go if I weren't sure. Now, let's go over everything one more time. I'm putting my helmet on so we can talk to each other."

Maddy felt stares and looked over at the porch. Clayton was watching, and he nodded yes at her. "Your dad thinks I can do this?"

"Yep, he's the one who told me to let you try; he told me I couldn't keep putting this off."

"Alright, get the straps in place. I'll hold the jetpack for you, start the engine, just tell me when to let go."

"Oh, Michael, I'm scared," she whispered.

"You… scared?" He sarcastically questioned. "Think of some bad guy, get mad, and go after him. You like speed, go for it, girl."

"Alright!" Maddy gulped and took in a deep breath. "Let go," she yelled pushing the throttle soaring up into the air, but she missed the tree branch. She pulled the joystick and maneuvered the jetpack close to the ground. Her head leaned back studying the limb, quickly pushing the joystick forward. She missed again. "Shit," she yelled into the helmet, "this helmet is blocking my view."

"You'll have the helmet on when you fly back into the pond when we leave Aionios. Take a look at the limb before the tree gets close."

Maddy maneuvered around for one more try, looking up at the limb in the tall tree. The joystick wiggled forward and she flew straight up again. "Yes!" Her helmet hit the limb. "I did it," she yelled into the microphone.

"I hear," chuckled Michael shaking his head. "Take some time to get the feel of maneuvering the jetpack. You can fly around, but don't go very far."

"Oh, this is so much fun," she called out.

She looked down and could see Clayton. His hand rose in the air with a big thumb's up. She flew near Michael. He had a warm smile with relief showing on his face.

"Time to come back. You can fly later on in the week. I might join you so we can get a feel of both of us flying together."

"Sounds good," she said nervously. "Since your Dad's watching, I just have to make a graceful landing."

"Slowly, let off the throttle and push the joystick back. Gradually, there you're doing it. Let me grab the jet pack so it doesn't pull you down."

"I'm doing it!" she insisted. "Sorry, didn't mean to yell."

"That's okay. Shut it off," he called back holding onto the pack. "Now, hit the quick release button and get out as fast as you can."

Her finger pushed the button and the straps fell to her side. She lifted the helmet off. "I did it!" she screamed, jumping into the air.

"Yes, you did," replied Michael setting the jetpack in the truck. "Come on, let's take a break," he said closing the truck doors.

"Bayle, Jackson… you two can come out now. They're fine!" Clayton yelled. He leaned over near Maddy. "They didn't want to watch you fly."

Jackson sat down in his rocker gripping the arms tightly with his fingers.

"Daddy, I flew the jetpack all by myself and it was even fun. You should've watched."

"He did, from the window," Bayle added grinning.

"Bayle, ya didn't have to tell her," Jackson remarked. "I've been spying on her since she was little always watching to be sure she…well, she's not bitten off more than she can chew."

"Sir, she'll be fine now. I'll watch over her and keep her safe," Michael said, pushing the swing with his feet.

"I can take care of myself," Maddy protested giving Michael a look. "Daddy, I always knew you were keeping an eye on me. I've seen you watching me for years."

"Let's eat," Jackson suggested, trying to change the subject.

Maddy stood from the kitchen table. "I'll be back in a little while. I need to send an email to Terry. I forgot to tell him that I need more vacation time."

She sat down on her bed. The laptop came on. Her eyes pulled to the picture of Ryan making her feel guilty that she cared for Michael. She picked up her camera from her nightstand, pulled out the chip, and inserted it into the laptop. There, in front of her were the two pictures of her and Michael. She raced downstairs to the living room, plugged her laptop into the printer, and printed out the pictures. She could hear her daddy and Bayle in the kitchen cleaning the kitchen, and Michael talking to his father on the front porch. Quietly, holding on to the pictures she made her way back upstairs and placed them next to the one of her and Ryan. A tinge of guilt made her shudder, but she had to smile knowing she was going to see Ryan soon, or at least she hoped so.

Chapter 18
The Khoranans

Early Thursday morning, Maddy woke and quickly dressed. The house was quiet since everyone was sitting on the porch. Grabbing a cup of coffee and a leftover biscuit, she pushed the screen door open and stepped out on the porch.

"Good morning," she said sitting down in the swing. "Is Michael still asleep?"

"No," answered Jackson, "he took some carrots and went out to see the horses. I think he needed time to think and the horses don't converse."

Maddy nodded her head, slowly sipped her coffee, and began to ask Bailey questions about Aionios.

"I guess my parents could be dead now, but my brother Sabian could be alive," Bailey added sighing.

"When we arrive in Aionios, we'll go into town and see if we can find Sabian," Maddy assured. "Sabian should know that you're alright and he should meet his nephew."

"I don't want you to get into trouble and you need to find Ryan, get done and come home," insisted Bayle.

"We can do both," answered Maddy, "and it would be good for Michael."

"What would be good for Michael?" asked Michael walking around the corner of the house.

"To meet," Maddy paused, "your Uncle Sabian."

"Sure, that'd be nice. I'd love to meet my uncle and my grandparents."

"Michael, they might not want to meet you," Bayle added moving her head from side to side. "They may still be upset with me for leaving. I didn't tell them I was leaving. I knew they'd try and stop me. I did leave a note on the kitchen table."

"You did?" Clayton questioned leaning over in his chair gripping his hands together.

"Yes," said Bailey somberly, "I explained to them I was in love with you, leaving, and going back to your world. I told them to please forgive me and I hoped someday to see them again."

"I'm not worried if they're still upset with you, Mom," declared Michael. "It'd be their loss."

Bayle began telling stories about growing up in the world of Aionios and she explained they'd need to find the cave near town, so they'd have a place to hide.

"Bayle," Maddy questioned, "what does *polis* mean?"

"Each section of land is grouped in clans or nationalities. Our city, or polis, has evolved and blended from other clans, kind of like people emigrating from other countries to the United States. But a few clans haven't changed over the centuries and have even reversed in their society. The government where I grew up is named Quanoid, and they could still be in control. There is one clan in the north that the Quanoids won't even mess with called the Khoranan," she said anxiously.

"Bayle, let me tell my story of the first time I met a Khoranan," Clayton chimed in. "Right before Bayle and I left Aionios, we flew out early one morning before the sun became too hot to see the Walden family. I needed to practice flying the craft with no one around to watch. The craft landed with ease and my mind was consumed tinkering with the gages on the craft.

Bailey screamed. My heart stopped. I spun around. In front of her stood this burly, blueish-skinned man standing about seven feet tall. Bailey slowly began to step backwards toward me. She tripped on a rock and fell to the ground. The massive man took a couple of huge steps forward. He grinned, squinted his gray eyes, raised his tight fist, and swung at me. I ducked missing the punch. Not being from Aionios, I was more agile and able to maneuver away from him. I grabbed Bayle's arm to pull her up and was ready to get the hell out of there, but the man wasn't going to let us leave. He stepped up blocking our escape route. Without thinking, I grabbed my knife from my belt and it flew into the man. The blade penetrated deep into his flesh. He thumped to the ground. Bayle and I raced to the craft and flew to the farmhouse. Later that morning Jeffery and I buried the Khoranan. Not wanting him to be discovered we added rocks on top of the grave."

Maddy gasped.

"Yes," Bayle added, "that ghastly man was from the Khoranan clan. They're a cold-blooded group of people. It's horrible, when a Khoranan kills someone they cut out their heart to prove they're dead, some kind of a ritual. We were very lucky that Clayton knew how to throw a knife."

"Oh," Maddy's voice rose looking at Michael, remembering Rufus.

Clayton leaned back in his chair. "The man was nothing I'd encountered before. I was sure glad my Uncle John taught me to throw a knife and told me to always carry one. He said you never know out on a farm when you might need it." Clayton moaned. "I'm sure my uncle never in his life would have believed the story of what I did with that knife."

"Dad, you need to show me how to throw a knife," urged Michael.

"Me too," Maddy assured worriedly her eyes glaring at Michael.

They became quiet. Michael stopped the swing. A vehicle was driving on the dirt road getting near.

"Terry must be here," Maddy called out jumping up from the swing, but stopped. "Oh, it's Johnny."

"He's the sheriff around here, isn't he?" asked Clayton nervously wringing his hand together again.

"Yes, stop worrying; he's a good guy," Maddy added moving over to the edge of the porch. "Hey, Johnny, what brings you out here?"

"Sorry, I didn't know you had company?" The curly-haired man said getting out of his patrol car.

"It's alright! Come and meet them," called out Maddy. "They're from Savannah, old friends of Daddy's. Johnny this is Clayton, Bayle, and their son Michael."

"Nice to meet you," nodded Johnny as he shook Clayton's and Michael's hands. Johnny turned around. "How you doing Jackson?" he asked.

"Doing, just fine," Jackson answered shaking Johnny's hand.

"Well Maddy," Johnny said his eyes on Maddy.

She bit her lip staring back at Johnny seeing worry on his face.

"Old Theodore, who lives about five miles down the road," Johnny began, "was killed last night."

"Oh," Maddy moaned turning her eyes to Michael.

"Yep, stabbed and his heart was cut out just like Rufus."

"It must be the same drifter!" exclaimed Jackson staring at the young man in front of him.

"It's gotta be."

"I was sure he'd be long gone by now," Jackson added nodding his head. "Theodore lived alone, so how did you find him?"

"Mrs. Tate checks on him and brings food every few days. It wasn't a pretty site and now everyone in town is speculating. It sure is stirring people up."

"That's not good," Maddy chimed in.

"No, it isn't. I better be getting back to town. I just wanted to let you know. It's nice to meet you, Clayton," Johnny added as he nodded to Bayle and Michael.

Maddy followed Johnny to his patrol car.

He turned to her. "Maddy, did you ever find out anything about the pond."

"Not much. It's still a mystery, but who knows, one of these days. I might find something."

"If I can help, let me know."

"I sure will. Bye, Johnny," she said moving back to the porch.

"Well, my heart is pumping again," said Clayton, as Maddy stepped up onto the porch.

"He doesn't suspect anything," assured Maddy. "We just don't want Johnny to know about our plan since that'd be difficult to explain."

Maddy's eyes peered over at Michael. Both were wondering the same thing: had Johnny been spying on them along with the Khoranan, Brennan, and maybe Deputy Sanders?

"I'm going to check on the horses," Maddy said stopping the swing.

I'll come with you," Michael replied hurrying to the steps.

"Now what do we do?" questioned Maddy opening the barn door. "We have a Khoranan killing people, Brennan checking things out, and now Johnny and Deputy Sanders looking for the so called drifter."

"Maddy, we have to stay focused, but I agree we need to get rid of the Khoranan so everyone will leave us alone."

"Right, I hope you have a plan," she added.

"No, not at the moment," he said staring at the horses. Without saying words, they knew what had to be done.

Chapter 19
Help

After lunch, the group sat on the porch talking, but they became quiet when they heard a vehicle approaching.

"Now, that's the FBI truck," Michael said smiling. "Its motor is a lot louder."

The truck pulled to a stop. Terry opened the door and climbed out stretching his arms. Maddy ran to him and he grabbed her spinning her around in a circle. "Girl, you look good. I guess planning to see Ryan is setting well with you."

"I'm doing great and I'm glad you're here to help. Come on." Maddy grabbed Terry's arm and they stepped up on the porch.

"Jackson," Terry said, leaning over shaking his hand, "nice to see you."

Clayton started to stand. "Sir, nice to see you; you don't have to get up," Terry assured shaking his hand, looking at the old man who had started this mission. "Bayle," he said as he nodded, "it's nice to see you again."

Jackson stood. "I need to start supper. Nice to have you home, Terry."

"It's nice to be here, especially with the meals you serve," laughed Terry.

"Jackson," Bayle stood, "I'll help you."

"Terry, tomorrow we are going to have a dry run and check out all of our equipment we need," explained Michael. "Maddy has learned to fly her jetpack, and we're both going to put on our suits and fly around."

"Wow! Maddy," Terry questioned, "you can fly one of those things?"

"Yep, and I even helped build one," Maddy responded proudly.

"Our biggest issue," Michael continued worriedly, "is…Maddy can't stand with her jetpack on, which makes jumping into the pond difficult for her. Dad and I have been discussing the problem. When we leave the other world to come back here, she'll be fine turning the motor on and soaring up into cloud and into the water, but we don't want to waste gas with them on when we dive into the pond."

"What did you come up with?" questioned Terry, stopping the swing staring over at Michael.

"We could throw the jet packs into the pond first, and then we would jump in after them."

"Would they be alright falling through to the other world on their own," asked Terry?

"Yes, when I went into the pond," Clayton answered. "I went right through the sand. If you send them into the middle of the pond, they won't have any problem sinking and they're built to withstand the fall into the other world. But, I'm not strong enough to help throw them into the pond."

"Well, Michael can't throw them in, because the pond's gravity pull is too strong for him. He'd be pulled in with them before he is ready. I can try and help, or maybe Daddy would be strong enough to help, I don't know."

"I think I'm strong enough to help," came, a voice from the side of the porch.

They all gasped. Johnny stepped up the steps. Maddy leaped out of the swing. Clayton started to stand.

"Sir, you're fine, please, sit," Johnny said in authority voice as he moved over to one of the rockers and sat down.

"How did you know something was up?" asked Maddy.

"It wasn't hard to see how nervous y'all were with me around, so I decided to run your guests' license plate. So tell me Maddy, how is a dead man sitting on your porch?"

"It's a long story and one I didn't want you involved in. You could get in trouble," Maddy replied.

"It's too late now. Tell me the story."

"C'mon," she said grabbing Johnny's arm, "let's go for a walk. Where's your car?"

"Parked by the paved road." He slowed down and looked at her. "When I saw the FBI truck coming back to the farm, I wanted to see what you were up to, so I decided to check things out."

Maddy and Johnny slowly made their way along the dirt and gravel road. She began the long story of Clayton and Bayle. The story of what had happened to the Walden boys, the Confederate soldiers and all the ones that had drown in the pond. She gave in and told him about the Khoranan that had come through the pond. He was the one killing people. "Alright, Johnny that is the entire story, now what?"

"And Ryan, you believe he's still alive?" Johnny anxiously asked kicking the gravel with the toe of his boot.

"Yes, and Michael and I are going into the pond Saturday morning to check things out. We may not be able to find him, but we're giving it a try. Johnny, we think Brenan is watching the farm?"

"Girl, we need to keep Brenan away and we have to find that person, what did you call him?"

"Khoranan. Johnny, one more thing, he is wearing a grey shirt, but he is also around seven feet tall and..." she sighed, "has bluish skin."

"What!" he shouted nervously rubbing the sweat from his brow. "He should be easy to spot."

"Stop worrying; we'll get him."

"I can't believe Ryan could be alive after all these years and living in another world below that pond."

"You can't tell anyone not even Paula. This can't get out. We have to find Ryan first."

"I understand. If it were Paula in the other world, I'd be going for it too. You have my full corporation. This is so dangerous. I don't know how to protect you."

"I'll be fine, don't worry."

"You know," said Johnny overwhelmed, "maybe I should go into the pond and help Michael?"

"No, I'll be fine. You have a family to consider."

He nodded his head yes as he furrowed his brow worriedly.

"We better get back; they're all dying back at the house." She smiled. "Wondering what you're going to do."

"Get in the car and I'll drive us back."

Maddy opened the passenger side door, sat down, and studied Johnny hoping she could trust him as they drove to the farm. The patrol car pulled next to the FBI truck. The doors closed on the car and Johnny and Maddy walked to the porch.

Jackson stood next to a post with apprehension on his face. He cleared his throat. "Son, what's it going to be, ya going to arrest us? Ya…turning us all in?"

"No, sir," said Johnny shaking his head. "I'm going to help you find Ryan. He was one of my best friends and I'm not stopping any efforts to bring him home."

Jackson patted Johnny on the shoulder taking in a deep breath. "We're getting ready to eat. How about joining us?"

"If Paula doesn't mind you staying," Maddy added. "Oh, are you on duty?"

"Nope, I'm off duty, if a sheriff can ever be off duty. Paula's at her mother's tonight. She needed to rest. These last few weeks of her pregnancy have been hard on her, and her mom will watch the other two."

"Then it's settled, come on in. It's not fancy just home cooking," Jackson explained, pulling Johnny inside the home. "I cooked a ham, mashed potatoes, and vegetables."

"I hope some cornbread," called out Clayton following Jackson.

"Yes, and some cornbread," Jackson laughed. "Oh, Bayle made a homemade apple pie that smells really good."

Terry grabbed Maddy's arm. "Maddy, I need to talk to you."

Michael, Maddy, and Johnny stopped and turned toward Terry.

Terry drew in a deep breath. "I just got word that there has been another stabbing here."

"Yes," affirmed Johnny. "It isn't a good thing that the FBI knows about these cases."

"No, it's not," replied Terry.

"Terry," Maddy turned to him, "Bayle told us about a story of a clan that lives on Aionios known as the Khoranans. They're coldblooded…and get this, when they kill someone, they cut out their hearts to prove they're dead, like a ritual."

"So, our drifter must be one of them," Terry concluded. "We were right about the material."

"Yes and we have to really be careful. Khoranans are not normal."

"I don't believe the Khoranans are smart with electronics. They're very primitive," Michael assured, "but they're dangerous and we need to be on the alert."

"And, with blueish skin they'll be easy to spot," added Maddy

"Blue skin?" questioned Terry.

"Yep," Maddy said nodding her head. "Light blue skin."

"Maddy," added Johnny walking back to the front door, "you do need to hide Clayton's car. It was too easy for me to run his plate and put two and two together."

"I'll get Dad's keys and put the car in the barn," Michael said hurrying into the downstairs bedroom.

Maddy stepped outside on the porch while Terry helped Michael hide Clayton's car in the barn.

The meal was busy with conversation, and this time they were eating in the dining room. It'd been years since Jackson had pulled out the beige tablecloth with small pick roses embroidered along the edges, Katy's favorite. Seeing the beautiful tablecloth made Maddy remember times of the past when her Daddy would sit at the head of the table and her mama would be busy serving everyone. Katy loved having people over, and it wasn't just holiday's when she would invite her friends to the farm. Maddy smiled seeing Jackson as excited as Katy used to be.

The strong stare of Michael pulled her eyes across the table as he smiled at her. She could see the isolation growing in his eyes because Johnny kept telling stories from the past about Ryan. Ryan had been an exceptional young man, and Michael started to wonder if he could ever measure up to the good memories people had stored up about him.

Jackson sat at one end of the table and Clayton the other, both men joking, enjoying talking, and telling old stories of living on the farm.

"I need to get back to town and stop by to see Paula and the kids before it gets too late," offered Johnny standing. "What time should I be here Saturday morning?"

"We're going to get started at daybreak. As soon as the sun comes up, we'll be out at the pond," Michael responded.

"Then, I'll be here early." Johnny leaned over shaking Jackson's hand. "Thank you, Jackson and Bayle, for the meal."

"You're welcome, son, and thank you for helping us," Jackson said standing, patting Johnny on the back.

"No problem, and I won't tell a soul," Johnny added, turning to leave.

Maddy scooted her chair back and followed him outside.

"Maddy, I'll also ask around town about Brennan and any information that I can find out."

"Thanks, Johnny."

"I do hope this works for you and Ryan and he comes home," sighed Johnny, with a worried look on his face.

"It will, don't worry. See you Saturday."

Johnny nodded his head, stepped off the porch, and got into the patrol car.

Michael leaned in next to Maddy with his face touching her face.

"Oh," she said startled smiling up at him. "I didn't hear you come outside."

"Maybe you were too busy thinking about Ryan."

"Michael."

"It's alright; I know with all this talk of Ryan and all the stories from your past it's bringing back a lot of memories."

"I don't want to hurt you."

"I know."

"There you are," called out Terry. "Let's sit a while out on the porch; it's such a perfect night."

"Yes, it is," Michael called back taking a deep breath as he tried to hide his feelings.

Clayton walked out onto the porch and sat in his chair. The subject changed and they began to talk about Johnny being involved. Jackson and Bayle joined in the conversation, but Maddy sat there quietly looking into Michael's sad blue eyes.

"It's a quarter to eleven and I'm tired. This has been a long day," Clayton admitted.

"Yes, it has been a long day, Dad, and the next couple of days are going to be even longer," Michael said leaning over putting his arm around his father giving him a hug.

"Well, I think," Jackson stood and stretched his arms out wide, "I'm going to join you. Terry, ya know where your room is. Ya make yourself at home."

"Thank you, Jackson."

Maddy stopped the swing hurrying over to Jackson with tears building in her eyes giving him a hug.

"Good night, honey," he said hugging her back. "Everything will work out. Don't overload and stress out about all this."

She wiped a lone tear escaping from her eyes before turning around to Terry.

"You're thinking about Ryan?" he questioned smiling down at her.

"This whole mess! Oh, it is so complicated," she snapped. "I don't know what I'm thinking. Terry, thank you for being here to help, but I have to admit I'm getting scared and worried."

"Nothing's wrong with being scared," he sighed. "That's normal," as he tightened his shoulders, "especially in this circumstance."

"You're tired and so am I," Maddy said. "Maybe I've thought enough and need sleep."

"Yep, tomorrow will be interesting," said Terry, trying to smile. "Tomorrow, I get to watch you fly around in a jetpack."

"Yes, and I have to say I like flying the thing. I feel so wonderful rising up into the sky and for a little while I don't think of the mission, but soaring free like a bird."

He stood. "Good night, Maddy."

"Good night, Terry," she said pulling the wooden door closed locking it. She didn't move leaning her head against the cool wood of the door. "Michael," Maddy whispered in a very quiet voice, "I love you." She stepped slowly up the stairs going into her bedroom.

There in her dark bedroom sitting on her bed was Michael.

"Oh," she said pushing the bedroom door closed. "You're going to get us in trouble."

"Live dangerously," whispered Michael pulling her near letting her fall onto the bed beside him.

She snuggled close to him feeling his heartbeat. "I'm sorry this evening hurt you so much. This is breaking my heart."

"I know. It's not you, but the situation. Let's not think about anything right now. We have a few minutes alone."

Her eyes closed when his arms tightened around her. She leaned in caressing him resting her face against his shoulder feeling the heat of his body. Her feelings were like an avalanche flowing from a mountain. She knew fate was about to take over her life. Now, would she surrender to it or be able to fight.

Michael's hand softly glided along her body and for a fleeting moment she didn't think of anything or anyone except Michael lying beside her. This is what her life could be and should be. But would fate allow this to happen? They didn't talk in the silence of the room. The only light in the room was from the clock on the nightstand. She cuddled next to Michael, just letting time click on.

Chapter 20
A Bad Feeling

Maddy shuddered when she woke and realized she was lying in her bed all alone. Michael had left during the night. The clock's red eyes said six o'clock. It was Friday, one more day. She took in a deep breath and climbed out of bed. She stopped by the dresser and looked into the face of Michael in the picture that was staring back. She picked up the picture of Ryan. The image of Michael wasn't a dream or a fairytale. Her life had become a complete mess.

Her eyes moved to the music box. Tears dripped from her face as her hand slowly lifted the lid. This was a love story that wasn't going to end well. The music box's lid snapped closed and the music died. She hurried to the bathroom, stepped into the shower, and let the water rinse the tears flowing down her face, but it couldn't erase the pain.

She shivered. "No," she whispered, "it can't happen again." She knew the clear blue water in the morning would bring more pain with it, but now she had the bad feeling that something was going to go wrong. It was the same feeling she felt right before Ryan fell into the pond. She kept trying to forget last night's dream but it wouldn't go away. The dream of Michael! The dream of his falling and her screaming; it terrified her. What was going to happen when they entered the other world?

She stepped out of the shower, pulled the towel off the rack, and dried her body. She looked into the mirror. Her face was red and blotchy from crying. She scooped her long hair into a knot on top of her head. *Maddy, you can do this; you have to stay positive.*

The kitchen was busy with everyone talking.

"Hi, Honey, how did ya sleep?" questioned Jackson with a worried look on his face.

"I guess too much to think about, nonetheless I did fall asleep with some nice dreams," she said looking over at Michael. His face was impassive, trying not to show his feelings.

"You need a good breakfast, and then you'll be fine," Jackson offered moving to the stove.

Terry stood. "Michael, let's go and get to work. I want you to show me what you've been working on."

"Sure." Michael answered as he scooted his chair back. He smiled his crooked grin at Maddy showing his dimples.

"Where's Clayton?" asked Maddy watching Michael and Terry leave the room.

"He's out front. He loves that porch. He can sit there all day and look out over the farm," Bayle said. She walked over by Maddy reaching over touching her face. "Honey, don't let this eat you alive. Michael will help you get through this."

"Thank you, Bayle, and I know you can see the pain in his face. It's driving me crazy knowing I'm the cause."

"No, sweetie, this isn't your fault. He fell in love with you knowing you loved Ryan. He was willing to take the chance. Now, you have to concentrate. This mission isn't going to be easy. I want you to come back safe and that also includes Ryan."

Tears swelled in Maddy's eyes as she nodded her head yes.

"I'm going out front with Clayton," Bayle added. "He's as anxious as you are."

Jackson handed her a plate full eggs, biscuits, and gravy. He pulled out his chair at the kitchen table and sat gazing into his cup of coffee, as if it might hold some answers.

"Daddy, I'm sorry. I'm upsetting everyone I love."

"Honey, it's not you. I feel responsible…I encouraged Michael to go after you."

"Yes, and I'll always be grateful for that. You know he'd have stepped back without your encouragement. Daddy, I don't know how I'll feel seeing Ryan."

"Honey, it's not going to be easy."

"I know that we've changed so much. My love for him was when I was a teenager. My love for Michael is real, right now," she smiled. "I hope he's listening to me."

"I have noticed that boy shor' can hear very well."

"Yes, he can and I love him so much."

"Then, get your butt in gear and go work on your mission bring Ryan back and get this dilemma over with."

"Thanks, Daddy," she said overwhelmed, jumping up wrapping her arms around him. "Now are you going to watch me fly today from the porch or the window?" she teased.

"I don't know. The window is safer for me, but I might have to watch from the porch. Ya just be careful and do as Michael says."

"I will," she called out heading out the front door. She stopped with her hands on the screen door. "I love you, Michael," she whispered before she pushed the screen door open seeing a smile grow on his face.

"Okay, Maddy let's get to work," called out Terry climbing out of the back of his truck.

"What's first Michael?" Maddy asked.

Michael lifted out the suits. "Get your gun and everything you're going to take with you and put your things on before you put the suit on."

"Michael, here are your guns," said Terry reaching into a box. "The small one fits around your leg as a backup and here are some knives. One fits in your boot and one for your belt."

"Son," Clayton called out motioning with his hand. "Come over here. I picked up two Swiss army knives with everything on them. I had one with me when I went into the pond, and it sure came in handy."

Michael picked his suit up putting his shoes carefully down into it, drawing it tight around his neck. "Maddy, clip the walkie-talkies on your belt loop." He smiled at Maddy when she did a little robot dance.

She began to laugh as he pulled her hood over her head tightly around her face.

"Now, we need our tanks. We have to attach them to the belt on the suit and let the hose hang. I'll show you later how to secure the hose to your helmet. We're just slipping the helmets on, not securing them so we can breathe normally. Gloves are next; get them snug so they're water tight."

"This is a lot of equipment," Terry offered, watching them.

"Terry, you'll have to help Maddy with her jetpack. Scoot it to the end of the tailgate and let her get it strapped on her back. She can't hold it. When she comes back to the ground, you'll have to grab the jetpack and help set it back in the truck. She's going to practice unsnapping the harness to get out quickly. When we fly back into the pond and after we go through the sand, we will have to unsnap the harnesses and let them fall back to the other world. We have to swim quickly to the surface to keep from being pulled back in."

Terry grabbed hold of the jetpack. "Alright, Maddy, you just give me the signal when you're done and let me know when you're coming back to the ground."

Maddy looked over to the porch seeing Jackson standing at the edge of the porch his hands nervously twisting on the railing. She gave him a thumbs up and he tried to smile.

"You ready?" asked Michael as he slipped on his helmet.

"Yes," Maddy called back, pushing the on button with the jetpack gearing up. She pushed the throttle and the joystick and soared up into the air simultaneously with Michael.

"Hey," he called over to her.

"What?"

"We can talk and they can't hear us."

"That's great. Maybe we could fly away and not come back for a while and spend some time together."

"Don't tempt me; last night was great."

"I didn't know when you left," she called back circling the house following him.

"I left about four o'clock. I didn't want Terry to notice your door was closed when he got up."

"I missed you when I woke up, but I did like your being there when I fell asleep. How about tonight?"

"It's a date. I guess we better do some practice hitting the limb."

"Maybe we could keep the helmets on the rest of the day so we could talk. I miss hanging out with you," she added laughing

"So do I, but like Mom and your daddy said, let's get this mission over and figure out what our lives are going to be."

"I hope great," she whispered.

"I can still hear you," Michael called back.

She pushed the throttle pulling the joystick back hitting the limb. "Yes," she shouted.

"Give Terry the signal that you're landing. Don't forget to quickly unbuckle."

She began her decent and Terry grabbed the jetpack.

She jumped in the air. "Daddy," shouted Maddy, "how was that?"

"Ya did great, honey, just fine." Jackson's hands gripped the railing tight and then he used the back of his hand to wipe his eyes.

Michael slipped his suit off laying it by his jetpack and Maddy did the same.

"We need to practice with the walkie-talkies," Terry added.

"Terry," Maddy whispered. "You know someone is still watching us."

Terry scowled. "Yep, I remember."

"You'll have to be on the alert when we go into the pond. Johnny knows someone may be around and he can help you."

Terry's head nodded.

"We'll be fine, don't worry," she said patting Terry on the arm.

Terry turned back to the truck with a grim face helping Michael put things away.

"After lunch, Michael, we need to practice shooting your gun."

"Absolutely, sounds fine with me," Michael said closing the tailgate.

"Boy, the morning zoomed by fast. I thought time would go slowly today," Maddy assured taking a big bite of her sandwich.

"It seems things are moving on just fine," Clayton added.

"Yes, the plan's coming together," said Michael taking small bites of his sandwich not eating much.

"Alright," said Maddy putting her plate in the sink. "Michael, let's go and practice shooting your gun. You do need to get used to it."

Terry stood from the table. "Maddy, I need to go out to the pond. All right, don't give me that look. I'm just curious about a couple of things. I won't be out there long and I'll be careful."

"You keep your gun close, and you better be careful," Maddy snapped. "Maybe you should wait until we're back."

"I'll be fine, stop worrying," assured Terry.

Michael pushed open the screen door and Maddy followed him out to the pasture.

"Okay," said Maddy grinning, "You do need to fire your gun a few times and get the feel of it, and then we can go find a spot to sit and talk."

Michael slid the clip into the gun and fired hitting every can.

"Well, that didn't take long."

"Nope, I was motivated to get done. Now where can we go to have some time to ourselves?"

"Let's go to the creek."

Maddy sat on the large rock throwing small rocks into the water. "Well, it's less than one day."

Michael leaned back his body heaved taking in a deep breath of sweet smelling air. He looked up at the tall pines soaring into the sky then back at Maddy. "Time has gone by way too fast, but it seems like I've known you my entire life."

"My mind keeps going over everything I've learned. I know I'll be alright with you," she said softly, leaning in next to him.

"Tomorrow, we have to stay focus and can't let our feelings get in our way or distort our judgment."

"I understand, but we do have tonight…at least part of it," she whispered.

"Yes, indeed. Oh, it's so quiet here," he said. "I hate to leave, but we do need to get back.

"Yep, I'm worried about Terry going to the pond alone, so let's go check on him."

Michael wrapped his arm around her holding her tight as they walked to the barn.

The horses galloped through the pecan trees. A gunshot rang out… Maddy's heart pounded in her chest. Without a second thought, she raced toward the old oak.

When Maddy arrived at the pond, there in front of her was Terry struggling with a man twice his size, a man with blue tinted skin wearing a grey shirt. She leaped from Nutmeg and the horse darted off in the opposite direction. The man's huge arm swung and plunged a knife into Terry's left shoulder. Terry wobbled falling to the ground. Maddy lifted her gun and fired at the man. He flipped soaring into the center of the pond disappearing into the clear water.

Michael ran to Terry. He pulled his shirt off using it to put pressure on Terry's knife wound.

Terry looked up. He whispered in gasping breaths. "There were two of them. They were talking on the other side of the pond. One left going north and this one came back to the pond. I pulled my gun, but the man moved in supersonic speed and knocked it from my hand just as I fired."

"C'mon Maddy!" Michael exclaimed. "We need to get him back to the farmhouse and to a doctor."

"Maddy," Terry gulped, "the man was way too strong. You've gotta be careful."

"Shush, stop talking. We're taking you home." Maddy cringed biting her lip as she looked at Michael.

"Maddy, can you find my glasses…"

"Sure, now lie still." Maddy said placing the bent glasses on Terry's face.

"Help me lift him into the back of the truck and you keep pressure on the wound," said Michael in a calm and authoritative voice.

Maddy climbed into the FBI truck and helped Michael lift Terry. Michael tied the horses to the truck's bumper, jumped into the driver's seat and drove quickly down the path.

Michael honked the truck's horn not letting up as he pulled into the driveway. Jackson ran out of the house letting the screen door slam.

"Daddy, Terry's been stabbed! Call Dr. Smith, and get him out here fast," Maddy shouted.

"Let's get the boy in the house, and then I'll call," shouted Jackson.

Michael and Jackson lifted Terry out of the back of the truck and Maddy held the screen door. They placed him on the couch in the living room. Blood gushed from the knife wound.

"Dr. Smith'll be here in a few minutes. He doesn't live very far," Jackson hollered from the kitchen.

Bailey squatted next to Terry putting clean rags on his wound. Maddy stood by the front door twisting her hands together nervously watching for Dr. Smith's car. About five minutes later, a Le Sabre Buick pulled up beside the FBI truck. A statuesque, bald man wearing glasses stepped out of the car carrying a black bag. He moved to the porch and Maddy swung the door open.

Bailey scooted back giving Dr. Smith room as the doctor bent down next to Terry. "Well, let's see how bad this is," Dr. Smith said in a calm voice. "It's deep, but a clean cut, must have been a sharp knife."

"Yep, I'll bet the drifter used my old paring knife," said Jackson rubbing his white hair from his face.

"Well first, I don't want any infection, so I'm going to clean the wound real well and give you an antibiotic injection."

Maddy paced back and forth. "I knew something bad was gonna happen. I had that same bad feeling," she snapped gripping her hands into fist. "I knew it and I didn't do a dag burn thing to stop it."

"Maddy girl, you just calm down. Your friend is going to be fine. I'll put a few stitches in, and cover it with steri-strips, and it'll heal in a couple of weeks," Dr. Smith added, patting Terry on the arm. "He's a lucky man. Just a few inches more, though, and things would be very different."

Dr. Smith pulled a sling out of his bag and helped Terry get it on and adjust it. "I'm going to leave you some triple-antibiotic ointment and bandages. Take Tylenol if you have pain. Leave those steri-strips on for three days; try not to get them wet, and then remove the strips and wash the wound with soap and water when you shower. Then put the ointment and a clean bandage on every night before you go to bed. If it gets red and puffy, call me immediately." Dr. Smith started putting his bag back in order and continued, "I'll have to report this to the sheriff; it's just one of those formalities with this kind of wound.

"Do what you have to do, Doc," Jackson stated and then smiled extending his right hand. "Thanks for coming right out and helping. Send the bill to me; I'll handle it," said Jackson as the two men shook hands.

"I heard down at the coffee shop that there's a drifter up to no good around here," continued Dr. Smith.

"Yep, I recon so. I've already told Johnny about someone pilfering through my house," Jackson affirmed.

Dr. Smith and Jackson moved toward the front door and Jackson thanked him again and continued, "Tell your Amanda hello for us. My wife loved having her for a Sunday school teacher."

"I'll do that," Dr. Smith promised as he walked to his car.

Jackson watched as the doctor got into his car and drove away. "A good man," Jackson stated under his breath.

Jackson turned to Maddy. "Now, Maddy, what's this about a bad feeling?"

Michael moved over near Maddy.

"Daddy, it's like the day Ryan fell into the pond. Last night, I kept dreaming about something happening to Michael. It's starting again," she said in a quiet voice. She sniffed, "I can't have it happen again."

Michael stepped closer. "Nothing is going to happen to me. Stop worrying. Terry's going to be alright."

"I don't know," she answered with her eyes staring at her daddy.

Jackson's face was tight and he kept nervously pushing his white hair back with his fingers.

"I'm going to call Johnny and tell him what's going on," Maddy said as she left the room and stepped outside onto the back porch. She stopped moving and looked around remembering that day when Ryan was sitting in the green rocker. The day of the broken shoestring, splinter in her hand, and the chicken feed: such small things that led to the most horrendous day in her life. Now, Terry was hurt, and a Khoranan was still here on the farm. What else could go wrong?

She explained to Johnny about the Khoranan attacking Terry and gave him the bad news that there had been two and there was another Khoranan roaming around.

He was as worried as she was when she told him about her intuition, knowing most of the time even when she was a child, she was correct. She clicked end sliding the cell phone into its case attached to her belt. Her hand felt her gun that was hanging to the side.

She moved to the one old green chair and sat down. Her head leaned back and her eyes closed. "Maddy, how can things get more complicated?" she whispered to herself.

She couldn't sit and think any longer. She jumped up out of the chair hurried to the barn.

She whistled and Nutmeg came running. She quickly saddled the horse. Nutmeg wiggled when she leaped up into the saddle and took off out through the woods. There next to the thick pine forest was Ryan's and her old fort, the old boards leaning, but time had aged them ready to give way and fall apart. This was their deserted island, a pretend place. Thoughts swirled in her head, memories from when she was young. Pirates would be coming after them yelling and screaming, but Ryan would always fight them off. Ryan, her brave defender. A smile emerged on her face. This time she would be saving Ryan…if he wanted to be saved. That was the big question. What would happen when she saved him? Could she just let her love for Michael go? Nutmeg kept walking through the pasture. Maddy looked up, and there in front of her was the blue water.

She leaped off the horse and slowly walked by the pond searching the area. A shadow swayed behind a large tree on the other side of the pond. Her fingers clutched her gun pulling it out of its holster. Holding onto the gun she ran, but the shadow darted with speed that no man on this planet could have. That thing had disappeared into the forest. Her arm relaxed and fell to her side, but she kept a strong grip on the gun. She crept closer as she walked around the pond. Her feet crunched the dead leaves, her head throbbed, and a sense of despair was taking over her mind. The shadow was real; she had seen the grey shirt, the other Khoranan. Was she letting her love for Ryan blind her of the real danger; this wasn't just about her, but finding another world.

She crouched on her knees and whispered into the clear water. "Ryan, can you hear me and have you been able to hear me all these years? I miss you so much. You have been and will always be my best friend."

It was odd she could see her reflection in the pond staring back at her, and then the reflection turned into Ryan's face. Her love was memories of a young boy. What was it going to be like to have Ryan and Michael stand next to each other, two grown men? The odds were great that was going to happen soon. She closed her eyes and could see Michael's face nodding his head to tell her everything was all right and go with her heart. He was too kind and giving, just wanting her to be happy. Would she ever be happy?"

She stood. "You damn pond! You've caused enough pain!" Then she laughed; without the pond, she wouldn't have met and fallen in love with Michael. How could something be so horrible bring so much happiness?

She turned to the old oak and jumped up onto Nutmeg's back, galloping, and then racing through the pasture feeling the wind blowing her hair and the strength of the horse beneath her. She kept the horse running. Finally, she pulled on the reins and caringly rubbed the horse's sweaty mane.

"Thank you, Nutmeg. I needed to get away from everyone and everything," she declared, letting the horse unhurriedly walk back to the barn.

"Maddy, where have you been?" yelled Terry standing on the front porch with his left arm in a sling. "We've been looking for you."

"I just went for a ride, Terry. No big deal. I needed some time alone," she shouted back jumping from Nutmeg. "I have to put Nutmeg out in the pasture. I'll be in the house in a few minutes."

Terry shook his head, turned and went into the house, and mumbled, "Yea, right, no big deal. There's just a big, blue monster on the loose from a parallel universe. Why should we be worried?"

Michael grinned at Terry's sarcasm. Then he walked out the door and stood on the porch with his arms crossed. Maddy smiled at him whispering, "I love you."

Michael nodded understanding she'd been to the pond.

Maddy pulled open the kitchen door and could hear everyone in the dining room getting ready to eat.

Jackson put his arms around her. "I heard you went for a ride this afternoon, all alone without telling anyone."

"I just needed to get away."

"I know, I remember when ya were little right after your momma died…ya did the same thing. Ya'd just disappear and then ya'd come in from riding Wild Spice. It seemed to help. Did it this time?"

"Yes, it did, I was able to sort out some issues. Daddy I have made my decision, and it's not one that will please everyone, but I'm not saying anything else until I come back home."

"It's your decision and ya do what ya need for yourself, honey, no one else." He sighed giving her a hug wondering what the decision was. "Oh, honey, Terry told us about the blue duo and that one's still around. That's why we were so worried about ya."

"We're being stalked, for sure. I think I spotted him again, but when I pulled my gun, he went off faster than a bell clapper on a cheetah's tail."

Jackson snickered at Maddy's expression. "We'll keep an eye out for him," Jackson affirmed. "All right, I do believe I have some hungry folks 'round here, so I better get busy."

"Let me carry some of the food into the dining room." She stopped. "Daddy, it's been nice eating in there."

"Yes, it has, honey. Your Mama'd be proud and she'd had a good time with everyone around." He handed her a big bowl of black-eyed peas and smiled.

"How was your horseback ride this afternoon," Clayton asked showing the same grin as Michael.

"Very enlightening. I love to take off and ride through the pasture all alone."

Clayton chuckled patting the table with his hand. "That's something Winfred would do. He'd just disappear and come back after a long ride on his horse. He said it cleared his head. Judith would get mad as a hornet, but she didn't stay mad long. It did seem to help to ease his mind."

"It seems Maddy did inherit something from Daddy," Jackson agreed.

"Alright, a toast," Terry said, holding his glass up with his right hand. "Here's to a successful mission."

"Yes," they all shouted clicking their glasses.

After supper, one by one the friends adjourned to the front porch listening to Clayton tell stories about living on the farm with Winfred. He became quiet for a few minutes. "It's getting late and tomorrow will come early," Clayton said standing.

"Yes," Michael said, "we do have a full day ahead of us."

"I have a few emails I need to check on," said Terry following Clayton, "and my shoulder is hurting some. I think I'll take some Tylenol. Goodnight, everyone."

"Goodnight," Maddy said looking over at Michael.

"If you need anything Terry, jus' holler and I'll come and help ya," Jackson said holding the door.

Maddy followed her daddy and Terry upstairs. She took a quick shower, but stopped for a few minutes staring at her reflection in the mirror. She smiled. She was backwards in the mirror like Michael. She went to her room and there was Michael standing in front of her dresser holding the pictures of himself and Ryan. She closed the door reaching over grabbing him.

"So," he said quietly setting the pictures back on the dresser. "You cleared your mind?"

"Yes," she whispered scrunching her eyes together not saying anything else.

He pulled her to the bed reaching over turning the lamp on the nightstand off. She lay back with his arms wrapped around her. Smelling his fresh clean scent caused a delicious shiver to run along her back.

This is what she wanted, for him to hold her. She sighed knowing tomorrow her world literary would be turned upside down.

He whispered, "Maddy relax. Don't think about anything. Tonight you're mine and I'm yours. I will follow my heart until the end of time, you are my love, and you are my life."

"Sounds wonderful, our night."

"Yes," he said softly caressing her, snuggling close, "but this isn't going to be easy for you."

Her fingers combed through his curly hair. "No, but you'll be there for me."

He leaned in kissing her giving her his answer.

Each knowing that tomorrow they would be going into Unktehi Pond.

Chapter 21
Unktehi Pond

The clock's alarm began to beep. Maddy glared at its steely eyes in the dark morning. It was four o'clock and once more she was lying alone. Somehow, Michael had quietly slipped out of the room, not waking her. She knew he hadn't slept all night and that he was as anxious as she was, maybe even more. Her body shuddered. Saturday morning had come too soon.

She didn't move as her body tensed. She was going into Crystal Pond. The pond she had feared all of her life, the Devil's pond. Closing her eyes tightly, she tried to hide from the thought. How was she going to be able to jump into that pond? She wasn't even near the pond and her body began to shake. Could she overcome the fear that was growing inside of her? It hadn't seemed real until now. It was easy to say yes with days away, but now, surrealistic. She had to leap into that clear water not only for Ryan, but also for Michael. He'd go without her into Aionios, but she couldn't let that happen.

Her mama's voice became clear in her mind, *Honey, the water isn't your enemy, but fear is.* She had conquered fear many times. "Okay, Maddy," she whispered in the quiet room. "Don't think of the water; remember you can overcome your fear." She'd never be afraid if she were jumping into another pond. "I can do this," she said softly. She closed her eyes and could see her mama smiling at her standing on the beach with the waves splashing at her feet.

Maddy opened her eyes. Her feet wiggled as she kicked the quilt off her legs and climbed out of bed hurrying to the bathroom. She slid to a stop and stared into the mirror over the sink. Shaking her head from side to side, she exhaled a slow, cleansing breath. Her eyes were swollen and red, now matching her hair. Her shoulders slumped. *Maddy, you might see Ryan today*, she thought feeling even more nervous. She lay a cool wet cloth over her face, closed her eyes, and took soft breaths. The damp rag fell from her face and she saw that it hadn't help. It had only increased the redness. It was too late now to worry about her swollen eyes and the redness of her face. How she looked today was going to be the least of her worries.

She didn't move, but kept thinking and trying to remember everything she'd learned from the past week, all the intricateness of the jetpack and the unknown of falling into another world. She ran the hairbrush through her long hair detangling the long mass. Then she French braided it tucking it under. She moaned aloud with worry about her dream of Michael falling, a nightmare that was still playing over and over in her mind. It was like a movie blurb that wouldn't disappear from her thoughts. What did it mean? She shuddered when she remembered her premonition before Ryan fell into the pond.

She laid the hairbrush on the counter by the bathroom sink and went to her bedroom. She picked up the picture frame holding Ryan and her, the picture from so long ago. She gently slipped the picture out of the picture frame and then she picked up the pictures of her and Michael that were lying on her dresser. She slid the pictures into her pants pocket. Maddy looked around her room and saw a picture of her daddy, mama, and her at the beach. She unclipped the frame pulling the picture out of its frame. "I now have the pictures of all the people that I love with me, just in case I never come home," she whispered very softly in the quiet room. Her body began to shake, but her thoughts were interrupted when strong arms wrapped around her.

She spun around and her eyes looked up into Michael's blue eyes.

"Maddy, you'll be coming home, I promise. Stop worrying. I'm going to do everything in my power to make this mission successful." He leaned in kissing her. He wasn't worried what anyone might say.

She grabbed him, holding him tightly and laid her head on his shoulder. Her body was throbbing with pain and angst. "We both have to say goodbye to our parents. I don't know how your mom did it?"

"Love can conquer all."

She looked up into those blue eyes and understood what he meant.

"We better get downstairs. I know they are all as worried as we are," Michael added. "Stalling will only make things worse."

"But, you didn't sleep. You thought through the plan all night, too. Your eyes are as swollen as mine."

"Yes, I couldn't sleep." He pulled her to him very tenderly. "We only have a few seconds before we go. Maddy Sayers, I will love you forever until the end of time. You are my Aionios."

"I love you too Michael Montgomery." Her hands dropped by her side. "Let's go and get this mission done."

He led her out to the hallway. It was dark and the ceiling lights glowed downstairs in the kitchen of the old farmhouse. Everyone was sitting at the table including Johnny.

They said, "Good morning," in unison then the room became eerily quiet.

"Honey," said Jackson grabbing his daughter's shoulders spinning her around to face him, "you need to eat something. It might be a while before you get some more food."

She smiled at her father wanting to remember everything about him. She understood that he was always worried about her and eating breakfast was his way of taking care of her. "Yes, Daddy, I'll eat an egg and a biscuit."

He turned back to the stove. Staying busy and cooking was a way for him to relax.

"Jackson," Michael added, "I'll take a fried egg too."

"Yes sir, son," Jackson said happily turning his eyes toward Michael. He continued to break two eggs into the old iron skillet.

"Michael," Terry began, "we've been going over a schedule for each of us to stay at the pond. We'll take turns listening and waiting for your call."

"Oh, I hadn't thought about your having to stay out by the pond. Terry, we'll be fine coming back out of the water. We don't know how long this is going to take."

"Well, one of us is staying and guarding the pond. One of us will be the gatekeeper of Crystal Pond," he said trying to smile. "If our communication works, then you can let us know what is going on," Terry added.

Michael started to speak, but Clayton gave him a look, nothing he said was going to deter the group. He looked over at Maddy as she nervously scooped the last of her egg with her biscuit.

"Well, one more trip to the bathroom, then I'll be ready," she offered, standing with all eyes on her.

In a few minutes, she came downstairs. Everyone except her Daddy was outside waiting. He stood at the foot of the stairs staring up watching her. She stepped from the last step, reached in, and grabbed him. "Daddy, I'll be back soon. I won't ever leave you."

"Honey, I want to believe that, but we don't know. I want you to know how much I love you and how proud I am of you."

She sobbed laying her head on his shoulder.

Michael came into the living room. "Maddy, we need to be going."

"Michael, I give her to you, to see to and care for. That is a lot of responsibility," Jackson added trying to smile.

"Jackson, I'd give my life for her."

"Thank you," Jackson relinquished as he rubbed his wild, white hair away from his face. He didn't bother shaking Michael's hand. He just pulled the young man to him and gave him a hug. "Please stay safe, son, and both of you come back."

The three walked out the front door and stood on the porch. Clayton, Bayle, Johnny, and Terry were in the FBI truck. Jackson walked to his truck, but Maddy stopped and leaned over by the ole dog lying on the porch. "Gordon T, you take care of Daddy," she whispered. She stepped off the porch, turned around, and took one more look at her home. Michael held the truck door as she slid in beside her father. Then he sat down in the seat beside her and pulled the door closed. Jackson started the truck and followed the large truck down the bumpy tree lined path.

"This is the time for you to say what you need to each other," Jackson offered.

Maddy leaned in next to Michael. They kissed their last kiss on this earth. "I love you," she whispered.

He squeezed her body tight to his. "I love you, Maddy. Remember, forever."

The old truck pulled next to the old oak and Jackson shifted to park. They stepped out of the truck and walked over to the FBI truck.

Michael grabbed his Dad. "I'll come back just like you did. Take care of Mom and remember I love you."

"Yes, I know you'll come back and I'll see you again. Son, be careful," Clayton said. He let go, moved back, and wiped his eyes. "I love you," he said quietly knowing his son could hear him.

Michael stepped by his Mom. "Mom, I'm just going to visit family. I'll be fine," he said smiling wiping her tears flowing down her face.

"Yes, you are, but don't stay long. You never want to visit family too long," Bayle added, trying to smile.

Maddy gave them hugs, and then turned to Johnny. "Thank you for helping. Please don't get in trouble and do not go into that pond after us, not for any reason. You have your family to see to and my Daddy."

"I'll take care of Jackson and my family," Johnny answered. "I'll also take care of that strange person from the other world and that snoopy Brennan."

"I know you will. You and Terry stand guard. Michael heard someone near the house last night. They're getting braver and if they're from Aionios, they're probably mean and cruel."

"You just come back to us, and we'll take care of things here," Johnny assured.

She walked over to Terry. "You do the same. Don't ever go into the pond. Thank you for helping. Oh, this is so difficult to say goodbye, but I'll see you again."

"Yes, you'll be back before we know it. That pond and world can't keep you, Maddy Sayers. Be careful, my Maddy, and I'll guard the pond, I promise. I will be your gatekeeper until you come home."

"Thank you," Maddy puckered her mouth trying to hold back tears as she looked at her daddy. She ran and grabbed him. "I love you, Daddy, and I'll be home before long."

"I love you too, my little Madeline Jean. Come home soon." Jackson heaved a sigh with tears swelling in his eyes.

She walked back to Michael. He handed her the walkie-talkies and they prepared their guns and everything that would go under the suit. She felt her pants pocket holding the pictures of everyone she loved. She slipped her shoes into the suit and pulled it tightly around her head, just as she had done in their practice. She slipped the belt around the suit and clipped on the small tank. Michael attached the long tube to each of the helmets.

"Now, when we arrive," Michael began, "I will try and radio you as often as I can." He shook Terry's hand. "Thank you, my friend."

"You both come back; that'll be my thanks," answered Terry.

They each slipped their helmets over their heads, securing them, turning on the small tanks. Their gloves were pulled tight and secured. Michael nodded his head. Johnny and Terry with Jackson's help sat the jetpacks next to the pond. Maddy held onto Michael's hand as they walked close, but they both stopped for a second looking back at their parents. Jackson and Clayton both were giving them thumbs up.

Maddy's throat tightened and tears swelled in her eyes. Her mind replayed Ryan's face as he fell into the pond that one beautiful summer day.

"Maddy, snap out of it and don't cry," Michael said, "You can't wipe your face. Hey, at least we are going to be alone for a while and can talk."

She grinned, looking over into those caring blue eyes. He always knew what to say.

Michael nodded to the men. It was time. They lifted the heavy jetpacks one at a time swinging them into the center of the pond. They all watched them make a huge splashed falling into the middle of the water, disappearing.

"You ready?" Michael asked.

"Yes."

"Jump high and into the center of the pond," Michael said as he gripped her hand tightly and they leaped into the water. In a matter of seconds with no time to think, it became dark. Michael's hand slipped from hers. She felt the sand rubbing the suit as her body kept going deeper into the blackness, but just as Clayton said, suddenly she was in a foggy mist with light glowing brighter. She blinked from the brightness. Her arms spread out wide. She was soaring in a blue sky.

"Michael," she called out panicking searching the area down below for him. Maybe her dream had come true with Michael falling. "Michael!" she yelled, "Where are you?" It was still quiet.

She screamed again and again, "Michael!"

"Maddy," came a soft voice, "don't scream. I'm right here. Look down."

She looked to the ground and Michael was standing directly below her. "Dad was right the gravity pull was strong. I landed hard and it knocked the breath out of me, but I'm fine. Pay attention and enjoy."

"Oh, I can see for a long way. I see the farmhouse over to the side and there are mountains to each side."

"Don't get distracted, you're getting close."

She didn't have time to think. Michael grabbed her.

"Did the jetpacks make it?"

"Yes. Shut your air tank off and let me help you with your helmet."

She grabbed him. "We made it! I jumped into Crystal Pond! We're on Aionios!"

"Yes, now get you suit off and let's place the jetpacks over by that group of trees. I placed some rocks at the point where you fell through. I did have one advantage of falling first."

"Michael," she began, placing her suit by the jetpack. "I jumped into Crystal Pond, I jumped into Crystal Pond…I did it!"

"Yes, you did! Now, we need to try and contact, Terry." He lifted up the walkie-talkie clicking it on.

"Terry," he called out, but only static continued. He changed channels hoping one would be strong enough. He stopped for a second; hearing voices. "Terry," he called out again.

"Michael," the crackling voice came back.

"We're safe," Michael shouted.

"We hear you!" came, cheers from the group.

"We'll try and talk again soon. Bye, over."

"Good, over!" Terry's voice rose with the static growing and his voice disappearing.

Michael turned toward Maddy, "Alright I made a mental note. I found them on J 12. We need to find our own channel for the walkie-talkies."

"I can't believe you talked to Terry. How?"

"Dad, I don't know, but he's a genius, it's something. Now, let's check out this world and find Ryan and go home."

"Sounds good to me," she said still whispering, "I jumped into Crystal Pond."

She took a deep breath as she looked around. The trees were similar to Earth's. They were soaring up into the sky, but they were different. They were all thin with a hint of green tone bark and fern like leaves from the top to the bottom. The ground under the trees was covered in brownish thick moss, but a red-like clay was on the ground out in the sun. She wiped the sweat from her brow; the heat from this sun was stifling.

Michael grabbed her arm. "Come on, get a grip," as he began to walk toward the old farmhouse.

"Wow," she called out spinning around pulling away from him, "this world is unique for sure, so like ours, but so different. I can't believe there are mountains around us. It isn't like our farm. We don't have mountains this close.

"Maddy, don't worry about this world. Remember, we have to be careful and concentrate. First things first. We don't know who lives in the old farmhouse or who might be around."

"I know and I have my gun ready. I'm prepared. You need to let me go first. I know what I'm doing, but it sure is quiet around here and strange. This place is uncanny; it gives me the creeps."

The wooden-planked, two-story farmhouse looked just like an old farmhouse on Earth, but it was made from the tall tree's unusual wood. She knew that the Confederate soldiers had built the house just like their homes on Earth that they'd grown up in. But, it was too quiet. There weren't any animals, like squirrels running around or dogs barking. Plus, there wasn't any movement around for such a large home. They circled and moved to the backside of the home so no one would see them coming up to the back door. Maddy stepped up the steps and peered inside the back door's small window, nothing. A dim light was shining from the ceiling in the kitchen and she could see a pot was simmering on the stove.

"Someone's in there," she whispered softy. "They're cooking. We need to be careful." Her hand turned the doorknob on the worn wooden door. It was unlocked. She opened the door slowly but it squeaked as it opened. She stepped silently inside the kitchen holding her left hand up for Michael not to move and stay behind.

He whispered, "The hall closet."

Her head nodded yes. She moved to the side of the closet door. Gripping her gun tightly with her right hand, she slowly turned the doorknob with her left hand. The door flew open and a young girl, tall and very slim about nineteen, stood in front of her holding a gun aimed right at her. Maddy leaped to the side. The gun fired hitting the frame of the door!

Maddy grabbed the girl's arm jerking the gun out of her hand.

"Maddy are you alright!" yelled Michael running into the kitchen.

"Yes, she shot the doorframe," called out Maddy. "Who are you?" she questioned looking at the young girl.

"I'm Jacie Walden. Who are you?" she questioned in a trembling voice.

Maddy grinned. "Then you're related to Tom and Jeffery Walden?"

"Yes," the young girl answered her voice calming.

"We're from Unktehi or Crystal Pond," Maddy assured trying to relax the girl.

"But, you're not wet?

Michael stepped up near the girl. "No, we wore suits."

"You wanted to come into this world?"

"Yes."

"Why."

"My father," Michael began, "fell into the pond years ago and met Tom and Jeffery. He also met my mother and they were able to get back to Earth, his world. I'm Michael Montgomery.

"Oh my, then you're Clayton Montgomery's son. I've heard stories about Clayton and that he was the only one to ever go back to his world or at least everyone hoped he made it back." Her eyes turned to Maddy.

"I'm Maddy Sayers."

"Your farm has the pond on it in the other world that's next to my great grandfather Walden's farm."

"Yes," Maddy said.

"Why are you here?"

"I'm looking for a friend, Ryan Beardsley."

"Ryan."

"You know him?" Maddy asked getting excited.

"Yes, he fell into the pond when I was little; he's lived with us since he came here."

"Where is he now?" Maddy exclaimed.

"I don't know," assured Jacie anxiously moving back to the kitchen stirring food sitting on the stove.

"Do you have any idea where he went?" questioned Michael watching Maddy's reaction.

"No, he left with my brother about six months ago."

Michael stepped forward. "Where are your parents?"

"They were taken prisoners in town over a month ago," she sighed, "after the battle."

"What do you mean battle?" Maddy's asked worriedly.

The war between the Insurgents and the Quanoids started about three years ago. Ryan called it a civil war. He said your country had one a long time ago. The war didn't bother us until last year. My parents got word that the Quanoids were taking prisoners. They went to town to get my aunts, uncles, and cousins to bring them back to the farm so they'd be safe. Back then no one came out this way; everyone stayed away. But my family became prisoners. Ryan and my brother Bristan got so angry that they left to join the Insurgent army. The last I heard from them, Ryan was moving up in the ranks. They knew he was different and that he understood war. Bristan said in his last letter that Ryan might become the leader of the Insurgent army."

"Michael," Maddy sighed, "a war, how will we ever find Ryan and will he leave with us."

"I don't know. This isn't good, and it's going to be dangerous to get around in the city."

"I can give you the name of the town where the last letter came from, but Bristan said they were headed back here to Macrobi." Jacie went to the old desk and pulled out a letter handing it to Maddy.

"This isn't Jeffery's old desk, the one he hid the journals in?" Michael asked, rubbing his hand across the smooth wood.

"Yes, the journals are right here." Jacie pushed the backboard inside the desk and it dropped forward revealing papers.

Michael lifted the papers. He smiled seeing his father's handwriting. "This is Dad's journal and the letter from the Confederate soldiers."

"Yes," Jacie said smiling.

Maddy looked up as she finished reading the letter from Bristan. "We need to read over all of the journals. They may help."

"Maddy, this one you'll be interested in," Jacie said handing Maddy a piece of paper.

She didn't have to read who it was from. She saw Ryan's handwriting. Maddy brought the paper to her chest for a few seconds hugging it.

Michael began to read his father's journal. He sighed when he read how scared and terrified his father was coming into this new world. He wrote about how the days were so lonely until he met Bayle, but even with her love, he had a longing to go back to his world. Michael smiled looking over at Maddy as he read how Clayton added the love he felt for Bayle, every detail and how his heart was being torn apart thinking of leaving Aionios.

"Dad added all the details of the QLR." Michael looked up. "I'll read the specifications on them. I might have to steal one, so I want to know how they're built and how they run." He continued reading how Clayton prepared to leave and difficult it had been to say goodbye to Bayle.

He smiled, knowing his mom had gotten her way and left with him.

"Tom added the last paragraph," said Michael reading it out loud.

My friends, I was terrified, a coward and I wasn't able to watch Clayton and Bayle leave this world. Later in the day, I went back to the spot where Clayton had entered Unktehi Pond. I found the QLR, but no sign of Clayton Montgomery. My brother and I stood looking up in the same spot we'd entered into this world and prayed that they'd made it safe from our world back to the Sayer's farm. We miss Clayton, but we hoped he and Bayle would have a long and healthful life. God bless him and keep him safe. Tom Walden.

Michael laid the journal in his lap looking over at Maddy. "I'll add my father's story of how he made it back to his world. How he lived his life with Bayle and how I'm a mixture of both worlds, just as the Walden's children."

She held up the piece of paper, Ryan's story he'd left for others to read.

Well, I am told that I need to leave a journal of my life, so I shall begin. I am Ryan Allen Beardsley from the world known as Earth, a young boy entering into this world at the age of fifteen, July 11th, 1989. I, like the others, am uncertain where I am or what happened that July day on the Sayer's farm. I remember flipping and diving into the pond, a real dumb ass thing to do, going deep into the clear blue water. Then I hit and penetrated the fine sand thinking I'd never survive, but I didn't stop with my body going deeper and deeper. My will to survive was strong, just as the others who'd come before me. I went through the sand coming out into a beautiful sky. Suddenly, I was able to breathe, relieved, since I hadn't had a chance to take in a deep breath before falling into the pond. I took a sharp breath, gulping for air. My body was like a kite floating from the sky. It was so amazing. That warm summer day the Walden family discovered me wet, scared, and homeless. They took me in: fed, dressed and gave me a new home.

Oh, I miss my family, and Maddy; sweet Maddy, my heart breaks thinking of the pain I've caused her and my parents. She warned me about getting close to that pond, always knowing how to take care of me, but I, being stubborn, didn't listen. Maddy, I am now sixteen, but didn't get to spend my sixteenth birthday as I had hoped with you. I am sorry for the heartache I have caused.

I considered trying to go back to my world like Clayton Montgomery. But I, not being very mechanically inclined didn't grasp or understand how to work the strange, winged cars, and I didn't have an alternative plan. So, I'm doomed to stay here the rest of my life. I've worked on the Walden's farm day by day, just as I'd done in my world. I hide when someone comes to the farm. I've gone into Macrobi City a few times with the family, never alone. I do stand out, being different. My lonely life here is a punishment, just as the Confederate soldiers believed, not until eternity, but until I die. I will continue the journal of my life as years go by, I'm sorry to say, not with answers for you. Good luck and God bless, Ryan Beardsley

Tears glistened in her eyes. "Ryan has felt the same pain I have for all these years, but he had to live with them alone. Michael, what would that do to a person?"

"Most people would've become cold. I'm afraid if Ryan is working his way up to the head of the Insurgents of this country, he isn't worried about dying. He doesn't have anything to live for, so…" He took a breath, "Maddy, I don't believe he's found anyone else in his life." Michael leaned back understanding the consequences of his statement.

"We have to find him before it's too late. I can't let him destroy himself, out of loneliness."

"We will," Michael said in a soft voice.

Maddy sat in the overstuffed chair rereading Ryan's letter over and over. She touched his words with her fingers knowing how close physically she was to him.

Michael picked up a pen and began his own story of his father's life, a long and healthy life back in his world of Earth. He then read how to build a QLR.

Jacie walked back into the room. "So, you're really Maddy, the one Ryan talked about all the time. He sure does love you."

"Did he ever find someone else? You aren't going to hurt my feeling. I need the truth."

"He's been dating Cory who's from the farm up the road," answered Jacie. "They did get close. Cory is a sweet girl, but…"

"What?"

"She was taken prisoner by the Quanoids over six months ago, and it has almost driven Ryan crazy. He said he couldn't lose someone again. That was when he decided to join the army to try and find her. My brother and he were planning to come back here and find where the Quanoids were keeping the prisoners. I'm so worried that those two will do something dangerous."

"We," Maddy proclaimed, "are going to find them and maybe we can help save your parents and Cory."

"You'd save Cory?"

"Yes, of course. I'd do anything for Ryan, no matter what."

"I see you love him, as much as he loves you," added Jacie.

When Michael heard what Jacie was saying, his eyes peered up over the paper he was writing and they stayed fixed as he watched Maddy's reaction.

"What do you think, Michael?" asked Maddy. "Should we go early in the morning to the city?"

"Yes," he said in a quiet voice, "Maddy, I'm not trained to fight, but we'll do what we have to. I also need to check on my mom's family and be sure they're all right. We can't take on the entire army of the Quanoids."

"You'll learn their technology very fast, and with my training, we'll be fine." She leaned over giving him a hug. Jacie cocked her head to the side intensely watching them with a wondering look.

"If you're going into town tomorrow, I'm going too," Jacie declared. "I," cutting Maddy off by putting her hand in the air stopping Maddy from saying anything, "Please don't stop me. I can't stay here by myself any longer. I'm going to go crazy."

"Why don't you have the house open, it's hot in here," asked Michael fanning himself with a sheet of paper as he laid the journal back inside the desk.

"The Quanoids have patrols out here daily looking for people hiding out. If they find you, they take you as a prisoner or just shoot you. Nothing can change from one day to the next, no open windows or lights turned on at night. I'm running out of food and sitting each night alone in the dark is too much on me. I do get out during the day, but I have to hide if I hear them coming. I've been too scared to go into the city, but with you, I'll be fine."

"Jacie, it's too dangerous for us to take you with us," Maddy explained.

"Wait a minute," Michael interrupted, "Jacie, do you know how to get to the city through the woods without being noticed?"

"Yes, sure, I know these woods. I've played with the neighbors, and I used to sneak off with Bristan and Ryan to the old cave near town."

"All right, Michael, I see your point," Maddy agreed. "Jacie, looks like we're going to need your expertise to help us sneak into town. I'll help you prepare. You'll need a small bag with one change of clothes and some food. You can't take much. We'll also need flashlights and some water to take with us. We'll leave before sunrise in the morning."

"I've cooked a stew; it's a little weak. There's not much food left, but it's food. I'm sure glad my mom liked to can vegetables," said Jacie going into the kitchen. "Mom had learned over the years how to grow certain foods in her garden and recipes from your world. Now, we need to eat and clean things up. We can't leave anything out on the table or counters. In the morning, we want everything turned off."

"Well," offered Michael, standing to follow Jacie into the kitchen, "let's eat and get the place cleaned up." He stopped moving.

"What is it Michael," whispered Maddy.

Michael moved to the back door. "I heard something moving around."

Maddy peered outside from the kitchen window. "I don't see anyone."

"They're gone now, but we need to be careful," said Michael moving back to the kitchen table.

Jacie didn't say anything. She nervously dipped the soup into bowls and placed them on the table along with some stale bread.

Michael scooted out a kitchen chair and sat down. "Don't my grandparents own a bakery in town?"

"Yes," said Jacie her eyes studying Michael, "their bread is delicious. My Grandpa Jeffery used to visit Bayle's parents a lot."

"I heard from my mother that the bread is comparable to our bread on Earth." Michael took a sip of soup, his face puckered. "Do you know if my grandparents are still alive?"

"Sorry about the soup," said Jacie with a smile growing on her face. "Your grandparents were safe last time I visited a few months ago. Sabian, I guess he's your Uncle Sabian," Jacie said with a laugh. "Has taken over the shop with his son, Joshua, your cousin…alright," she sighed shaking her head, "your family is getting complicated. Joshua is a couple of years older than I am. He used to meet me out by the cave, but I haven't talked to him for a long time." She looked at her bowl and got quiet.

Michael looked at Maddy. He smiled, nodded his head seeing the look on the young girl's face when she was talking about Joshua.

Jacie didn't eat much. Too much hurt with her world turned upside down, just as Ryan's world. Busily, Jacie began cleaning the kitchen, a reparative chore she did each day before dark. She straightened everything so it didn't look like anyone was home.

Darkness was taking over the house giving it a chill. Jacie went to the stairs. "Let me show you were you can sleep. If we're getting up early, we need to get rest."

Maddy looked at the Jacie's swollen and red eyes, sleep wasn't something she'd had a lot of. "It's been tough on you living alone in this big house, especially at night."

Jacie ducked her head. "Yes, I can't sleep at night. I hear noises and believe the soldiers are coming inside. If I do sleep, I dream horrible dreams. Maddy," said Jacie stopping by a bedroom door, "here's Ryan's room."

Maddy pushed the door open. She stopped by the dresser looking around. The green and black checked curtains matching the covers on the full bed were pulled together tight letting the red setting sun's rays glow, flowing around the edges into the room. She lifted up a hairbrush that was sitting on the dresser. She could see that Ryan's hair color was the same, a dark blonde color. She smiled. There, sitting at the end of the dresser was a pointed white rock, glistening in the evening sunlight. Ryan's passion was collecting rocks and he wanted to become a geologist and a petrologist. She lifted the rock up by the window watching it sparkle in the light. Ryan used to tell her he was going to find gold and treasures.

She opened Ryan's closet door, not many clothes were inside the closet. He'd never worried about things like clothes. She went back to the dresser and pulled open a small drawer. Peeping out from under his clothes was a small black journal. She picked it up and her fingers rubbed the soft leather. "Oh," she sighed, as she began to read the words that were written in the journal. Tears flowed. She heard a noise and spun around. Michael stood quietly by the door staring at her.

Maddy lifted the journal in the air. "This is Ryan's diary, he tells of how much he loved me and how much he misses me. Each night he writes the same over and over." She sobbed wiping tears away with the back of her hand.

Michael grabbed hold of Maddy bringing her close. He knew only one person who could help her.

"I'll read the journal later," she said laying the diary back in its hiding place. "I'd like to take a bath; we won't have that opportunity for a while to clean up and soon it's going to be dark."

"Sure, it'll relax you. This has been some day. Maddy stay on the alert, I think someone still may be watching the house."

She reached up touching his face bringing it close, kissing him. "I'll stay alert. Thank you for helping me find Ryan."

He was quiet.

Maddy turned from Michael hurrying to the bathroom. The bathroom was astonishing. Everything else in the house was like her old farmhouse. But, the bathroom was computerized like in a science fiction movie. Buttons replaced handles and the water flowed directly from the wall into the smooth rock tub. She hoped tomorrow morning she would have time to take a shower, but the tub at the moment was so relaxing. She leaned back in the huge tub and could read the buttons in the shower. It seemed you stepped into the shower and it was like a car wash with water jets and spray heads all around. She hated to leave. She could almost forget the danger that the three would be facing tomorrow. She grabbed a towel and stepped out of the tub. Enough relaxing, she wanted to get back and read the diary. She hurriedly dressed and went to Ryan's room.

She pulled the diary out of the dresser drawer clutching it as she sat on the bed by the window. She carefully pulled the curtain open, but not enough to be noticed from the outside.

Maddy began to read page after page, day after day of Ryan's story, his life for the last eleven years. Her body ached remembering the same pain, thinking the same things repeatedly each day in her own mind. He even wondered what his life would've been like if she had fallen into the pond with him. She smiled when he said his life would've been worth living if she had been with him. The sun began to set making the bedroom dark. Marking her spot in the worn diary, she laid it on the dresser.

She looked up. Michael stood in the doorway. He had been watching her intently. "I wanted to say good night. I don't think I should stay in here with you, not in Ryan's room."

She moved over by him, even in the darkening room, she could see the hurt in his eyes, believing he was losing her to her past.

"Michael, I love you, and this'll all be over soon."

"I hope, for the best," he said quietly, leaning in kissing her holding her tight, but feeling her mentally slipping away. "I'm going back to the entrance to the pond early in the morning and try and contact Terry to let him know what we're doing."

"Do you want me to go with you?"

"No, I can find my way and you just stay here with Jacie. I'll be fine; it want take but a few minutes."

"You be careful and use that gun if you need to."

"I will, I love you, and I will love you forever. Get some rest." He turned around and walked out of the room, but stopped and looked back at her.

She sat on the bed staring at the diary.

"Maddy," came, a soft whisper from the door." Jacie came into the room. "I want to thank you for giving in and taking me tomorrow."

"I hope it works for all of us."

"I see you found Ryan's diary. My mother bought him the diary hoping it would ease the hurt of losing his family and you."

"It did."

"Well, if you want to read it some more, he should have a flashlight that was what Ryan called it, in his nightstand. You can go into the closet. I've sat many nights in my closet reading and writing in my diary with the light of a flashlight. It's not so lonely that way."

"That's a good idea; thank you, Jacie. Now, get some rest. This might be the best night's sleep you get in a while."

The young girl left the room and Maddy pulled open the nightstand drawer. There was a small flashlight, tiny, but with brightest light bulbs. She held the diary in her hand, pulled open the closet door, closed it behind her, and scooted deep inside. She clicked on the flashlight. Her eyes continued to read the words that Ryan had written year after year. She could feel his coldness growing. She sat there remembering the coldness in her eyes for all these years, but then the words began to change. A girl named Cory began to be mentioned. He wrote about how beautiful she was and how new emotions were stirring inside of him. At one point, she felt like an intruder and she didn't have the right to read his private words. His personal stories, like the night he made love to Cory, every detail immerged, but this was her life too and she had to know. His description of Cory was one of wonder and love. He'd fallen in love with her, but he still loved Maddy. He felt like he was cheating on her. She leaned her head against the wall and smiled understanding that was how she'd felt these last few days. The guilt was eating at her. They would always love each other. Nonetheless, each of them had found someone new, someone that brought life back into their lives.

"Oh, Ryan, I have to find you. We need to talk," she added sobbing. She knew he was trying to be loyal to her, but was it going to cost him his life. She couldn't let that happen. She had to find Ryan no matter what. This had to stop before the pain could go away. Her excitement grew and she couldn't wait until she saw his face. She flipped the pages in the diary coming to the last page.

Ryan Beardsley, fate has taking away your love again, and you are to be lonely the rest of your life. Oh, Maddy, how I wish you were here to guide me. You, my love, were always the strong one and knew what to say to keep me motivated in life.

Cory, my heart is breaking. My dear love, you are too sweet and naïve and they will destroy you, just as fate has tormented me. I can't lose you. I won't let you down, as I did Maddy. I will fight, but will I ever get to hold Cory as I did that one night, our night. I don't know what my future will be. I leave my soul in this diary, but I'm not hopeful of ever returning to this home. I shall die on the battlefield fighting for justice. If I can do one thing in my lifetime, I will set Cory free to live, maybe not with me, but to live.

Sleep won't come. I leave in the early light with Bristan to enter into a world of civil unrest. One, I'm sorry to say that I understand war, a war in my world that didn't end well, and I'm sure it won't end well here either. I say goodbye and good night. I've lost my Maddy and I can't lose my Cory. God help me.

Maddy closed the book. Her body trembled with pain. Anger was building; it felt like when she and Ryan were kids. He'd fight for her, just as he did that day at the creek, and she'd fight for him, never letting anyone or anything hurt the other. She now had to fight for Ryan and bring him home, to whatever home he wanted. Her hands squeezed the small book. She couldn't let her emotions interfere with the objective of the mission, finding Ryan. She turned the flashlight off, pushed open the closet door, and laid the diary back in its hiding place so it'd be waiting for Ryan to add to it when he returned. She climbed into bed; she needed rest and sleep. Tomorrow would be a new day to repair what fate had taken away.

Something caught her eye. She peered at the floor. She gasp. Sticking out from under her bed was a man's arm that was slowly inching its way out from under the bed. Her body stealthily moved in the darkness of the room. She gently slid her pillow under the quilts. Quietly, she slipped her gun out of its holster that was hanging on the post of the headboard. She scrunched next to the headboard on the other side of the bed. She sat barely breathing waiting holding the gun tight in her hands.

A small thin light flowed from around the window onto the floor showing a shadow of a body slowly begin to slide out from under the bed. A young man with dark, long hair noiselessly stood up from the floor. His weapon fired at the center of the bed hitting the feather pillow sending feathers into the room.

Jacie screamed and Michael came running into the room. The man spun around in a half circle pointing the gun at Michael. Not hesitating, Maddy fired at the man and his body thumped to the floor.

"Maddy," shouted Michael.

"I'm fine Michael. You were right someone was watching us."

Jacie stood holding onto the doorframe to support her trembling body. "How did he get inside without our seeing or hearing him?"

He slipped inside the house when we were busy getting settled upstairs. Michael couldn't tell which one of us was making the noise. If I hadn't seen his arm as he began to move, well…"

"We don't want to think of that," exclaimed Michael. "Now, we have to get rid of the body. Jacie get a sheet."

Maddy bent next to the dark tan man who was wearing a black uniform. He doesn't need his gun or knife anymore. She pulled out his ID from a pocket. She moaned. "His name is Al and he's only eighteen." Maddy looked up at Michael. "Why did he have to come inside? If he'd waited one more day, we would have been gone."

Jacie handed Michael the sheet and he flipped it into the air spreading it out. He squatted by Maddy and rolled the body onto the sheet securely tucking the sheet around the body. "You two get his legs and I'll take his shoulders. We have to take him out to the woods and bury him."

"Michael, the patrols will be looking for him," mumbled Jacie.

Michael stood. "That's why we don't want them to find him. Maybe they'll think he deserted."

The three grabbed the man carefully walking down the stairs and outside. Jacie lead them to a spot near the woods. She ran to the barn and hurried back with two shovels. When the grave was deep enough, Michael rolled the body face down into the small trench and filled it with dirt. Jacie and Maddy threw a few rocks on top, and then they covered the grave with dead foliage so the fresh dirt wouldn't show.

Tired, dirty, and bushed they made their way to the house. Jacie exhausted from the episode went to her room to rest. Maddy entered Ryan's room. She didn't move seeing the blood on the rug by the bed and feathers from the pillow strewn everywhere. She understood the blood could've easily been hers.

Michael walked into the room. Maddy turned to face him. "I've got to clean the room. We can't leave a trace that shows signs of anything happening."

"I'll do it. You go and rest; you're fatigued."

"No, I'll get the rags and cleaners. You start picking up the feathers around the room," she said.

She scrubbed the rug, made the bed and Michael finished picking up feathers.

"There, I don't think anyone will notice," she said quietly wiping the sweat from her brow. "Let's go downstairs. I can't sleep."

Maddy and Michael stepped slowly down the stairs. Sleep still wasn't coming as she sat in a recliner and Michael sat in the other chair not talking, just thinking.

She did fall asleep waking to noise in the kitchen. She sat up realizing it was morning. She looked down at her clothes covered in dirt, so much for being able to relax this morning in the incredible shower. She pulled in a deep breath. Worry was taking over. She had dreamed again about Michael falling and her anxiety was growing. What was today going to bring?

Chapter 22
An Uninvited Guest

"Good morning, Michael. Were you able to radio Terry?" Maddy questioned walking into the kitchen sitting down at the table studying Michael.

"No," Michael said as he stared at her becoming quiet.

"What's wrong?" she snapped back. "I see something has happened."

"That soldier last night caused us more problems than we knew. Our jetpacks and equipment are missing. I looked all around but couldn't find them, and for some reason, the walkie-talkies aren't working."

Maddy leaped from her chair and began to pace the room. "So, what do we do?"

"It will take me a long time to get a QLR ready for us to use to go into the pond." He grabbed her shoulders tightly. "It looks like you and I won't be going home soon."

Tears swelled in her eyes. "I have to find Ryan, but staying here and not going home wasn't a part of our plan."

"Well, we sure can't ask that soldier where our things are."

"C'mon," Maddy said staring out the window. "I'll help you search some more. He couldn't have hid them too far from here."

"We must be cautious. There are sure to be more soldiers patrolling this morning."

"Do you want me to help?" questioned Jacie.

"Yes, you can help keep watch," replied Maddy. "Sorry, but we will have to go into town later today or tomorrow. We have to find our equipment."

"That's all right. It's just nice not to be alone," Jacie added turning off all the kitchen lights.

Michael stepped down the back steps and stood quietly listening. "Come on, I don't hear anything," he said motioning with his hands for the girls to follow.

They walked through a group of tall trees searching for the jet packs. Maddy's eyes were pulled to the grave they had dug the night before and her anger grew. *Why did that guy have to ruin their plans?* She shook her head. Things were a mess! But, in some ways, she did feel sorry for the young man who forfeited his life for a ludicrous war, who wouldn't be able to grow old with someone he loved, and who would never have children or grandchildren. But, she couldn't think about that now; she had to regain her focus and work toward the objective at hand.

For the next hour, they searched the old barn, the fields, and the woods nearby. The heat of the sun was warming the morning making it almost unbearable to walk around.

Maddy stood in the field, looked around, and wiped the sweat beads growing on her brow. She shuddered. It was still so quiet, too quiet. No birds or animals were making any noises and the strange tree's leaves were silent. The world was unnatural to her.

"Maddy," called out Michael, "you and Jacie get back to the house! NOW. I hear a strange noise."

"I'm not leaving you," Maddy shouted back.

"Get Jacie to the house!" he yelled.

Maddy took off running. She had to leave Michael and get to Jacie. "Jacie get in the house," she yelled. The kitchen door swung open and the girls raced into the room. Jacie crouched in a corner her hands covering her head. Maddy's heart was pounding in her chest. *What did Michael hear? Why didn't he run?*

A few minutes later, that seemed like hours, the kitchen door opened and Michael stepped inside.

"Michael what's wrong? What did you hear?" Maddy insisted.

"This you won't believe," he answered shaking his head. He turned around, went to the kitchen door, and swung it open. There standing on the top step dripping wet was none other than Brennan.

"You have to be kidding!" Maddy shouted. "You idiot!"

"I'll get a towel," Jacie said as she quickly raced out of the kitchen.

"Come on in, Brennan," Michael said grabbing the man by the arm.

Jacie ran back into the kitchen and threw a towel to Brennan.

"Okay, Brennan, start talking," Maddy said as she sat down at the kitchen table staring at the man.

"Early this morning, I went to the pond and was confronted by a guy name Terry," Brennan began as his hands gripped the back of a kitchen chair. "Terry ordered me to leave and never come back. After he pulled out his gun, I didn't hesitate. I turned and started walking fast through the woods back to the dirt road where I'd left my car. I heard a noise, turned around thinking it was Terry, but it was an ugly, huge, light blue-skinned man pointing a knife at me. I ran as if the devil was after me and I think he was. I wasn't paying attention where I was going and ended up back at the pond. The blue-skinned man lunged at me with the knife in his hand. When I leaped backwards, something flipped me into the center of the pond. I kept going through the sand and somehow ended up here. Where the hell am I?"

"Well, Brennan, you have joined us in Aionios, another world similar to Earth," replied Michael.

"Another world, you're kidding right?" questioned Brennon.

"Nope," answered Maddy.

"Alright, how do we get back to Earth or back to the Sayer's farm?" Brennon said his hands turning white as he continued to clutch the chair's back.

"That is the big question of the morning," responded Michael, "and you have complicated matters greatly."

"You can say that again!" Maddy stood scooted her chair back from the table and started pacing the floor. "Do you know if Terry alright?"

"I heard a gunshot as I fell into the pond, but didn't see anything. Boy, it was strange. I just kept going through the water, then sand, and then there was a bright light." He stopped for a second and looked at them. "Okay, stop joking! Where am I? This is a dream, right? I must have hit my head."

"I told you that you have fallen into another world, named Aionios," snapped Michael.

"All right," added Maddy. "Things are just a little mixed up. Our first plan of action is to find Ryan, then find a way to get home. I can't believe we have to deal with you," she added giving Brennan a hard glare.

"Ryan, oh, he's the boy who drowned in the pond years ago. Right…You mean he's not dead? I guess we aren't dead, or are we?"

"No, we aren't dead. We are just like the others that came through Crystal Pond. We are stuck here unless we can find the jetpacks or a way back to the pond," said Michael.

"You really mean we have to live here?" Brennan asked trying to dry off. "What others do you mean, and where are they?"

"Don't know," replied Michael. "Some have left, died, and even been taken prisoner. However, you better get used to it, Brennan. This is our new home, the world of Aionios. Sorry it isn't a pretty one."

Jacie warmed the watered-down stew. They ate lunch and sat down in the living room. Michael told Brennan about the patrols and the soldier that snuck into the house last night that had tried to kill them. He warned him to be on the alert and keep his mouth shut, which he knew would be a difficult thing for a reporter.

Maddy left the three talking and made her way up to Ryan's room. The worn stairs squeaked as she walked up them. She felt like the weight of the world was on her shoulders. She sighed. It literally was.

The door swung open; however, she didn't move. Her eyes were glued to the woven rug at the foot of the bed. The one with blood stains. None of the cleaning products in the house could take out the reddish spots. This was real and she didn't have Terry or the FBI to help. She stepped over the rug and stopped at the dresser. Slowly, she pulled the drawer open and there where she had laid it last night was Ryan's diary. She brought the diary to her chest.

She flipped the diary open and gazed at the words, but her mind wouldn't let her concentrate on the diary. She stared out the window remembering that one day, that beautiful summer day, so long ago when she and Ryan were young. Now she was so close to seeing Ryan, but felt so far away. She grabbed a pen. She had promised Terry to keep a journal. Tears swelled in her eyes. *Terry, oh Terry, I hope you're all right*, she thought as she began to write her story.

She finally smiled thinking of Terry who was now the Gatekeeper guarding Crystal Pond. She decided to believe that he was alive and well. She caressed the diary. She knew what she had to do. *No small task,* she whispered into the dark room.

How did her mission of finding Crystal Pond's secret change her life? She just wanted to find the answer to Crystal Pond. Well, one mission down, but this new mission was already not going according to the plan. Her mission of finding Ryan had ended in another nightmare…war and killing. How was she going to find Ryan in a world she didn't understand that was as large as Earth? She not only had brought Michael and his family into this mission but also her dad, Johnny, Terry, and to top that off…Brennan. She took a deep breath. She closed the diary and placed it in her bag. She would continue to record episodes as they unfolded.

She slowly stepped down the stairs. She could hear the three talking in the kitchen and Brennan was even laughing.

She stopped on the stairs, closed her eyes, and could hear her daddy. *"Nothin's ever gonna stop you, my Madeline Jean."*

Maddy opened her eyes and whispered, *"I hope you're right, Daddy. There's no sense in stopping now. I'm seeing this through come Hell or high water."* Sadly, she had already had a good taste of both, but then there were the gatekeepers waiting and watching. She couldn't let them down.

About the Author

Diann Shaddox is a Native American Indian and a member of the Wyandotte Nation of Oklahoma and she has Essential Tremors. She's an award-winning author of *A Faded Cottage*, a SC love story about an artist with Essential Tremors; *Whispering Fog* a time travel romance; *Miranda* a love story, a journal of a young girl living in the late 1800's; and *Spirits of Sacred Mountain* a story about a young Native American boy who discovers a magical world hidden deep in a mysterious mountain.

Diann is the Founder of Diann Shaddox Foundation, a Non-Profit 501c(3) public organization fighting the battle to find a cure and bring awareness for Essential Tremor, (ET).

Diann was born on December 18th in a small southern town of Nashville, Arkansas, the youngest and only daughter of William and Mary Ann Shaddox. But, fate stepped in and William, a crop-duster, at the age of 25, died in a plane crash on November 20th, a month before she was born, therefore, Diann was never able to meet her father. Mary Ann, who grew up in Miami, Oklahoma, moved back to Miami after William's death, where Diann lived until her mother died when she was only 3 years old. Diann then moved to Nashville, Arkansas to live with her grandparents. At the age of 10, Diann's Granddad Holt died of a stroke, leaving her grandmother alone to see to her.

Diann learned from an early age about death and how life should not be squandered. Her Mamow Holt, who had lost her right hand in an accident at a factory in Nashville, Arkansas, taught her, you never give up. Her grandmother never let anything stand in her way. She taught herself to write, cook, and even how to sew and make quilts with her left hand, without any prosthetics. Being handicapped was a word she never used.

Growing up in a small town was wonderful, learning to fish, growing a garden and the most important thing, patience of a grandmother. Stories from the past evolved of family bringing many stories to life. Sitting out late at night on cool summer evenings, swinging on an old swing staring up at the stars helped Diann's vivid imagination grow.

On May 20, 2014, Diann's son Richard died of a brain tumor.

She has an enthusiasm for travel and living life to its fullest. You have only one life and shouldn't waste it. The zest for meeting and getting to know people is a very important component in her life. She is a believer of herbs, natural and organic foods, and a big supporter of Bio-identical Hormones and keeping our planet green.

Diann has resided in eight great states, Arkansas, Oklahoma, Kentucky, New Jersey, Virginia, Texas, and Florida. South Carolina. www.diannshaddox.com

Diann Shaddox Foundation for Essential Tremor

The Diann Shaddox Foundation for Essential Tremor is a Non-Profit 501 c(3) public organization committed to find a cause and cure for Essential Tremor, the largest and most common movement disorder.

Diann Shaddox Foundation is dedicated to educate and increase awareness to the world about people living every day with Essential Tremor and to donate research grants to doctors to find a cure.

Essential Tremor (ET) is the largest movement disorder and is a progressive neurological condition that causes a rhythmic trembling of the hands, head, voice, legs, or body. 42 million people worldwide have Essential Tremor, including children. Essential Tremor doesn't discriminate with age, race, sex, or national origin.

Quality of life is a big issue for people with Neurological conditions. Daily activities such as feeding, drinking, grooming and writing become difficult if not impossible. Many people with movement disorders are too embarrassed to go into public and depression sets in. Children and teens are bullied and teased in school.

With awareness, people with Essential Tremor can come out of hiding; live normal lives as anyone with a disability.

Please join Diann Shaddox Foundation to make a difference for millions of people around the world living with Essential Tremor and donate.

Diann Shaddox Foundation for Essential Tremor.

www.diannshaddoxfoundation.com

THE GATEKEEPER